Prologue

GUNNER

TEN YEARS EARLIER

My father came across as an unassuming man. If he paid attention to you, it made you feel like the only person in the room. Jonathan Youngblood could be warm, non-threatening, and a good listener. My mother said I had his smile, and when I got excited about something as a kid, my eyes would light up with the same brightness as when he used to look at her.

Used to.

I noticed from an early age that his smiles were never directed at her anymore, but his teeth and eyes shone brightly for pretty new fixtures—the socialites who came to his parties, daughters of his business partners.

It was jarring to me, seeing my father giving my mother the cold shoulder at their events. Mom held onto his arm, nails manicured and diamond jewelry throwing light all over the place like disco balls. Her smile was just as fake as his.

In contrast, my grandparents, who I spent more time with, only had eyes for each other. Gram would cackle with laughter, smacking Gramps' hand away when he pinched her behind as she walked by. They had touched all the time, bantering and bickering with smiles on their faces. Until Gramps passed away when I was thirteen, they slept in the same bed every night, and always retired to their bedroom together.

I couldn't remember a time when my parents ever went to bed together. One of my earliest memories was being carried by my nanny as I watched my parents walk to their separate, opposite wings of the house for the night.

All of these contrasting views rifled through my brain as I sat across from my father in his office. There were no family pictures, no touches of warmth or humanity in this space. Just polished wood and leather with the occasional shiny metal surface, reflections of him and his ego.

A massive taxidermy rhinoceros head jutted out from the wall behind him. The animal was completely extinct now, with no subspecies left except for those in zoos. Dear old Dad and his cousin, a US Senator, paid a fortune to hunt the last six wild rhinos remaining. He laughed at the activists, the public outcry, and the woe from environmentalists. This motherfucker was *proud* to have a direct hand in wiping an endangered species off the planet. That's the kind of man he really was underneath the smiles.

I kept this all in mind as I stuck my fingers between my neck and my shirt collar, the silk tie feeling like it was strangling me, while I waited for him to begin this charade.

Sometimes, even behind closed doors, he found it amusing to play the part of a father.

"General Arros sent me your final marks from McAlister today." Jonathan Youngblood folded his hands on his desk as if speaking to a business associate. "All perfect scores, as usual."

I frowned, shifting in my seat. "Grades don't come out until next month. I turned in my final project this morning."

"Don't be foolish, Gunner. You know the power I have over the entire academy board." A self-satisfied grin pulled at his lips. "You know the benefits of being a Youngblood."

I propped my elbow on the arm of the chair and lowered my head into my hand. I actually worked my ass off at McAlister Academy, and not just because I woke up doing push-ups at 4:30 am every day. I actually studied. I paid attention in class. Military history, battle strategy, it all fascinated me. I begged my teachers, and even met with the headmaster, to grade and evaluate me based on my own effort, not what my dad slipped them under the table. They all assured me they did, but apparently being in Jonathan Youngblood's favor was more appealing.

Dad began pouring a glass of Scotch—only one of course, for himself. This was a success for *him*, after all. I fantasized about breaking the bottle over his inflated head and gulping down the expensive booze myself.

"You'll receive a call from the Pentagon in two weeks' time," he said. "They'll offer you a job as a junior strategist. It's just above entry-level, you see. I couldn't place you in a higher-level position without…arousing suspicions." He chuckled, like that was a cute joke. "Keep your head down, do your job, and the pieces will move in your favor."

He paused to take a drink, swallowing while he looked me over, as if inspecting merchandise. "You'll be flying out to D.C. the following Monday. I suggest you prepare in the meantime, such as getting a haircut."

I scoffed, running a hand back through my buzz cut that had grown shaggy. During the last few weeks of the semester, I said 'fuck it' to my weekly haircuts. I was fucking sick of them.

"Yeah, about that..." I let my arm fall back down to the couch. "I'm not taking the job."

It was Jonathan's turn to scoff, not that he was surprised. He even humored me with a smile as he poured himself a second drink. "Don't be ridiculous, son. And sit up straight, you look like a fucking delinquent."

I slouched further down into the chair, spreading my feet wide on the floor, adding insult to injury. Only then did I see the first hints of cruelty he displayed when he didn't get his way. The pulse in his neck, the steely coldness in his eyes. Dad was used to me rebelling, that was why he sent me to live with my grandparents. If a five-year-old who poured ink all over his favorite ottoman while the nanny was distracted could be considered a rebel.

After that, he enjoyed toying with me when I said no. When I didn't want to come to his parties so he could show me off like a prized pig, he sent men over to Gramps' house, who punched and kicked me in the stomach until I agreed to come. When I refused to end things with Beth, the maid I was seeing, he sent her away and never told me where.

Like everything else he owned, he loved exerting control over me. He liked seeing me fight back until the moment I caved. But he never truly saw me stand up to him before.

"I'm not working at the fucking Pentagon," I told him. "I'm not cutting my hair. I'm not doing a *fucking* thing you tell me to anymore."

The snarl on his face used to scare me. Now he just looked like a tired old man. "I'm in no mood for your games tonight, Gunner. If I have to lock you in a room, strap you down, and take a razor to your head, I will."

"I'd like to see you try, Jonathan."

He slammed his hands down to push himself up and round his desk, but in the time it took to blink, I was already towering over him. My father's confident motions skittered to a halt, eyes wide with the first glimpse of uncertainty I'd ever seen him express.

"Didn't expect me to move so fast, did you?" I taunted, leaning down into his face. "From sitting like a *delinquent*."

"So you *did* apply yourself to your studies." His gaze roamed over me, as if noticing for the first time that his twenty-year-old son was taller and stronger than him. Shit, he probably never truly *saw* me this clearly in my whole life.

"I did," I breathed softly, squaring my shoulders. "I have to thank you for that, at least. Shipping me off to McAlister was probably the best thing you ever did for me."

"It was," he agreed with a vigorous nod of his head. "Because a Youngblood must always be in power. By the time you're thirty-five, you'll be the perfect candidate for president, son! The Pentagon is just the next step—"

"Yeah, see, that's where you got it wrong, old man." I crossed my arms. "I'm not one of your puppets, not anymore. McAlister didn't just test the limits of my body and teach me military strategy. I learned to think for myself, be my own person." A grin stretched across my face at seeing the rage forming on his. "And I love that, to you, that's the *worst* thing I could've become."

"You are a *Youngblood!*" he bellowed. "You serve no other purpose than to honor and continue our family's legacy! Do you understand? The *only* reason you exist is to follow after *me*."

I spread my arms wide and lifted my shoulders in a shrug. "Well, the world's about to end anyway, so doesn't seem like it would've lasted long. I'm riding off into the sunset instead. And if you try to stop me?" I leaned in even closer, making him shrink back. "I don't want to hurt your guys, but I can guarantee some broken fingers and ribs. Wouldn't want you to waste your money on some hourly workers' hospital bills."

Turning on my heel, I made my way to the office

doors, finally tugging the knot loose on my tie. I couldn't wait to trample this whole fucking suit under my motorcycle tires.

"Gunner!" Jonathan called out after me. "You walk out that door, you are dead to me, you understand? You won't see a penny from me. If you come crawling back, begging forgiveness, I will gladly kick your face in myself! See how many maids want to fuck you after you're broke *and* ugly."

"Don't worry, pops." I didn't even spare him a glance as I pulled open the heavy wooden doors inlaid with the Youngblood family crest. "Unlike you, I still have a personality."

I walked out of the room to the sounds of a grown man's temper tantrum, then down the long marble corridor to the front door. The cool night air was like a soothing balm on my skin, a gentle caress after a heated exchange. *I actually fucking did it. I stood up to the bastard and now I'm my own man.*

My jacket and tie were off by the time I made it to my private garage, where the only earthly possession I cared about waited for me. I hit the button on my keyfob and stripped down to my boxers and socks as the garage door lifted. Leaving my discarded clothes and the keyfob on the gravel path, I walked inside and started pulling clothes out the duffel bag I had ready.

Now this was more like it. Jeans and engineer boots. A simple fitted t-shirt and a leather jacket.

Once dressed, I turned to Old Rusty, Gramps' vintage Harley that Jandro restored for me five years ago. I kicked-started the ancient bike as gently as I could, my heart vibrating in my chest as he sputtered to life. Throwing a leg over the seat, my hands in place on the grips, I felt at home.

I kicked my feet up and accelerated forward, aiming a straight path over the clothes on the driveway. Running over my dad would've been more satisfying, but it was still a rush to grind the costume of my former life into the dirt. As the Youngblood family estate grew smaller and smaller in my rearview mirrors, maniacal laughter escaped me.

One thing I didn't tell my dad, was that McAlister only played a small part in my standing up to him and taking my life back for myself. No, that honor belonged to the two men waiting for me at the end of the property. The two *delinquents* who saw past my family name and wealth, and became my first true friends.

"Took you fuckin' long enough," Reaper growled when I pulled up at the crossroad.

He and Jandro sat on their idling bikes, the machines making gentle, purring rumbles. The cherried ends of their cigarettes lit their faces up in a red, ominous glow. It kind of made them look like demons.

"Yeah, whatever." I beckoned a hand at Reaper, unable to contain the grin on my face. "It's done. So gimme a smoke and let's ride."

GUNNER

PRESENT DAY

Thirty miles outside of Sheol, I slowly rolled through a town that had seen better days. Bullet holes lined the sides of buildings and abandoned cars. Plywood covered up some of the broken windows—those that hadn't been pried off by squatters, at least.

Horus sat perched on my handlebars, beak clicking and eyes darting around, not missing anything about our surroundings. I stroked the feathers on his back idly, ignoring the few remaining residents of this town who were drawing their curtains shut and hurrying into alleyways off the main road. No one wanted to get in the way of the patch on my back.

I pulled up to my destination, a squat, one-story brick building, and cut the engine. Horus flew to my shoulder as I swung a leg over my seat and went to unstrap my cargo.

"Heard you carried Reaper's ass in midair," I

scratched under my bird's beak. "Where's my help in carrying this shit?"

He chirped in reply, puffing up and shaking his feathers out.

"Yeah, that's what I thought."

Grabbing the metal case in both hands, I heaved it up off of my bike seat and headed for the front door. Thankfully, Arty left it unlocked today so I was able to push it open with my shoulder. I crossed the stuffy, dimly lit room in two steps and dropped the case with a heavy clang on the counter.

"You're gonna throw your back out, swingin' heavy shit around like that," Arty yelled from his back room.

Behind the counter, his office door was barely cracked. I couldn't see anything through it except flashes of light from sparks, accompanied by the hiss and crackle sounds of welding.

"How'd you know how I swing it, old man?" I yelled through the door.

"I have cameras, dipshit. What'd you bring me this time, your whole damn armory?"

"Nah." I leaned against the counter, eyeing all the new clutter accumulating in his shop. Guns and unique weapons were his favorite, which was why we got along so well, but he also had a bunch of taxidermy animals piled into one corner. Ornate glass bongs littered another shelf and decorative cigar boxes piled up in another.

"Whatcha got, then?"

"A few things," I called back dismissively. "Also a special request, of sorts."

The flash of sparks stopped, and I listened to his groans of exertion through the door as he got off his work stool. When the back door opened, a short, rotund man with frizzy gray hair circling the bald crown on his head peered up at me.

"Special request, eh? What're you damn Demons up to this time?" He shuffled over to his stool behind the counter, climbing up to meet at my eye level.

I pulled open the lid of my case. "Moving, for one. What'll it take for you to liquidate these for me?"

"Aww, Jesus, Gunner." Arty reached in and pulled out one of my vintage revolvers, the beautiful thing polished to a high shine and still in its hand-sewn leather holster. "Don't tell me you're getting rid of these? You're breaking my damn heart."

I raised both shoulders in a shrug. "Can't take it all with me. Keeping my favorites, though."

"Where y'all headed?" Arty began laying my once-glorious weapons collection out on the counter.

"Dunno yet." I scratched my forehead. "Wherever the hell we can go without starting a fucking turf war."

"I take it you'll need fuel, then? And ammo? Standard rounds?"

"That'll work."

He nodded, then peered up at me expectantly. "What was this about a special request?"

I pulled a knife from the hidden pocket in my cut and laid it on the counter, removing the sheath to show the carvings on the blade.

"You ever make jewelry, Art?"

"Jewelry?"

"Yeah, like for a woman." I ran an index finger along the flat side of the blade. "How hard would it be to make this into a pair of earrings and leave the carvings intact?"

Arty patted at his chest until he found his glasses in his shirt pocket. He put them low on the bridge of his nose, then picked up the weapon to inspect it carefully.

"Well, the blade is real silver. That'll make it easy to cut and shape."

"Cool, let's do that."

He looked at me shrewdly over the top of his glasses, mouth tightening into a frown. "Gunner, this knife is somewhere around five hundred years old. You could buy all your wildest fantasies with this thing, and you want it cut into earrings for *one* woman?"

"My wildest fantasies have all come true already," I grinned at him. "So you gonna do it or not?"

"You youngins," he groaned, pinching his shiny forehead. "Always thinkin' with your dicks."

"Honestly, it was never my favorite knife." I shrugged. "I would've thrown it in the box with the other stuff, but my girl likes it. Figured I'd make it into a little keepsake for her."

Arty just snorted, turning the blade over in his hands like it was a precious relic.

"So you gonna do it or not?" I asked him with a harder edge to my voice.

"Yeah, Gun. I got you," he sighed longingly.

"You've got plenty of weapons here to fawn over." I leaned both forearms down on the counter and snatched one of his pens and notepads. "Now here's what I'm thinking for the earring design."

————

WITH THE LOAD on my bike now twice as light, I made the ride home in half the time. I felt a lightness in my chest too, picturing Mari's face when I gave the earrings.

Knowingly or not, Reaper and Jandro set a precedent with their gifts to her. She only took off her necklace and ring in the bath or for work, and I wasn't about to be the odd man out that *didn't* have something for her to wear. I just hope that she liked what I came up with.

As the Steel Demon flag waved at me on the horizon, I sat upright, relaxed on my ride, taking one hand off the handlebars to rest at my hip. Only a few more runs to liquidate assets, and then I wouldn't have this homecoming view again.

For nearly four years, we had called this place home. I never expected it to be ours forever, but having to leave had crept up on us sooner than expected. And just when I found someone I could make a permanent home with.

The thought of Mari brought my hand back to the grip, the machine accelerating with a gentle thrust between my legs. After spending so much time pushing her away, I stuck to her like velcro now. I soaked up every beautiful laugh, sigh, and kiss, and then took every opportunity to fill her up with more. There was no undoing the hurt I caused her already, but I swore I'd never be a source of pain for her again.

Horus screeched above me, his shadow running

along the ground just to my left. As we approached the gate, I glanced up just as he dived. Wings folded back, he hurtled through the air, almost faster than my eye could follow. I squinted, watching him, and slowing the bike down as I met up with Benji at the front gate.

"Welcome back, captain. Your bird hunting?" He shielded his eyes as we watched Horus's missile-like form together.

"Shouldn't need to. He ate this morning."

I spotted Horus's target as soon as the words left my mouth—a black-feathered bird roughly the same size as him and nowhere near as fast. Panic stole my next breath as the realization hit me.

"Oh shit! Is that T-Bone's bird?"

"Sure as fuck is."

We both whirled around to find the Sons of Odin Sergeant at Arms staring at us through the gate. Unlike Benji or me however, he didn't seem at all concerned about his raven becoming a snack for my falcon.

Tattooed arms crossed as T-Bone leveled his gaze at Benji. "Mind if I have a word with your captain?"

The kid scurried away without a breath of argument. I wondered if he'd run to get Reaper or Jandro. If T-Bone was out for my blood, I wasn't about to go down without a fight.

He leaned in close to me, wrapping his hands around the wrought iron bars that separated us. "Haven't been inside your bird's skull in a bit, have ya?"

I bristled at the question, a knee-jerk reaction. I wasn't used to people knowing about my ability to see through Horus, much less meet someone who could do the same thing.

"I don't fly and ride," I huffed. "Been on the bike running errands all morning." My head cocked to the side. "You don't seem all that concerned, though. Confident your raven is still alive? It's been a minute."

A grin tugged at his lips. "See for yourself, Youngblood."

The dude was testing me. If his ability was anything like mine, he lost control of his body while seeing through his raven. He could stab me through the gate right now if I *saw for myself.*

Except for the few times Horus seemed to pull my consciousness into him himself, which I had no control over, I only looked through him when alone or with those I trusted most.

I still didn't know T-Bone from Adam, but he and his two fellow Sons proved to be trustworthy at every opportunity so far. The Sons of Odin killed my uncle—something he deserved, but I'd probably never have the balls to do—after he violated their contract and kept them prisoner. They stopped a drone attack on us, then allowed themselves to be detained, tied up, and questioned by us. All the while, dealing with the loss of their clubhouse to a fire that spared no one.

So even my skeptical ass was willing to put a tiny bit of trust in T-Bone's hands.

My eyes rolled back, my consciousness leaving my body as easily as a breath. The next thing I saw was the entire compound from five hundred feet in the air.

I was light as air and just as free. No dead prey in my

talons weighed me down. A black blur caught my eye and then Horus was diving again.

No, don't kill that bird! I yelled silently as the wind rushed past my feathers.

Horus ignored me, zeroing in on the raven like a target-locked missile. The bird cawed and beat its wings hard, but it was no match for the sky's fastest predator.

Stop! Stop!

My, our, *his*, talons stretched out, wings spreading out to brake hard. One more second and those glossy black feathers would be in our reach.

Ah—fuck!

At the last possible moment, Horus twisted in midair. We veered off course, wings spread wide and floating on the momentum. Chirps and screeches left my beak, Horus's happy sounds. The raven followed me, cackling as we began to fly in tandem.

Like a slingshot, my awareness slammed back into my human body. I grabbed onto the gate for support through the vertigo, blinking my eyes rapidly while T-Bone looked at me expectantly.

"They're…playing," I breathed, when I finally found my feet under me.

"Like a couple of kids on the playground," T-Bone chuckled. "What do ya make of that?"

"I think," I grinned back, "you should open this damn gate and I'll pour you a drink."

MARIPOSA

"What in the fucking hell is this shit?" Jandro's voice floated all the way through the house from the backyard. "Foghorn, what the fuck did you do?"

Sitting together at his home tattoo station, Shadow and I exchanged a look. We could do that comfortably now, look at each other without that bolt of terror in his eyes or the apprehension in mine.

Everything to do with the tall, scarred man, from small talk to eye contact, was easier now. We went from no words exchanged, fear and distrust on both sides, to sitting comfortably in close proximity. As comfortable as one could be while receiving a tattoo, anyway.

The fear of crossing his tripwire-like boundaries had evaporated at some point, although I was still careful about touching him. I only did so when it was absolutely necessary. To be honest, it was more about me not feeding the simmering tension I felt in his presence than it was about making him uncomfortable.

The gentle pressure of his hand on my arm only exacerbated my blooming crush on him. It amazed me how he had no true awareness of how sweet he was. He inked the outline on me so carefully, dark brows knitted together in concentration. Even now, he asked several times if the pain was too much.

The Rod of Asclepius, an ancient symbol of medicine, on my arm was nowhere near as painful as the Demon covering the top half of my back. Plus, all my tattoo jitters disappeared the moment he first touched that needle to my skin. I cherished this new warm, friendly territory with him, and the age-old dilemma of potentially ruining the friendship if I pursued more, took over the forefront of my mind.

"I should probably see what that's all about," I said apologetically as Jandro cursed up another storm from the backyard, this time in Spanish.

"I think you better." Shadow's lips curved in the echo of a smile as he set his tattoo gun down. "We can stop there for today."

Looking down at the fresh black outline on my arm, I tried, and failed, to swallow my disappointment. "But we just got started."

"You're bleeding a little." He wiped gently at my sore, freshly inked skin, the contact stinging. His uncovered eye brightened as it returned to my face. "Had a bit to drink last night?"

I stared hard at him before breaking out into a grin. "What's this I hear? Are you *teasing* me, Shadow?"

"No. I never tease." Still, his lips quirked up again as

he taped a thin bandage to my arm. "I'll make sure to finish it before we move. But no drinking the day before."

He didn't cap it off with a *missy* or *young lady*, but the playful sternness in his voice said it all.

I bit back my laugh as I stood from his chair. "Whatever you say, boss."

He huffed, snapping off his gloves before organizing his supplies. "I'm not your boss."

"Hey so, uh..." I raked my hair back, feeling like I was thoroughly killing the mood as I lowered my voice to a near-whisper. "How are *you* doing with the whole drinking thing?"

His hands paused as he looked at me slowly. "Good, I think. I have a few with the guys now and then, but I've still cut way back."

"Still sleeping well?"

"Yes." His gaze dropped. "Thank you."

"Just checking on you." I resisted the urge to touch his massive shoulder as I scooted past him toward the backyard. Aside from starting my tattoo today, we'd had no physical contact since I cried into his chest outside of Andrea's house. "If I'm being too nosy, just let me know."

"You're not," he said, so softly I almost didn't hear before sliding open the back door.

"What's going on, *guapito*?"

Jandro was shirtless out in the direct sun, raking up chicken manure. I crossed my arms and gave him a piercing stare from the doorway. He *knew* I didn't want him pushing his range of movement, nor exposing his back to the sun, while his burns were still healing.

"I thought you were getting tattooed," he said, pointedly ignoring my glare.

"I thought you were following my care instructions," I retorted.

"Babe, look." He turned around, showing his back to me. "Am I high, or does this shit look almost fully healed?"

My mouth fell open at the sight of him, and I stepped off the porch to get a closer look.

The healing tissues were still tender and red in many areas, but the top layer of skin had definitely hardened in record time. None of his muscles or deeper skin layers were exposed to the elements anymore. He'd have a large burn scar covering most of his back, but I'd never seen such accelerated healing in my life.

Wait, yes I had.

Hades, back at the Sandia outpost after I pulled the shrapnel from his flank.

"Do you feel this?" I poked Jandro between his shoulder blades.

"Ah. Little tender, but yeah."

"What about here?" I poked two more spots on his back and received the same confirmation. Without warning, I slapped his fine ass so hard that my palm stung.

"Ow!" He rubbed the spot I hit, spinning around to face me. "What'd I do?"

"Your nerves have reconnected!" I laughed, grabbing his face and reaching up on tip-toes to smack a kiss on his lips. "You didn't have any feeling in those places when I touched them two days ago."

"Well, shit." He returned my grin, pulling me in by the waist for another kiss. "My girl fixed me up good, huh?"

"Not me," I shook my head. "It's all your body. This healing is ridiculously fast. You're at least two weeks ahead of where you should be."

We looked down at the same time to find Freyja winding around our ankles. She met our eyes with a green gaze, bumping her forehead against Jandro's shin with a loud purr as she weaved her body between our legs in a figure-eight pattern.

"After my narrow brush with death," Jandro's forehead slid against mine, "I'm not about to question things that are supposed to be impossible."

"Someone's watching out for us," I agreed, nudging the black cat with my foot.

"A few someones." Jandro rolled his shoulders back, then his head around his neck. "Still feels weird, though. Like I'm a snake in a new skin."

"That's basically what it is," I said. "I'm amazed you didn't need skin grafts. You should still keep it covered when out in the sun and moisturize—"

"I know, bossy medic," he chuckled. "I just came out for a couple minutes. I felt like a caged rat inside all the time."

"So what were you yelling about earlier?" I asked. "I could hear you all the way from inside the house."

His cheerful face fell into a scowl that I barely recognized on him. "Come look at this."

He led me to the chicken coop, which he'd built out of scraps from his auto shop and leftover lumber soon after bringing the birds home. It wouldn't win any beauty contests, but, knowing him, it was solidly built.

Foghorn, the rooster, and two of the hens, I think Leti and Chela, milled about outside the coop. As Jandro approached, Foghorn stuck his neck out and crowed loudly at him.

"Yeah, I got my eye on you, cocksucker," Jandro pointed at him. "I know what you did."

"What the hell?" I followed Jandro around to the back of the coop. "Did he hurt one of them?"

"No, worse." He leaned down and opened one of the nesting box doors. "Look!"

The third hen sat in a clean nest of hay. Nothing seemed unusual until Jandro reached in and pushed some of her feathers aside.

"Oh my God!" My hands pressed to my chest as I saw four tiny beaks and beady, dark eyes peering out from under the mother hen. "Baby chicks! Jandro, they're so cute!"

"They're gonna grow up and multiply," he groaned, slapping a hand to his face. "Not thrilled about transporting more animals as we move, but I guess we'll have more to eat soon."

"What?" I stared at him in horror. "No! They're your pets!"

"Mari, we're gonna end up with a flock of five-hundred if we don't do something."

"Then get the eggs as soon as they're laid. It's not Foghorn's fault, he's just going off of instinct."

"Yeah, it is," he muttered. "Damn cock fertilizing my eggs."

I snorted, earning a sheepish grin from him. "That came out wrong."

"Sure it did." I patted his arm. "Congratulations on the new babies, *papi* Jandro."

"It's not me, it's that motherfucker!" He pointed accusingly through the coop to Foghorn on the other side, strutting around proudly like the pimp he was.

"What are you gonna name them?" One of the chicks wandered out from under its mother, and I reached out to pet its fuzzy down feathers.

"I can't name them or else I'll get attached," he groaned, extending a finger to pet another one that emerged. "Seriously, we'll probably have to trade some of them for supplies while on the road, if you won't let me cook 'em."

"I guess that's better than watching them die with us," I sighed.

"You're already attached," he teased, pressing a kiss to the side of my head.

"How can I not be? They're so cute."

"Yeah, just wait 'til the males grow up and start competing with King Foghorn over here." Jandro rose to his feet, pulling me with him. "Guess I should let you get back to your tattoo."

"Shadow told me we'd pick it up another day," I sighed. "Those *anejos* last night thinned my blood enough to make me bleed during the inking."

"So?" Jandro lifted an eyebrow.

"He said no drinking the day before," I shrugged. "I assume it interferes with his work."

"Never heard him give anyone that stipulation before." Jandro scratched his head. "But whatever. What are you up to now?"

"I say we get you," I poked his chest, "back inside before you burn and undo all that healing."

"Hmm, now that you mention it." I heard the grin in his voice as I turned back toward the house, Jandro following me with his fingertips on my waist. "I haven't gotten anywhere near enough sexual healing."

I giggled while sliding the door open, his plush lips already teasing the back of my neck. "That is a bold-faced lie. You get all of that in spades."

"That's the thing, *mi Mariposita.*" His mouth skimmed from my neck to my ear. "I'll never get enough of you."

———

JANDRO WAS FAST ASLEEP a half-hour later, lulled into utter relaxation by me rubbing healing ointment into his back. He looked incredibly adorable hugging a pillow, lips parted slightly. I knew he'd never say it outright, but he seemed to relish his afternoon naps. He protested at first when I told him to take time off from the shop, but a sensual back rub with soothing balm shut him right up.

As luck would have it, the three remaining members of the Sons of Odin MC were competent bike mechanics and eager to make themselves useful. With the three of them helping out Slick and Larkan, Jandro wouldn't even fall behind on his work while he recovered.

I slipped out of the bedroom quietly, Freyja following me with a high tail and her loud purr still rumbling.

"Do I have you to thank for that?" I cocked my head toward Jandro's sleeping form as I closed the door softly behind me.

Which part, the healing or the deep sleep?

The warm, omniscient voice made me stop in my tracks. It came from no discernable direction, but stroked over every inch of my skin like a hug. *Oh, don't look so bug-eyed. You've heard me before.*

"Guess I wasn't really expecting an answer." My feet started moving again, heading downstairs with my companion cat goddess at my side. Shadow was nowhere to be seen, which left the whole bottom floor empty except for me and Freyja.

I answer when a question piques my interest enough. Which is more than what can be said for Hades. She ran ahead of me and jumped up on the couch. Despite the complete lack of human gestures, I knew it was an invitation to sit and have a conversation.

"I thought you and Hades were practically the same." I lowered to the couch, keeping a few feet of distance between me and the cat.

Goodness no, child! What ever gave you that idea?

"Jandro said," I frowned, "when he was...uncon-scious, that you and Hades talked to him. You both convinced him to keep fighting and not let go. And from what Reaper explained to me, you're both gods of death from different pantheons."

Did it feel weird to be speaking those words out loud as part of a conversation with an actual deity? Abso-fucking-lutely. Did I still care about how crazy and unexplainable this all seemed? Not in the slightest. In the months of my life with the Steel Demons, I had seen and experienced too much to write it off as anything else.

Hades and I represent different aspects of one of humanity's many mysteries—death. And that's where our similarities end. His culture made him masculine, a stern overlord of a dark, cold after-life, so that is the lens through which humanity perceives him.

"And how do we perceive you?" I asked.

The cat rolled onto her back, twisting her spine as she looked at me. I didn't *hear* laughter, but got the sense that she was amused.

You tell me, Freyja challenged.

I thought for a few moments. "Feminine," I began. "Nurturing, affectionate, independent."

Yes, go on. Say what's really on your mind.

I waffled over which adjectives to use. "Sensual. Loving."

Also sexual. The amusement bled through her voice. *And fertile. I represent the sacredness that is femininity. Both a woman's gentleness* and *her fierce strength.*

"That's why you were with Tessa," I realized. "You eased her pain and turned her baby while she was in labor."

I was always with her, Freyja said lightly. *As I was always with you. Just not always in this form. The gods are the tether that bind humanity into one universal existence.*

"So why are you here now?" I asked. "In a cat's body, with a voice? Why was I pulled to find you?"

Humanity is on the verge of breaking beyond repair, Freyja's voice turned solemn. *It is not just your civilization that has collapsed, but your collective spirit. To turn against each other as you have, you destroy yourselves. And if humans fall, so shall gods.*

THREE

SHADOW

I left the house silently before Mariposa made it to the backyard, closing the door behind me without a sound.

Her bleeding was a lame excuse to stop the tattoo, but there was no way I could tell her the real reason. Not that I *ever* wanted to stop. I made the Rod of Asclepius as large as she would allow me on her arm. Once finished, it would be a great piece with lots of detail.

I couldn't help but feel like a thief. Her smiles, her warmth, her time—none of it was meant for me. So I stole it. I wanted to steal every second she sat with me. The soft laughs and the glances, I collected every one and kept them tucked away in my memories like a dragon hoard. She may have thought she gave them to me willingly, but the fact remained that we were never meant to share anything between us.

She had three men who gave her everything she needed. I was never supposed to be the one who held her as she cried into my chest.

Hands shoved deep in my jeans pockets, I headed down the street toward the clubhouse while my fingers itched to wrap around a bottle and drink. When the urge came on strong like this, I knew the outcome would be one I'd regret. So I ignored the alluring thirst for numbness, bypassed the kitchen and headed for the stairwell.

It was the middle of the day, not anywhere close to sunset yet. But the first view of the sky from the roof eased the tight clamping in my chest just slightly. The air was cooler lately and I welcomed the chill on my skin.

I leaned over the balcony and allowed the breeze to blow my hair freely. No one could see me up here. It was one of the few places I didn't have to hide.

Around *her*, I wanted to hide everything. Everything that was wrong with me, I wanted to bury and shove away. Being around her made me feel like all my faults were on display, out in the open to shame me. I made sure to keep my facial scar hidden, and to speak at appropriate times. I never cared about being normal before. Now I wished for nothing else.

But at the same time, she made me feel normal—despite my freakishness being painfully obvious to me. I felt like I could grow an extra head and she would just smile and ask me how my morning was.

Her warmth and kindness shined an ugly spotlight on how fucked up my upbringing was. The pain from a blade slicing my skin used to be the only physical contact I ever knew. After touching her during a tattoo or our few brief hugs, my skin felt like it was starving for more contact.

I'd never felt anything remotely like that before, like I *needed* to feel the touch of another person.

Violence and alcohol used to be my drugs of choice. I kicked them, but found a new addiction in Mariposa, and couldn't begin to understand it.

Horus and the raven, Munin, circled each other in midair, diving and chasing each other. Watching them distracted me from my own thoughts, at least for the moment. Their aerial acrobatics must have done the trick, because I didn't even hear the Son of Odin walk up until he was right next to me.

My pulse shot up but I didn't react. Distracted or not, no one had been able to sneak up on me in a long time.

The silent man to my left was the one they called Grudge. His hair was pulled back into a ponytail at the base of his skull. The wiry whiskers of his beard nearly reached the top of his chest. I'd only ever seen Dallas with a beard that rivaled that one.

I gave him a nod of acknowledgment but otherwise ignored him. He kept his distance and seemed to be up here for the same reason I was—to get away from everybody else.

Commotion on the pool deck drew my attention below. Gunner and T-Bone walked up together from the front gate, talking and laughing. Those two seemed close lately, but Gunner was always good at making friends.

The smell of fry batter hit my nostrils. It was nearly lunch time, and we were trying to use up our perishable food before moving. If my senses were correct, fish tacos were the main menu item today.

Just as I was debating heading down for a bite, a nudge at my arm nearly startled me out of my skin. Fuck, I'd have to learn some things from this Grudge guy. I thought I was silent, but he took it to a whole new level.

Turning to face him, I saw that he held a small pad of paper out to me, which was what had touched my arm. Written across the paper were the words, *Sisters of Bathory?*

Fuck.

Fuck. Fuck. Fuck.

I felt like a child again as I stared at him, the shadows deep in my psyche rising up to darken the sky and sun that I found freedom in. It had been nearly a decade since I'd seen or heard the name of that community.

"You too?" My question came out a choked whisper.

Grudge gave a single, tight nod. He pointed at my arm, indicating my scars, then hovered that same finger in front of his face and opened his mouth.

The man had a small, moving muscle in his lower jaw toward the back of his throat, but nothing where his tongue should have been.

"Holy fucking shit."

He closed his mouth and nodded.

"But," I narrowed my eyes, "I was born there, and the only male they kept long-term. No one else survived. I would've remembered you."

Grudge quickly wrote across his notepad, *NV, outside of Old Vegas. You?*

"Here in Arizona," I answered. "I don't know

where, exactly. The community got invaded by the National Guard and they sent me to a mental health ward at a prison."

"Hm-hm-hm!"

Grudge seemed to be laughing, but it was hard to tell from the limited amount of sound he could make. He pointed his pen at me, then at the notepad to ensure I was watching. Slowly, he wrote the word *COMMU-NITY* in large, all capital letters across a fresh sheet of paper. Then he took the pen in his fist and dragged it through the word, making deep black lines across the letters.

He dragged the pen back and forth until the word could barely be seen underneath. Then underneath, he slowly wrote the word *CULT*.

"I know," I sighed. "Trust me, I'm still catching on to how fucked up they were. Especially after finding a brotherhood like this." I allowed myself a small smile. It was getting easier to do. "I guess we lucked out in some ways, Grudge. I didn't even know Bathory had other locations."

He nodded and flipped to a fresh page in his notepad. *Nothing wrong with your "mental health", yeah?*

"No," I shook my head. "I don't understand a lot of things, but nothing's wrong with my brain. The medic hasn't given me pills for that, at least."

Grudge made his odd chuckling sound again. *Medic's pretty. Yours, too?*

"No, she's not mine." Tightness enveloped my chest and throat in a painful grip. "She's the president's, VP's, and Gunner's, who you've met."

You two are close.

"We're…friends." The word felt strange in my mouth, but I knew it would be the one Mariposa used to describe us. "She's the only woman I'm comfortable around. You know, considering…"

I trailed off, no need to elaborate. Grudge nodded to show that he understood. I could barely wrap my head around the fact that another man had been subjected to the same life as me, and lived to talk about it.

"How did you get out?"

It was the first question that left my mouth, although dozens more piled up in my brain. He couldn't have been a blood bag like me, but why else would they keep a male alive? Why remove his tongue? Grudge wasn't all scarred up like me, but my torturers never felt the need to silence me. I had a feeling they enjoyed my screams, and had become dissatisfied when I stopped feeling pain, stopped reacting to anything they did.

They would never kill me, so a big reason for my silence was to spite them.

Grudge chuckled again, the pen in his hand moving quickly. *A longer story than I got paper for. T and D can tell you, though.*

"They're good men, huh?" I asked. "Helped you make sense of the outside world? Made you feel more normal, useful, like you had choices and a purpose?"

"Mm." Grudge nodded sharply. *Learned what trust meant. Loyalty. Respect. Being a person.*

"Being in a brotherhood," I agreed.

He laughed again and continued writing. *Wouldn't call 'em my brothers. Love them, but not like that.*

I looked at him. "I'm not sure what you mean."

Smirking, he huffed out an amused breath. *We're brothers like you and the medic are "friends".*

"I don't *lov*—" My mouth clamped shut as my face burned. I couldn't even bring myself to say that alien word.

No, that definitely wasn't why the need for her touch had replaced my drinking habit. I was just a shell of a man, trading one vice for another to escape the past. It definitely wasn't the reason I purposely ended her tattoo sessions early, just to ensure I'd see her again. I was nothing but a thief, stealing time and attention from a woman who would never be mine.

Grudge gave me a knowing look. *Tell her how you feel.*

"There's nothing to tell." I shook my head. "Even if there was, she has *three* men. All of which know how to actually be with a woman."

You a cherry?

"No," I sighed. "Just service girls, that's it." *And her, who I was never supposed to have.* "I know what hole I'm supposed to go in, but nothing beyond that."

"Hmm." Grudge just stroked his beard as he smiled at me, laughing at some internal joke I wasn't privy to. *Some advice?*

I shrugged. Whatever he wanted to tell me wouldn't apply to my situation, as nothing would ever happen between me and Mariposa. But being able to listen and relate to someone who'd been through what I had was not likely to happen again in my lifetime. He understood me. And in my situation, that was incredibly rare.

He thought for a moment before returning to his notepad. *Be yourself. Don't hide who you are. Not even from her.*

The bitter scoff left my mouth before I could contain it.

"I appreciate it, Grudge. But I still have no idea who that person is."

FOUR

MARIPOSA

I stared at the cat long enough for her to grow bored of me and begin grooming herself.

"So we're on the brink of a full-fledged apocalypse, huh?"

Yes. Not exactly the nuclear meltdown your fictional stories presented, is it? Freyja's tail flicked. *Although the political unrest and slaughter of citizens is not far off.*

"So where do you come in?" I asked. "Have the gods come to save us?"

Oh, we were always here. You just stopped listening. She yawned, revealing more teeth than I ever remembered seeing in a cat's mouth. *As for the saving business, that's on you to do yourselves.*

"Then why *are* you here?"

To remind you. Her sharp, feline gaze returned to my face. *Me, specifically, I'm here to fuel the love stories. I'm the magic you feel in the smiles of children. The celebration of life. I'm here to kindle the flames of desire, to accelerate that muscle beating in your chest. I'm here to remind humanity of the beautiful vulnerability that happens when you give yourself to another. And when a life ends due to a selfless act of love, I reveal my true form and guide that soul to peace.*

I sank into the couch, small moments with my men over the last few months flickering through my mind like a highlight reel. Everything, from a sweet touch and tender words spoken, to the roughness and heat that my body craved with the most primal desires.

"So how many thanks for my three-way love life do I owe you?"

None. An amused chuckle laced the goddess's voice. *I only steer with gentle guidance. I do not manufacture what is already there. The success of your relationships has everything to do with your compatibility, and the strength of your human hearts. However,* Freyja walked across the couch to me, bumping my hand with her forehead, *I sense some resistance in regards to a certain tattoo artist.*

"Shadow?" His name burst out of me so loudly that I straightened up and looked around to make sure he was really gone.

The sexual attraction is palpable. Your care and affection toward each other is clear. You have clearance to take another lover. So what stops you? She lowered to her belly next to me, tucking her front paws in toward each other as she stared at me expectantly.

How to explain why I didn't pursue a man who nearly drank himself to death to avoid nightmares? Who, when he *did* have nightmares, was uncontrollably violent to the point of needing to be locked in his room?

The answer seemed obvious when putting his most glaring flaws at the front and center of my mind. But I couldn't ignore what the medic in me knew—those flaws were only symptoms, not the cause.

Even thinking of him purely as a patient, without feelings clouding my judgment, I knew kindness and compassion were the best measures to counteract the root cause of his issues. To be treated as a person and not something *other.* He just needed practice and exposure to forge new neural pathways in his brain—pathways that told him women were just people too. That we weren't so different.

What Shadow *didn't* need was me selfishly projecting my own desires onto him. Of course I was attracted to him on a deep, primal level, but as his medic, I was also responsible for his well-being. To pursue things physically or romantically, especially while he was healing and still learning social norms, would only be looking out for *myself.*

"I don't want to scare him." It seemed to be the easiest way to sum up my feelings to Freyja. "His trauma with women runs deep and I don't want to trigger anything that could set him back."

His ability to adapt is stronger than you give him credit for. The cat goddess almost sounded like she was chastising me. *You don't need to be a god to see that he doesn't associate you with his painful past.*

"I don't even know if he likes me like that," I said. "He's easy to be around in just a normal context, but I have no idea what's going on in his head."

He doesn't know how to express his desires, because these desires are not something he's ever felt before.

My eyebrows lifted. "So he does like me?" I felt like a teenage girl gossiping with a friend.

Your presence soothes him. He finds comfort in you. He's finding it easier to communicate in general, now that he's realizing he won't be punished simply for existing.

A twisting pain rolled through my chest. "What happened to him?"

The cat blinked slowly at me.

That man has wounds only love can heal.

I STEPPED out to Jandro's front porch after that bizarre conversation, then turned to close the door behind me. Freyja acted completely normal, so nothing alerted me to the figure behind me until I felt arms wrap tightly around my waist and throat.

"Break my hold, baby girl." Gunner's warm breath tickled my ear.

"And slam you straight into this door?"

"Well, pretend to."

I tapped the side of his knee with my boot, just hard enough for him to feel, then drove my elbow back toward his gut before surging my weight forward. He followed my momentum, catapulting over me until he slapped a palm against the door.

"Nice job!" His smile beamed through the hair in front of his face before he raked it back. "You're getting faster, babe. Don't forget, you can also swing a fist down to hit 'em in the crotch. That might be more effective than the elbow."

"I'll try it next time," I grinned coyly, running my hands up his shoulders. "Thanks for the warning," I directed down at Freyja.

She stared back at me, then began licking a paw.

"Your kitty's smart, she knows I gotta train you to react on your feet." Gunner's hands laced at my lower back.

"Mm-hm, I'm sure that's what it is." I gazed up at him, playing with the hair at his collar. "Where's Horus?"

His sunshine-bright smile nearly split his face. "I'm glad you asked. He's doing an errand for me."

"An errand?"

"Let's go to the pool." He slid his grip from my waist to my hands, tugging me in the direction of the clubhouse.

"Gun," I started to whine, but followed him nonetheless. "It's getting too cold to swim."

The fall and winter months seemed to get colder every year in the Southwest. Back in Texas, I hadn't noticed much of a difference in climate, but in recent weeks I felt the humidity creeping up, which seemed unusual for Arizona. Maybe it had to do with the oceans being closer than they were fifty years ago.

"We're not going swimming, baby girl." He tugged me to his side, throwing the arm with our laced hands over my shoulder. "What we are doing is making a dent in the booze and perishables to lighten our load for when we move."

"I can't drink too much," I protested, "Or I'll bleed through my tattoo session and piss Shadow off."

Gunner's sky-blue eyes narrowed at me. "Since when does Shadow care about a little blood during a tattoo? I bled like hell through mine. Hell, I'm pretty sure I was drinking *during* my session."

"You're the second person to ask that question," I muttered. "Anyway, what's this errand Horus is doing for you?"

"You'll see." The wily grin never left his face. "You hungry? They're frying up fish tacos to use the last of the stuff."

"I am, actually."

Jandro and I hadn't had our usual lunch dates together since he got injured. Most of my time was spent tending to his burn and making sure he rested enough.

Freyja ran ahead when we reached the pool deck, and I could quickly see why. Hades had his back to us, sitting like a good boy, looking up at Reaper for a piece of food. After moving in closely behind tables and chairs, and then some strategic butt-wiggling, she pounced on him.

Hades yelped and whipped around, but she had already taken off to hide under one of the couches. Reaper saw the whole thing and laughed so hard he nearly choked and started coughing.

"Careful, or you'll need mouth-to-mouth," I said as Gunner and I walked up.

"Are you suggesting I shove things down the wrong pipe more often?" The president cleared his throat and grinned lazily as he drew me into his lap on the deck chair. "Hey, old lady."

"Hey, old man." I circled my arms around his neck, curling up against the hard planes of his body. "Chew your food or I'll look at getting you a set of dentures."

"Watch your mouth or I'll put something in there to keep you quiet," he returned, low and rumbling, with his thumb on my lower lip.

I melted like an ice cream cone under the sun. No one else could get away with talking to me like that. It would be crude, disrespectful, annoying, and definitely *not* hot. But coming from Reaper, the quiet threat of dominance revved me up like the roar of his bike.

And he knew it. The delighted hum from his chest was like a purr as he placed a smoldering kiss at the corner of my jaw.

"Gunner's up to something," I mumbled the first thing to pop into my flustered brain.

"I know."

We both watched the blond demon make his way through the taco line, piling fixings onto a plate of tortillas while grinning and chatting with the others milling about the patio. He and T-Bone seemed particularly chummy today.

"Are you in on his scheme?" I dragged my fingers along Reaper's scalp, admiring how my ring caught the sunlight through the dark strands.

"Nope," he chuckled, picking up his whiskey from the side table. "But he's got a shitty poker face. He's grinning bigger and dopier than usual."

I let out a frustrated groan and nuzzled my forehead into the side of his neck.

"How's Jandro?" Reaper's fingers skimmed across my back in a hypnotic pattern.

"Good. Better than good, even." I lifted my head to look at him in the eye. "He's healed super fast, weeks ahead of schedule."

"Like Hades did."

I nodded. "That, I still can't explain. But I think Freyja being around helped this time." I blew out a breath. "Not that that's a real, medical explanation."

"It might be. Just not one that you're satisfied with, medic." Reaper's teasing expression turned thoughtful. "So we might be able to move sooner than we thought. We're liquidating shit fast enough." He chuckled at my whining groan. "I know, sugar. But the sooner we're out of here, the safer we'll be, away from Tash's eyes."

"Have you decided where we'll go?"

His mouth tensed. "Still working on that part."

I rested my head on his shoulder again, my fingers running over his chest in a way that I hoped was comforting. Gunner meandered back to us after a few moments of quiet. He held a plate out to me, then quickly pulled it out of reach when Reaper made a grab for it.

"I was gonna give it to her," Reaper laughed.

"Like fuck you were." Gunner stayed out of arm's reach, then jerked his chin at me. "Come here and let me feed you, baby girl."

I smiled against Reaper's neck and kissed him there before standing up. "Can't say no to that."

"Get, woman." He swatted my ass and stood after

me, heading toward the kitchen, presumably to refill his drink.

Gunner laughed lightly with a small shake of his head. "Still throws me for a loop."

"What?" I followed him to a small table near the pool, just outside the overhang.

"That the president's girl is also my girl," he grinned. "And he doesn't want to slice my dick off and feed it to me over you."

"And you're still okay with seeing us together?" Reaper warned me that Gunner might need some extra reassurance about our relationship, considering he was resistant to the idea for so long and wasn't familiar with a multi-person dynamic.

"More than okay." Gunner squeezed my knee under the table. "I thought it would be harder, like I'd have to figure out how to tolerate it. But I actually really like seeing you with them."

"You do?" I folded up my tortilla around its filling and took a cautious bite of my overfilled taco.

"Yeah, it's like Jandro said," he mused thoughtfully. "It's weird how *not* weird it is. I just love seeing you happy and taken care of. And when you're with me—" His eyes flicked away from my face for a moment, then back to me. "It doesn't diminish anything between us. When we're together, it feels like I'm the only guy in your life."

"Aww, Gun." I reached for his face, leaning over the table to kiss him just as a screech and a whoosh of air warned me to duck my head.

"Shit, Horus!"

Gun pushed his chair back to the sounds of thumps and ruffling feathers. I looked up to see that Horus had crash-landed on one of the couches, and everyone on the patio had ceased their conversations to see what had happened.

"Is he okay?" I rushed over to where Gunner had picked him up and inspected his wings.

"Yeah, he's fine." He looked sheepishly at me. "I guess he didn't expect you to touch me right then. It's hard enough grabbing onto my shoulder with only one foot."

I stared at him. "Why would he grab you with one foot?"

Gunner looked down at the bird on his lap, now seeming nervous. Everyone was still staring. "Because," he sighed, "he was supposed to land on my shoulder and then hand you this." He lifted Horus to show that the falcon held a small box in his talons.

A jewelry box.

A giddy laugh escaped me as I gently took the box from those fearsome claws. "This was his errand?"

"Yeah," Gunner frowned. "Tried to have it all planned out and romantic—"

I leaned in, kissing him to the sound of whistles and cheers from our spectators. "You're the sweetest man ever. Thank you."

His smile touched mine, one hand reaching up to stroke my cheek. "You haven't even seen what I got you."

"Doesn't matter." I kissed him again. "You're still the

sweetest." His face was flushed, throat working nervously as I sat back and opened the lid on the box.

"Gunner!" I gasped and looked up at him with my mouth open. "Are you serious? Are these…"

"From the dagger on my wall, yeah." He swallowed again. "It didn't mean that much to me, was too old to be used as an actual weapon. But I knew you liked it, so—"

This time, he saw the kiss coming. My ears recognized Reaper's sharp whistle, the only hint that there was a world outside of my gunman's beautiful smile.

"They're perfect." Both of us were smiling too hard to really kiss properly.

"Put 'em on," he whispered, his grin reaching up to his sky-blue eyes.

The earrings were shaped like two daggers, the sharp end pointing down with a slight curve like the original weapon they came from. The silver had been polished to an almost mirror-like finish, while the carvings had been etched and blackened to show them more clearly.

It felt like putting on a unique kind of armor as I slipped the hooks into my earlobes. I realized the gifts of each of my men represented the nature of my relationship with them. Gunner helped me find my own strength. Jandro filled my life with laughter and color. And Reaper's devotion promised I was never alone.

"They look amazing on you." Gunner's eyes moved from my ears to the butterfly necklace at my throat, his gaze then lowering to rest at the ring on my finger. "All of it does. It's a complete set."

"Because I'm completely yours." I was all but crawling over him now, him leaning so far back he was nearly reclining on the sofa. "I love you." I made sure to say it low enough that none of our audience could hear.

His grin, however, was telling enough. "Love you so much, baby girl."

My next kiss did send him lying back, Horus squirming to get out from between us. Gunner grabbed my upper arms to pull me closer, and a throbbing pain shot up to my right shoulder.

"Ow!"

"Shit, sorry." He released the bandage covering my newest tattoo. "Forgot that was there for a second."

"It's okay."

The ache throbbing up my arm was a stark reminder of Shadow, how the tattoos were his own, unique kind of gift. Not in the same way as my guys, but…

I pushed the thought away and melted deeper into Gunner's kiss.

REAPER

The maps in front of me blurred into meaningless squiggles and lines. I rubbed my eyes, leaning back in my chair with a groan. Trying to decide on a route for the whole club was tedious enough, but after a full belly of tacos and maybe a *little* too much whiskey, working on anything was a chore.

I couldn't help that last drink though, not after seeing Mari and Gunner all wrapped up in each other. Before giving her my ring, I thought about having Hades give it to her. Although entertaining to watch, that crash-landing by Horus made me feel good about my decision *not* to have animals involved in my proposal.

In any case, I was glad to see that Gunner had fully embraced his place at Mari's side, symbolizing his devotion with a gift in the same vein as me and Jandro. An extra celebratory drink was the only logical thing to do.

Celebrating could never last, as I knew all too well. Mari went to check on Jandro and bring him food, Gunner rode off to liquidate more supplies, and I came back here to my study. To stare at fucking maps again, and try to guess the least dangerous route through the desert, to some unclaimed place we could settle. Away from General Tash and his spies.

Naturally, I'd rather be doing just about anything else. So when a knock came to my study door, I welcomed the distraction. Hades, in a food coma of his own, barely acknowledged the sound—just an ear twitch from his sprawled out position in the dog bed next to my desk. At least I knew whoever was at the door posed no threat.

"Come in," I called.

The door swung open and I regarded my visitor with cool indifference from across the room.

"Prospect," I greeted, refusing to address Larkan by his name. "What can I do for you?"

"President," he returned just as coolly. "Mind if I sit?"

I gestured to the armchair across from my desk and watched him stride over to it. The kid was not lacking in confidence, I'd give him that. It was him who gave us the information that Tash turned against us. I thought he was just a rat at first, flipping on his employers in the hopes we'd spare his life. It turned out, he was an accomplished marksman and bike mechanic, and had wanted to become a Steel Demon since he heard about us nearly a decade ago.

I was man enough to admit my first impression was wrong, and we took him on as a prospect. If he continued being loyal to us, he might even become a fine

Demon one day. Only when Larkan sat down did I notice the nervous swallowing of his throat.

"President," he began. "I know I haven't been with this club long, but I want you to know you have my steadfast loyalty and respect—"

"Skip the ass-kissing, prospect." I waved my hand in a *move along* motion. "Just tell me what you need."

His throat worked again, Adam's apple bobbing as he swallowed his nerves.

"I came to ask your permission to make Noelle my old lady."

My gut feeling told me this was about my sister, but I felt no victory at being proven right. Instead, I felt the heat of my temper curling under my skin, shaping my hand into a fist. I beat Larkan's ass at the last Fight Night for being too damn handsy with my sister, and the fucking kid just seemed eager for more.

"No."

He had the gall to look confused. "No?"

"I'll be clearer—absolutely fucking not."

Larkan sucked in a breath, his own hands curling into fists at his sides as he fought to control his own temper.

"With all due respect, Reap—president, I love her."

"I'm sure you do." I reached for my cigarettes and stuck one in my mouth. "I don't give a shit."

"President, I—" He stopped himself and tried again. "I'm not new to this. I've been committed to a woman before, faithfully. I have and will continue to treat her well. I'm not the kind of guy who will—"

"I'm sure you're a fine man, Larkan," I said. "I'm not

refusing on the basis of your character, but on the simple fact that you're just a prospect, and she's the president's sister. By club law, you're not worthy of her. Not until you're a fully patched-in member."

Knowing better than to argue, his lips clamped shut while I lit my cigarette. In all honesty, I had no doubt he'd be a full-fledged Demon within a year. The right time to patch him in would be at my discretion, sometimes preceded by nomination from one of the other guys. But he would only receive that honor if he breathed and bled Steel Demon loyalty, not because he was in love with my sister.

"Was there anything else you needed?"

Larkan sighed, unclenching his fists on his knees. "I was hoping you might be willing to look past club politics and see what really matters."

"Keep talking along those lines," I pulled the cigarette from my mouth and pointed at him with it, "and I guarantee you'll never earn a fucking patch. You've got some big, heavy-swinging balls to come in here asking *me* to circumvent the laws of *my* club."

"Noelle wants this too." Larkan's jaw set, hard and determined. "We've talked about this and want to be together, officially."

"And you know why she's not here?" I didn't give him a chance to answer. "Because she's not a fucking fool. She already knew what I would say. Let me guess," I paused for another drag off my smoke, "she tried to talk you out of coming to see me. Told you it was a bad fucking idea."

His face told me everything without having to say a word.

"If you really love my sister," I said, not bothering to hide my smugness, "you might want to listen to her more." I tapped my cigarette over the ashtray. "You can leave now."

He walked out without a word, and moments later I was stubbing out my smoke and rubbing my eyes while groaning again.

I needed space. Open road and fresh air. Sitting here would just keep me stewing over young punks who wanted what they hadn't earned yet. After sparing Larkan's life, giving him a home, and an opportunity too. Thinking any more about his ungrateful ass would leave me sour for the rest of the day if I didn't do something.

Hades' ears perked up as I scraped my chair back noisily. He got up from the dog bed with a few lazy stretches and followed me out of the study and into the garage.

I hit the button to open the garage door, and turned the ignition on my favorite steed as light from the outside world filled the room. I didn't notice the booted feet standing in my driveway until the garage door was waist-high. At first, I thought Larkan was still hovering around and squared up toward the door. If he didn't get the message with words, I'd teach him another lesson with my fists. At this point, I didn't care about waiting for the next Fight Night.

But the garage door continued rolling up to reveal one of the Sons of Odin standing on the other side.

"Dyno." I lowered my fists cautiously to my sides. "What are you doing here?"

"President." The tall, slender man noticed my stance and did not appear the least bit threatened. "I was on my way over for a quick word, but looks like you're heading out."

"Seems I'm popular today," I sighed, walking toward him so as to not yell over my bike idling. "What do you need?"

"Just to say thank you, and uh, apologize." He scratched one side of his shaved head, a few dark strands coming loose from the topknot at his crown. "I didn't appreciate your men tying us up, nor you keeping us locked in a room for three days, but I understand your caution. And aside from that, you've been a very generous and hospitable host. So, I thank you and I'm sorry for my earlier remarks." He stuck his hand out and waited.

After a moment to collect myself from the surprise, I clasped his palm in mine and shook it firmly. Now there was another lesson in respect that Larkan could afford to learn.

"Apology accepted." I released Dyno's hand and crossed my arms as a thought came to me. "You got anywhere to be right now?"

"Ah, no." He looked puzzled. "Why?"

I jerked my head toward my rumbling steed in the garage. "Ride with me."

"Me?" He raised a hand to his chest. "You're sure, president?"

"I was gonna go alone to clear my head, but

someone with a fresh perspective might be even better." I shrugged and turned toward my bike. "Come or not. S'up to you."

Five minutes later, I was roaring out the front gate with Hades at my side and Dyno right behind me. For a moment, I regretted not dragging Mari out with me. The sun was just starting to lower, casting long shadows and bathing everything in a golden light. The sky would explode into colors in a few short hours, before being swallowed by dusk.

I thought of how I woke up in bed that morning, the first thing I saw was her turning her hand over as she admired my ring.

"Still like it?" I had murmured groggily.

"Of course I do." She looked over at me with a sleepy smile. "I love it."

"Still love me?"

She pursed her lips together and her look became playfully stern. "What do you think?"

"I don't know." I pulled the sheet back and rolled over, tucking her beneath me where she fit so perfectly. "Tell me," I whispered, kissing my favorite spots to elicit those soft sighs and giggles. "Show me."

"I love you, Rory," she told me with the sweetest whimpers while we did serious damage to the head-board this morning.

It was hard to believe I'd have a lifetime of those mornings ahead of me. Plus a lifetime of sunset rides to take with her, my wife. As long as I found my club some-where safe to resettle.

That last thought was sobering, like a face full of ice

cold water. I leaned forward on my bike, accelerating hard, knowing Hades and Dyno would stay with me.

The three of us cut across the landscape, leaving a trail of dust behind. Originally I didn't have a destination in mind, but with Dyno joining, I led our small, merry band to my favorite place to think.

A half-hour of riding took us to a ridge overlooking what was once the Hopi Indian reservation. We cut our engines, the silence of the land swallowing the roars of our bikes. Dyno looked over the ridge, his foot on a boulder as I poured water for Hades from my canteen.

"Did you realize our old clubhouse was on Hopi land?" he asked.

"Suppose I didn't," I muttered, joining him to look over the expanse of red rock down below.

"Here, the markers are obvious." He pointed out the stone dwellings that remained of the tribal homes. "But when you ride up directly from the south, everything on that end's been destroyed."

"How does that work, having a Norse-devoted MC on tribal land?"

Dyno shifted his gaze toward me. "The Hopi were never a warring tribe. They were peaceful, harmonious." He released a scoff. "Guess it doesn't really matter. Most of them fled or were killed when General Tash rolled through."

"You grew up on the reservation," I realized.

"My mother's family was Hopi," he replied. "Our clubhouse used to be a visitor's center for tourists. Our president, Bash, and T-Bone, suggested it so my home with the club would be near my ancestors."

His throat worked, jaw clenching as his gaze jerked back to the landscape.

"I'm sorry for what happened," I said. "That's just further proof that Tash is right outside our door, and we've got to get our people to safety."

Dyno sucked in a shaky breath and nodded, quickly composing himself.

"Four Corners is your best bet," he said. "There's not much there yet. You'll be living rougher than you do now, but it's well-defended and safe."

"And people have rights?" I asked skeptically. "No slave labor? Human trafficking?"

"That shit's strictly forbidden. If you're worried about your women and kids, you don't have to be. Governor Vance runs a tight ship, but he's fair. The Sons can vouch for him personally."

"It's not that I don't believe you. I'm just reluctant to trust anyone with enough power to call themselves a governor. Or a general, for that matter."

"We know Governor Vance's general too. He was a border war conscript who escaped his assignment, and now serves Vance willingly to keep the peace."

"Hmm," I mused, scratching Hades' ears. "I'll believe it when I see it."

"So you'll go?" Dyno's eyes brightened with curiosity, hands resting on his belt buckle.

"I'll pitch it to the club at church. This is something we should vote on." I cocked my head at him. "You and your boys are welcome to sit in and make your case. There will be questions, I'm sure."

"We'll be there." Dyno looked out to the stretch of

desert once again. "If you all do this, you'll have to go around the reservation, up into Utah. We know the area pretty well and can scout ahead for you."

"And what about when we show up at Four Corners' door?" I asked. "Is the benevolent governor going to welcome us with open arms? Somehow I doubt that."

"We'll vouch for you, too," Dyno assured me. "We've done dozens, if not hundreds, of contract jobs for Vance. He's solid. He doesn't have any preconceived notions about MCs like some rich folks do." Dyno clapped a hand on my shoulder. "Once he sees how well you look after your people, I don't think he'll have any issue letting you stay."

"It'll be temporary," I reminded him. "Until we find someplace permanent, that's ours alone."

An eyebrow lifted. "When do you think that'll happen?"

I lifted my water canteen to my lips. "When General Tash is wiped off the map."

SIX

MARIPOSA

I fumbled blindly in the dark, woken up by my bladder screaming at me to be emptied. Reaper's chest was usually a solid wall behind me, but tonight it wasn't there at all. Carefully maneuvering around Gunner and Jandro, loosely piled around on the mattress, I made it to the bathroom in time.

After finishing my business, I paused, standing next to the bed and allowed my eyes to adjust to the darkness. Jandro and Gunner both splayed out on their stomachs, their back muscles rising and falling with their steady breaths. As tempting as it was to fall back asleep in the cuddle pile, I felt a nagging need to know where Reaper was.

I found him on the balcony just off of the master bedroom, leaning over the railing wearing only his jeans, and a cloud of cigarette smoke surrounding him. But he wasn't alone—Freyja and Hades lounged on the floor nearby. Neither of them looked surprised as I shrugged a robe on and pulled it closed around my waist. Reaper's head cocked at the sound of my bare feet padding over to him.

"What are you doing up, sugar?" he asked, his voice rough.

"Got up to pee and saw you were missing." I slid a hand along his lower back and he lifted an arm to tuck me into his side. "What are you three doing?" Freyja's tail flicked playfully, and Hades padded over to lick my hand.

"I think these two are just making sure my dumbass doesn't fall over the railing," he laughed dryly.

"What are you doing, then?" I laced my fingers with his hand draped over my shoulder.

"What you all said I should do." The words came out softly as a whisper, but with a bite of frustration. "Trying to let my brother in so we can talk."

I squeezed his hand. "And?"

"Nothing," he growled. "I think Daren's given up on me. Or more likely, I'm a fucking idiot for trying to talk to a dead man."

You are not truly letting him in. Freyja's voice hit us both at the same time. *You are allowing your doubts to create barriers.*

"I *am* trying, okay?" Reaper grumbled. "Of course I have doubts. I haven't talked to my brother since he fucking *died* in my arms."

Would it help to remind you that death is not an end? Freyja rubbed her head against Reaper's leg. *It's a transformation. A new chapter for the soul. Daren isn't gone. He's on a different plane of existence.*

"Sounds like a bunch of horse shit to me."

This is what I'm talking about. Freyja's voice seemed to sigh with exasperation.

"Well, what are you doing out here?" I ran a hand up his back, fingers digging into the knots of his muscles. "Noelle said he comes to her in dreams."

"According to them," Reaper's hand flung out to indicate the animals with us, "I should talk to him while I'm awake, to let him know I'm listening. He's supposed to respond in my dreams after I go back to sleep."

"And nothing?"

He shook his head. "I've been having a bitch of a time falling asleep as it is, with the move, Dallas, everything. So I keep coming up here to clear my head, get shit off my chest, and—"

His arm tightened around me with a sigh. "There's so much I want to say to him, but it feels stuck. It's not that I doubt him being out there, but everything I say feels forced. Like I'm fucking faking it, 'cause I am."

"You're too hard on yourself." I brought our linked hands to my lips and kissed the back of his palm.

"I'm not hard enough, sugar." He squeezed me harder with the confession. "Dallas died within our own walls. That never should have happened."

"There was nothing you could have done. You had no way of knowing what would happen." I leaned my weight into his side. "No wonder Daren can't get through, your mind is all over the place. You're not focusing, love, except to blame yourself."

"One of the things I do best," he grumbled.

I released our hands and moved in front of him,

blocking his view of the compound and surrounding desert as I looped my arms around his neck.

"Come back to bed." I lifted onto my tiptoes and pressed a kiss to his frowning mouth.

"I probably shouldn't. I'll just keep you and the guys up with my tossing and turning."

"No, you won't." I traced his collarbone in the dark, my finger following the length of bone to the hollow of his throat. "If you don't fight me for once, and relax."

Even in the dark I saw his smirk, and a soft huff of breath left his mouth. "What are you scheming, sugar?"

"I'm good at following your rules when you set them." My finger dragged slowly between his pecs. "Now I'm asking you to follow mine."

"And what rules do you have for me?" His voice turned husky as my hand drifted down his abs to rest at the waistband of his jeans.

"To relax." My thumb flicked at the button on his pants. "To lie back and let me do everything that *I* want to you."

"Hmm." Heavy, calloused fingers pushed my hair aside to caress my neck and shoulder.

"And when I'm done with you?"

"Yes?" he mused, thumb on my lip.

"You will go right to sleep. No touching me or getting me off."

"Not fuckin' happening, sugar."

"Reaper, come on." Only while arguing with him, attempting to assert myself and take control, would I find myself pleading. "You need to sleep. You need just a few hours of having *nothing* run through your mind."

"Maybe, but I ain't about to be a damn pillow prince to get it."

"Just tonight," I begged, rubbing my palm shamelessly against the front of his jeans. He was getting thick and hard with each passing second, so I knew he wasn't completely opposed to the idea. "Let me take care of *you* for once."

His head tilted up, facing the star-filled night sky as he blew out a breath. "Fine."

"Oh yeah?" I wrapped my arms around his waist, bringing my chest to his. "I thought for sure you'd take more convincing than that."

"Don't push your luck, sugar." He tapped a finger to my nose. "Or I might change my mind."

I could have skipped with giddiness as I led him back inside. A smile stretched across my face, but I bit my lip to halt any noises tempted to escape. Our sneaky footsteps to the bed, and Jandro and Gunner's deep breaths, were the only sounds in the room.

Careful to avoid the two sleeping men, Reaper sat on the edge of the bed and pulled me roughly into his lap.

"Hey!" I whispered harshly. "This wasn't the deal. I call the shots, remember?"

"Just let me kiss you first." His mouth was already dragging a fiery trail along the side of my neck. "And let me take this off."

He reached for the lapel of my robe, aiming to slide it off my shoulder, when I grabbed his hand. "No. I see what you're doing, *Rory*."

"What?" He feigned innocence, but his shoulders

shook with the laughter he kept inside. "You want to please me. I'm pleased by seeing you naked."

"You're trying to be sneaky." I pulled on his bottom lip with my teeth. "*I'm* doing the seducing here, not you. Now lay back."

"Damn bossy wife," he sighed while my insides turned to jello at hearing him call me that. But he obeyed, lacing his fingers behind his head as his back hit the mattress between Jandro and Gunner, somehow still passed out. "Go ahead, have your way with me."

I remained straddling his thighs, loosening the robe so the sleeves fell just past my shoulders. Most of my chest and the swells of my breasts were visible, the lapels making a long V down to my navel. Reaper tried to look passive, but I could feel how his eyes watched me, cloaked in darkness with only slivers of light. Leaning over his stretched-out torso, I kissed him full of tongue and heat, while pinning his wrists in place—a wordless reminder not to touch me.

He groaned softly into my mouth, hips shifting beneath me, but otherwise remained still. My kisses trailed down his neck, moving leisurely over the lines of ink swirling across his chest. I held onto his wrists until my reach was fully extended, with my mouth near his navel. As I moved lower, my hands mapped down his body where my lips had just been.

I felt him hot and pulsing against my cheek by the time my fingers reached his zipper. As I started pulling it down, planting kisses on his hip bones and lower stomach, his caress of my arms had me yanking the zipper back up.

"No touching," I whispered.

"Fuck, sorry." He placed his hands back under his head. "Feels wrong not to touch you."

"Be quiet or you'll wake them."

"Yeah, yeah."

I unzipped him again and worked his jeans down his legs, watching the tension in his face and how his arms flexed with restraint. For a moment, I considered binding his wrists with his belt, but not even I had the patience to go without touching and tasting him for too long.

His cock rested on his lower stomach, angling to the left as I kneaded his thighs. My thumbs moved in steadily toward his balls, massaging all around his base without touching him directly.

"Sugar, please…"

A grin split my face as I leaned down, lips hovering over his stiff length. "Hm, I like hearing you beg." How many times before had he told me the same thing? Payback was sweet.

Reaper let out a growl of frustration, tilting his head back toward the far wall. I would have bet anything his fingers were curled into a white knuckle grip on his hair. Only then did I give him any relief.

I dragged my tongue in a long, slow trail, starting at his balls. His shaft pulsed under my tongue, smooth skin over concrete hardness, growing hot at the contact. When I reached the base of his crown he sucked in a sharp hiss, then moaned as my lips slid over him and took him within.

I circled my tongue around his head first, my hand wrapping around his base to assist. My other hand wandered up and down his body shamelessly, if even cruelly. Just feeling my man, the way his breath stuttered, how his muscles bunched and stretched in response to my touch, gave me pleasure too. I was still getting so much out of this, even while focusing on him. But I could see how much difficulty he had in not touching me in return.

"*Fuck*, Mari…"

My mouth slid down his shaft now, swallowing his head as my hand worked him from the bottom.

"Sugar, let me kiss you. Please."

I slid my free hand up his chest, finding his lips with my fingers as I continued dragging my mouth up and down his cock. He kissed my hand like a man dying of thirst, desperate to lick and nibble at any part of me that he could reach.

"Can I touch you with my hands? Please?"

"Mm-mm." I shook my head no as I pulled my fingers away from his mouth. Releasing his dick with a pop of my lips, I glided both hands along his shaft, now coated with my saliva. "Was this your plan? Go along with me, then beg to get your way? You're not as resilient as I thought, Mr. President."

"I have no resolve at all when it comes to you." His breaths were ragged, voice taut with the tension winding up in his body.

"You always need to be in control." I planted a small kiss on his hip. "Relax and let go for a little bit."

"I can't *not* reciprocate when you're doing that to

me. I'm going fucking crazy here, I have to please you too."

"Trust me." I ran a palm up his body again, lowering my mouth to lick at his crown again. "I am pleased."

"Ugh, not enough," he groaned as my lips sealed around him again.

With my head down and mouth at work, I paid no mind to the movement on the bed, figuring he was just squirming and thrashing as I sucked more of his thick length down my throat. When a hand grabbed my breast, I released him with a gasp of air. Ready to scold him again, I blinked with surprise in the darkness to see Reaper's hands still clasped behind his head. But he wore a cocky smirk, and the two sleeping bodies of Jandro and Gunner were no longer sprawled on the mattress.

A familiar pair of soft, pillowy lips dragged a kiss along my neck. "Put that dick back in your mouth, *bonita*," Jandro murmured as his hand found its way inside my robe.

"You traitor," I whimpered, my nipples aching as he rolled them between his fingers.

"What? You didn't want *him* to touch you, so he's not." He leaned in, his head nearly resting on Reaper's leg, to suck the sensitive peak into his mouth.

Before I could protest, the cool breeze of someone lifting my robe from behind sent a shiver wracking through me. Gunner let out an appreciative hum as his skilled hands roamed my backside. He kneaded the back of my thighs, cupped my ass, and then I felt his mouth press against the hot molten core between my legs. All three guys seemed to revel in the satisfaction of my moan that followed.

"This is so not fair," I complained, while pushing my hips back into Gunner's face at the same time.

"Do we look like we care?" Jandro dragged kisses alongside my ribs, his palm smoothing over my spine.

Gunner hummed his agreement, grabbing the sides of my ass as he buried his face in my pussy. I was already slick from playing with Reaper, now my golden man's skilled tongue was dangerously close to getting me off first.

"You seem a tad distracted, sugar." Reaper cupped my chin in his hand, his grin still cocky. "I thought you wanted to please me."

I stroked him from base to tip, squeezing his hard flesh. "How did you plot this out?"

"I didn't, I swear." He was terrible at looking inno-cent. "They woke up and saw what was happening. I can't control what they do."

"Uh…huh."

My noise of skepticism came out more like a moan. Gunner had just inserted a finger into me, his thumb rolling across my clit while his mouth continued to do magical things to my pussy. Jandro started kissing the nape of my neck, his hands still sweeping across my waist and breasts.

"Gonna finish what you started?"

I glared at Reaper. "Shut up and put your hands back where they were."

"Yes, ma'am," he grinned.

"You move a single finger, I'm stopping entirely." It was an empty threat. Infuriating as he was sometimes, he never left me unsatisfied. And he knew I would never leave him blue-balled.

"Mm, sure," he chuckled.

I descended on him again, taking him deeper down my throat than I had yet so far. With the other two awake now, there was no point in staying quiet. My head bobbed and my hips rolled, moaning loudly with every stroke of Gunner's fingers inside me.

"Holy fuck." Reaper's hips bucked underneath me. Jandro pulled back my hair as his teeth dragged over my earlobes and neck.

My stifled moans grew whining and desperate as pleasure coiled up tightly in my core. I made wet sucking sounds with my mouth as well as my pussy, Gunner hitting the perfect spot over and over, as Jandro teased all my nerve endings into a frenzy.

"Oh yes, yes, yes," came the husky whisper behind me. "Come for us, baby girl. You're so close."

I closed around his fingers in a rushing, sudden release. The convulsions of my orgasm rolled over me in hot waves just as Reaper spilled into my mouth.

"Fuckkk," he panted, fingers curling in my hair as I swallowed, squeezed his balls, and pumped my hand to drain him. I didn't even care that his hands were free now.

Gunner lapped me up, just as I did to Reaper, until we were a sweaty, panting pile at the foot of the bed. Jandro was the first to scoot back up to where he was sleeping and pulled me with him.

"Goodnight, bonita," he whispered with a fast kiss to my lips, then arranged his pillows for sleeping on his stomach.

Gunner slid up behind me, tilting my face to plant a kiss on my forehead. "Goodnight, baby girl."

"Night, guys." My eyelids were already drooping, searching for Reaper before I completely passed out.

He laid right in the middle, hands rested on his chest with his mouth parted softly. Deep, even breaths became gentle snores.

I crawled over to lay a soft kiss on his forehead before whispering, "Good night, my love."

JANDRO

"Tell me this. How the shit does he expect me to pack up a whole damn bike shop and fit it in the bed of a pickup truck?"

Shadow bent over his desk in the corner of the room. He didn't reply and likely hadn't even heard me, deep in drawing some tattoo design. It didn't really matter, I was just venting and talking to no one in particular.

"So we've unanimously voted on Four Corners, but aren't making it a permanent stop until we scope the place out. Fair enough. I understand we might be continuing on to fuck-knows-where and we gotta pack light for the road. But where does Reaper expect me to store all my tools and shit? And on top of that, I've got like a dozen chickens to pack now!"

A grunt floated over from the desk.

"He asked if I can bring the lift! The fuckin' two-ton hydraulic lift that took us three days to get here from down the road! Like sure, I'd love to hold on to that thing, but are you fucking kidding me?"

"So don't bring it," Shadow muttered distractedly. "We'll prop bikes up on blocks like before if we need to."

"That's what I'm saying! Reaper's all," I lowered my voice and added a growl to imitate him, "Oh, don't over-pack, bring just the essentials, like all the fuckin' machinery in the shop and my fuckin' mahogany coffee table."

"He didn't say anything about a coffee table."

"I know, man. I'm just picturing him trying to load that thing onto his bike as a taste of his own medicine. I bet he would too, he stole that out of some governor's office."

Shadow's shoulders shook with a light chuckle, but he otherwise remained steadfast on whatever he was working on. I didn't like to hover over his tattoo work, but curiosity got the best of me and I walked up to lean against his desk. He stopped immediately, straightening up with a stiff back, but didn't try to hide the design.

"Still tweaking Mari's design, huh?"

He had four separate sketches of her Rod of Asceplius arm piece, each the same base design with slightly different variations. One had smoke and flames billowing out from behind the snake. Another had the snake and staff emerging from a rose with a small butterfly on the petal.

"I just keep getting different ideas," he shrugged. "I want to make sure she gets something she likes."

"Like you do with all your clients?"

"Yes."

"Shadow." I cocked my head, giving him an intent look.

"What?"

"Bro, I saw your line work after her bandage came off. She was hardly bleeding at all."

"Yeah, well, I just didn't want to—"

"Come on, dude. Be straight with me." I crossed my arms. "I'm not mad. I know you two are on friendlier terms now. But is it more than that? Do you *want* it to be?"

He met my eyes for the first time since starting the conversation, and I was surprised to see it wasn't the confused, deer-in-headlights look when I usually asked him an uncomfortable question.

"I don't know," he admitted. "I don't know if that's what I want, what she wants, or even if I did know, what that would feel like."

"You like her, though."

He nodded carefully. "I like being around her. I enjoy it when she's here and it feels…strange when you're all at Reaper's house."

"You miss her," I said, the realization becoming clear. "You…long for her when she's not around."

"I…I think that's what it is, yes."

I released a sigh, lowering my head to pinch my brow. On one hand, I was glad to learn Shadow felt something toward a woman besides fear, resentment, and defensiveness. He was miles ahead of where he was just a few months ago, and it was all Mariposa's doing.

On the other hand, why did *she* have to be the first woman he developed feelings for?

I wanted the big dude to be happy, to have good experiences with women, but he was still years behind the curve emotionally. He'd make mistakes, like we all did, back when we were young dumbasses chasing girls for the first time. And I didn't want Mari to deal with any of that. She deserved better than that.

Maybe after a few years, when he got some real experience under his belt and had some time to mature, we could see about bringing him in our relationship. That was of course, assuming Mari felt the same way. Not to mention *if* Shadow would be able to handle a multi-person relationship. Gunner never had any trouble charming women and he almost missed out because of his own biases.

"I won't *do* anything, Jandro," Shadow said in a voice that was almost pleading. "I know what's off-limits and I'm not crossing that line. Really, what I enjoy most is talking to her."

That was exactly what I was afraid of. He was more emotionally attached to her than physically. I couldn't pinpoint what concerned me more, the emotional intimacy developing between them, or the physical act that had already happened—the proverbial elephant in the room.

"I trust you, man. I really do," I said. "But she's *my* woman and I'm feeling this protective…shit right now. Like my hackles are raised, but I can't pinpoint why. You won't hurt her physically, I know that. I believe that you won't touch her. And I'm not opposed to y'all becoming friends, I'm just…" I scratched at an itch on my chest, scrambling for words that got the point across, but weren't cruel. "I'm concerned about your lack of experience, I think is what I'm trying to say."

Shadow's posture didn't change, but I sensed the deflation in him, like air out of a balloon. His attention returned to the sketches at his desk.

"I understand. I'll finish her tattoo, and then I won't take up any more of her time."

"Dude, I care about you," I sighed. "And you've been doing great at being more social and all. But I love her, and—"

"You don't need to explain, I get it. I'm still behind in those areas. It's not fair to you, the other guys, or Mariposa. I won't overstep."

"I'm not saying *never*, you know. I'm jus—"

"It's okay. I'd like to finish this now, if you don't mind."

"Sure, yeah," I sighed. "Guess I gotta see about getting a lift hooked up to someone's truck."

With that, I took my leave, not feeling any better about getting that off my chest. If anything, I felt like an even bigger asshole.

MARIPOSA

"Good morning, Shadow!"

"Good morning, Mariposa."

I frowned a little. Shadow seemed distracted. He was getting better at eye contact and some semblance of a smile when we greeted each other lately, but today he mumbled it all while turned away, clearing his desk for tattooing.

He was the second man today who'd apparently got up on the wrong side of the bed. Reaper had slept well, but woke up in a foul mood. Three more nights had passed with no dreams or any contact from Daren, and he was getting frustrated. Seemingly satisfied that they'd given him enough guidance, the gods had also gone silent.

Freyja wriggled out of my arms to dart over to her favorite person, headbutting Shadow's leg hard before winding all around him like a furry black rope.

"Hi, Freyja."

He reached down with one hand to give her a

cursory pet along her back, but she wasn't having that. She jumped into his lap and got between his arms as she lifted onto her hind legs. Her front paws rested on his chest as she rubbed her cheeks on his neck and chin, purring up a storm.

"Just when I thought you couldn't get any more clingy," I sighed, taking Shadow's other seat. "Let the man work."

"I don't mind."

He never did. Setting his tattoo machine down, he curled his fingers into Freyja's fur on the sides of her neck. She stretched up higher, leaning her head back for more of his touch and undivided attention. Shadow huffed out a chuckle at her reaction and scratched her more vigorously.

I'm getting jealous of a cat, I realized, watching from my chair.

Touch was such an uneasy subject with him. Coaxing him into speaking to me, treating me like any normal person, was one thing. But physical contact could go from harmless and platonic to so much more. A wandering hand during a hug could easily turn into something else. Freyja said he needed love to heal, but was escalating touch okay to do? As much as the physical chemistry crackled from my end, I didn't want to do anything that confused him, or worse, that was unwanted.

He placed Freyja on the floor and, apparently satisfied with her daily Shadow fix, she shook out her fur and walked off with her tail high.

"I didn't have a single drink yesterday," I told him with a playful tilt of my head. "I hope you're proud."

He nodded, but otherwise didn't tease back like he did at our last session. "Ready?" he asked me with a shy glance.

"Yep." I forced a smile, shoved down the feeling of rejection, and scooted my chair closer. The heat from his large body seemed to engulf me even though I was still a couple of feet away. Or maybe that was the battery for his tattoo machine.

"I, um, came up with a few more background ideas, if you'd like to see."

He seemed nervous today, and I wondered if something happened. Did he accidentally say or do something that Jandro had to correct?

I waited until his gaze met mine and gave him my best reassuring smile. "Hell yes, I do. I always want to see your ideas."

His shoulders softened a little and he opened up his sketchbook to a spread showing variations of my Rod of Asceplius piece.

"Oh, wow." I scooted closer and leaned over until I was sitting right alongside him. My eyes bounced all over the pages. "I don't know what to choose."

"You don't have to choose any," Shadow murmured softly. "We can always fill the background in later—um, fuck!"

"What?" I snapped my gaze to look at him, brow pinched and jaw clenched. "Something wrong?"

"No, sorry. I, um…" He sat back, rubbing his forehead and teeth grinding in obvious distress. After a quick breath, his eyes flashed open, focusing on me for the first time that day. "If that's what *you* want. Getting the background filled in later, I mean. Only if you *want* to get tattooed by me again later."

"I mean, I can probably decide today after a minute to think." I watched his body language with curiosity. He seemed conflicted about something. "But I definitely want to get tattooed by you again. Why wouldn't I?" I smiled again, it seemed to make him feel better. "You're my favorite artist."

"I'm your only artist so far. You do have other options, you know."

"Why would I go to anyone else? I like *you*."

Three simple words that didn't hold nearly as much power as *I love you*, but in this context they felt heavily weighted all the same. My heart sped up and I wondered if Shadow picked up on the multiple meanings of those words. I liked his art, and I liked *him*.

"This doesn't bother you?" he asked. "Spending so much time with me?"

The question made me lean back in shock. "Of course not, Shadow. Why—" I stopped myself from demanding an explanation from him, reminding myself how outcast he'd been all his life, and still was.

He wasn't used to people spending extended time around him, and didn't need to explain his feelings of otherness to me. I realized he needed to *unlearn* what he'd always known and start at a new baseline— having a friend who simply enjoyed spending time with him.

"I like just sitting with you. Talking to you," I said. "I

love the tattoos, but honestly, I'd sit and chat with you while doing nothing."

"You *would?*"

"Yeah. We can just have coffee and let Freyja climb all over you. We can talk about books, the weather, whatever we want."

"What would your men think about that?"

I crossed one knee over the other, folding my hands in my lap. "I think they respect me enough to let me talk to, and form friendships with, whoever I damn well please."

The color deepened in his cheeks. "I just don't want to make anyone uncomfortable. Or put strain on your relationships with them because of…"

What we did.

His words trailed off, but I knew exactly what he referred to. My cross-legged position tightened at the memory of him filling and stretching me, the way he watched me as if hypnotized, but otherwise never touched me.

Heat flooded my skin, bringing a rush of sensitivity to the surface. My pulse pounded in my lips, gaze falling to the large hands still wrapped around his tattoo machine.

"See, I've made you uncomfortable already," he said, his voice pained.

"No," I said in a rush of breath, my throat tightening. "You haven't. I…" I raked my hand back through my hair, for a moment wondering how truly inappropriate it would be to run over to Reaper, get his approval, then run back and hop on Shadow right then.

"Whatever comes up between me and the guys is on us to work through," I said. "What, um, *happened*, was acknowledged and moved on from. I won't deny that it's awkward," I added with a forced laugh. "But we can't undo it. We can just move forward. And I'd like to do that by being your friend, Shadow."

I had told him this before. But like most people facing trauma, he needed gentle reminders of safety. He needed to know that I genuinely wanted this, and wasn't just giving empty promises.

Did he need to know about my ever doubling-in-size crush on him, and ridiculous sexual attraction? That was still up for debate. And putting my own desires aside for a strong, foundational friendship that made him feel safe, could only be a good thing.

"I…would like that with you, too." His eyes flicked to my face before adding hesitantly, "as long as it doesn't cause any problems. I don't just mean with your men, but I know I'm still learning socially—"

"Shadow, you have more social grace and tact than *many* people I know." I leaned forward and, after a moment's hesitation, placed a hand over his. "As far as I'm concerned, you're not behind socially on anything. You watch people, you learn and adapt. Considering we're in a *motorcycle club*, I'm a bit shocked you're as well-mannered as you are."

"You think I'm well-mannered?"

"You *are*," I laughed lightly. "There's no thinking about it. I've never heard you say anything rude or in bad taste. Your mood is more even-keeled than Reaper, and you've definitely never stuck your foot in your mouth like Jandro or Gunner."

He stared at my hand on top of his, dwarfed by his large palm. With the tiniest, hesitant movement, his thumb lifted to brush over the edge of my wrist. "No one's ever told me anything like that before."

I fought down the urge to touch more of him, keeping my hand still as I smiled. "That's what I'm here for."

"It's like…" He trailed off again, leaning back in his seat as he began to slide his hands out from under mine.

"Tell me," I urged through the ache in my chest as I sensed him retreating. "Don't be afraid to express yourself, Shadow. I *want* to know what you're thinking. This is just between us."

He touched the tips of his fingers together, resting his forearms on his thighs. With a deep breath, he began again.

"Everyone is always telling me I'm improving. I'm doing better. I've come so far." He swallowed. "Which is nice, I guess. But all of that implies that I'm still not good enough. I'm not there yet. I'm not *normal* yet." His fingers laced together. "Like you said, I keep watching people to make sure I'm not being weird. I read psychology, history, all of that, to learn how normal people behave. I exhaust myself trying to remember everything, only to keep hearing the same things. 'You're doing better, Shadow. You've improved so much.' You're the first person to tell me that—" He pulled in another breath, this one shakier, as he looked at me. "That I'm already good enough."

I leaned into him, my hands finding their way to his again, fingers nestling into wide palms that were surprisingly soft. If he didn't hiss in a breath of surprise at the contact, I can't say that I wouldn't have kissed him.

"You *are* good enough," I breathed, lips inches away from his. "As you are, right now. There is absolutely *nothing* wrong with you, Shadow."

His gaze dipped lower to our conjoined hands, moving his lips further away, but his forehead touched softly to mine. Slowly, his fingers unlaced from each other and closed around mine, thumbs rubbing down the backs of my palms.

"Thank you, Mariposa."

"You can call me Mari, you know."

"I like saying your full name." There it was, that glint of humor and personality dying to come out. "Saying longer words helps me practice speaking."

"You're a natural at it already." I leaned away and he released our hands.

His touch felt like it remained on my skin and I wondered if that moment felt anywhere near as intimate to him as it did to me.

"So." The confidence in him had returned, eyes bright and hints of a smile on his face as he turned back to the sketches on his desk. "Did any of these appeal to you? Or did you want something different?"

Biting back my own grin at his lifted mood, I leaned over his desk again. "Hmm, I kind of like this background," I pointed at a sketch with swirling smoke behind the snake, "and this kind of detail on the scales. Can you combine them?"

"Of course. That's easy."

I sat back in my chair, trying not to beam too hard as Shadow held my arm steady while he cleaned my already-started tattoo with an alcohol wipe. He didn't hesitate in touching me this time and I hoped that would only continue.

For his own comfort, not for your thirsty ass, I reminded myself.

We sat together in companionable silence as he worked on me, much like my first tattoo. I enjoyed this with him too. With my three guys, everyone was always chattering on about something. I'd almost forgotten how comfortable silence could be, too.

"Can I ask you a medical question?" Shadow said—completely unprompted—when my line work was done and he prepared the colored inks for the scales of my snake.

"Shoot," I answered.

"I guess I'm wondering," he mused, "if there's a medical reason why I can't feel pain."

"Ah." I tilted my gaze up toward the ceiling to ponder. "Most likely there is. Is it everywhere on your body, or just certain areas?"

"Yes, everywhere."

"All types of pain?"

"Um, yes. I think so."

"That tells me it's neurological," I said. "Your brain shut off the signals from those nerves for some reason, probably to protect you in some way."

He finished pouring the small pots of ink and turned to me, looking unsure of himself again.

"Something wrong?" I asked.

"I only feel it during those nightmares," he confessed. "I feel everything vividly. But while I'm awake, I only feel my skin coming apart, the blood spilling. All of the other sensations, but never *pain*."

"It sounds to me like your brain is trying to process your past trauma when you're asleep. And the feeling of pain is closely linked to that. But when you're awake, it gets buried again, to protect you."

"Protect me from what?" he muttered with a frustrated growl that was oddly adorable. "If it weren't for those pills you gave me, everyone would have to be protected *from* me."

"This isn't my area of expertise," I admitted. "But in simplest terms, when people confront their trauma before they're ready, it can make things worse. They can become depressed, harm themselves, or attempt to take their own lives. So sometimes the brain sort of locks traumatic memories away to prevent that from happening."

"I remember everything that happened to me," Shadow said. "And I can remember what pain feels like, if I focus on it. I just...wonder why it left and never came back."

"I don't have an answer for that." I looked at him sympathetically. "I'm sorry."

"That's okay." He returned to tattooing me, the buzz of his machine filling the silence between us.

"Maybe not right away, but at some point," I said softly, "you might want to talk to someone about what happened to you."

"No," he shook his head. "I don't like thinking about it, much less talking about it."

"I don't know if it would bring the pain sensation back, but the sleeping pills are only a band-aid on your nightmares."

"They work for me."

"They won't forever," I insisted gently. "You'll develop a tolerance, and another bad habit, if you're not careful. But if you want the nightmares to go away for good, you have to work *through* what's causing them."

Shadow paused to set his machine down and wipe away the excess ink on my arm. "I just want to move on. My past isn't something I ever want to return to." His gaze flicked up to mine for a moment. "The present is so much better."

NINE

MARIPOSA

"What a shame to have to leave this all behind."
I walked around Reaper's study as if noticing
it for the first time. Glass cases held mementos and arti-
facts like elk antlers, a skull carved out of quartz, and
motorcycle parts. A heavy, wooden bookshelf held maps
and weathered volumes.

"It's just stuff." Reaper moved behind me, fingertips
skimming over my waist. "It can all be replaced." He
pulled a slim, leather-bound journal from the shelf and
tossed it onto his desk. "We'll need that. All the Steel
Demon MC laws are in there."

"Have you made copies?" I opened the cover to find
an ink drawing of the Demon grinning up at me from
the title page. Shadow's work, most likely.

I traced the horns with a finger, picturing Shadow
bent over this book as he sketched the symbol of his one
place of belonging.

"Hard to do these days," Reaper sighed. "Can't
find a fucking copy machine in working order

anywhere, let alone a camera or a scanner. Jandro started copying it by hand, but got bored of that quickly."

I chuckled at the thought. "He just needs something complex, like a puzzle or an engine to keep him stimulated."

"Yeah, I don't blame him. No one is exactly lining up to volunteer. Gotta keep the book safe in the meantime."

I moved to the closed wooden box on his desk, running my hand over the varnished lid. "What's in here?"

Reaper cleared his throat and placed his hand next to mine on the lid. "My mom's journal, plus a few of her gemstones and other jewelry pieces." His hand moved to cover mine, squeezing gently around my fingers. "I still haven't brought myself to read it."

I pressed a kiss to his cheek, wrapping my free hand around his bicep. "She might want it back from you someday."

"That's what I tell myself, even though it sounds delusional," he said. "I feel like if I open it, I'm admitting that she's gone and all I'm reading are memories of her."

I turned to face him, sliding my arms around his neck. "You're a good son to keep hoping," I said. "And to hold on to her things."

He reached for my hand again, gazing at me with such warmth and love as his thumb caressed over my ring.

"I've never touched anything in that box since

Noelle and I left that place," he whispered. "Not until I knew I had to give you this."

The kiss that followed was cut short by a soft knock at the open study door.

"Yes?" he barked.

"Um, is this a bad time?"

"Tessa!" I untangled myself from Reaper and rushed over to let her in. "Of course not. Come in and let me hold that baby!"

She sent a bashful smile in Reaper's direction before holding her daughter out to me.

"Oh yes, come here, little lady!" I took her gingerly, supporting her head. "Did you decide on a name?"

"Vivian," Tessa beamed. "Aiden, my oldest, picked it out. We're calling her Vivi."

"Well, you're awfully calm, Miss Vivi." I watched her wide, blue eyes move around the study. "Not giving your mama any trouble, are you?"

"She's really good, actually," Tessa admitted. "Easier than my two boys were, by a mile."

"I gotta say, sugar," Reaper leaned over me to look at Vivi, resting his chin on my shoulder, "You look good with a baby in your arms."

"Yeah, right," I huffed. "Right before a massive move, perfect time to get pregnant."

"I actually wanted to talk to you, president." Tessa lowered her eyes meekly. "About, um, a family matter."

Reaper straightened, peering at her shrewdly. "What's going on?"

"Should I leave?" I asked, looking between both of them. "I'll watch the baby while you two talk."

"No it's alright, Mari." Tessa clasped her hands nervously in front of her. "Please stay. I'm glad you're here, actually."

"Do you want to sit down?" Reaper turned the armchair facing his desk toward her. When she nodded and accepted the seat, he knelt next to her. "What's on your mind, Tessa?"

Her eyes flicked to me for a moment before returning to my husband. "I want to separate from Big G."

I couldn't say I was surprised, but took in a sharp breath all the same.

"Has he hurt you?" Reaper asked. "Or the kids?"

"No, not physically, anyway." Tessa looked at me again. "I think you know this has been building for a while, but it all kind of came to a head last night."

"What happened?" I held Vivi against my shoulder as she sucked on her fist.

"I've been spending a lot of time with Andrea," Tessa explained. "You know, just helping out while she grieves. Big G wasn't happy about being left alone with the boys for longer than usual. So I started bringing them with me to hang out with Andrea's kids, and to give him a break. Then G got mad about none of us being home."

"Fucking Christ," Reaper grumbled.

"I was going to bring dinner over to her last night and, um," she swallowed, "he wouldn't let us leave the house."

"Oh my God, Tess." I went to stand next to her, rubbing her arm and shoulder as I looked at

Reaper. "That's awful. He can't be allowed to do that."

"He started screaming at me in front of the kids," Tessa's voice shook. "Blocking the doorway. He didn't touch me, but I was *scared*."

Reaper took one of her hands between his, as though trying to calm the tremors running through her. "Would you be alright with living at Andrea's for a while?"

Her eyes widened, blinking like she couldn't believe what she was hearing. "Um, yes. Yes, I would. She was even asking if I wanted to stay in one of her spare rooms…"

"I'll have Gunner and some of his guys move your things from Big G's house. The kids, too. Only the essentials, though. Whatever you're taking with you on the move."

"And," she breathed, "what about after we're moved?"

"That'll depend on where we end up," Reaper sighed. "But I'll keep guys posted on you if you feel unsafe. No one will force you to be near him, if you don't want that."

"He will want time with the kids, though," I pointed out. "And as much as I hate to admit it, he has a right to."

"I'm not even thinking that far ahead." Tessa rubbed her forehead. "I just want some fucking *space* for a couple weeks. To help my friend. To remind him of what it's like to *not* have me there doing everything."

"You have our support," Reaper assured her. "No

matter what you decide. Whether you're with him or not, you're one of our own, Tessa. You're raising three baby Demons, after all."

"In more ways than one," she muttered, then gave Reaper a relieved smile. "Thank you, Reaper. Honestly, I wasn't sure how this was going to go."

"This is the first time it's happened in the club," he admitted. "But it's not right for him to scare you and trap you in your house. I don't think any of the guys would disagree."

Tessa rose from the chair and held her arms out to take Vivi back from me. "Again, thank you."

"Go on straight to Andrea's," Reaper said. "I'll have Gunner and his guys escort you back to gather your things."

She nodded and left the study quietly, with a small smile back at me. Reaper and I just stood there for a moment, sitting with the weight of what she told us.

I broke the silence after a heavy few seconds. "Are you going to do anything to Big G?"

"I'll talk to him." Reaper rounded his desk in search of his cigarettes and lighter.

I stared at him. "That's it?"

"What do you want me to do, sugar? She said he didn't put hands on her. He was acting like an asshole. Guess what, he *is* an asshole. That's not news to anyone." He stuck the black cigarette in his mouth, but didn't light it, choosing to flick his Zippo open and closed instead. "Hopefully the mere threat of losing his woman and kids is enough to make him act right." He finally lit the smoke and dragged deeply, exhaling with a dreamy smile.

"What's that look for?" I asked.

"Just thinking about you holding that baby." He approached me, grabbing my shirt at the waist with his free hand to pull me closer. "When are we gonna make some, sugar?"

"No sooner than three years, when my birth control expires," I said. "And this," I snatched the cigarette from his hand, taking a quick suck before returning it to him, "can *not* be around me while I'm pregnant."

"Hm, making me give up my vices already." His eyes danced with amusement, bringing it back to his lips.

"Do it outside. On the balcony, I don't care. But the second I find out I'm pregnant, I can't be inhaling your smoke."

He grinned, turning to ash out the cigarette in the glass tray on the desk. "A lot can change in three years, sugar. That's plenty of time to kick a habit."

"We'll see." I crossed my arms, the skepticism plain on my face.

"Now whiskey, on the other hand," he pulled me into his chest by my belt loops, "I draw a line there," he said with mock seriousness.

"We'll talk when you're up at all hours of the night, changing diapers and bottle-feeding," I retorted.

"Have you forgotten you have *three* men?" he laughed. "We'll be rotating shifts, baby. You won't have to do a thing but whip these gorgeous tits out."

He pawed at my breasts, leaning down to kiss my

chest with a groan while I laughed and shoved him away. "You animal."

"Seriously, sugar." He stood upright, wrapping me in a protective embrace. "I want a family with you, and I'm here for all of it. Late nights, exploding diapers, projectile vomiting, banshee screaming, the whole thing."

I laughed, nuzzling into his chest. "Okay, at first I thought a baby sounded nice, then you said all that, and now I'm having second thoughts."

"Ah, come on. It'll be fun." He stroked my back, resting his chin on top of my head. "Can you imagine Jandro with a kid? Or Gun?"

"Jandro will never let the fun stop," I groaned. "He'll be like the big brother figure. I can see Gun taking on the daddy role well."

"And me?"

"You?" I laughed, tilting my face up to kiss under his jaw. "I worry for any girls we have. You'll terrorize every single boy that looks their way."

"As I rightly fuckin' should," he growled. "If they're anything like you, they'll put me in an early grave."

"Like me how, a pain in the ass?"

"That, too." He leaned down, lips hovering over mine as he kept me locked against his chest. "But I was thinking if they were anywhere near as beautiful."

Just when I thought I became used to him looking at me like that, the fluttering in my chest overwhelmed me. I got bashful, burying my face in his neck with a playful thump of his chest. "Stop."

"Never." He caressed my nape, massaging circles

into my hairline. "Really, though. Is it something you want, too?"

I nodded, my face still hidden from him. "I want to meet the people you and I would create," I whispered. "I want to teach them about what went wrong with us, our parents, and grandparents. How their generation can do better."

"Me too." His lips brushed across my forehead. "You know what else?"

"Hm?"

"Thinking of you with a big, pregnant belly, growing my kid inside you," he whispered, "it's so fucking hot. Damn, it's making me hard right now. "

"Reaper!" I slapped his chest.

"Just being honest," he chuckled, hands drifting lower toward my belly. "Three years feels like a lifetime from now. But I'll take that time to build a better home for us. A place where all of us can raise families in safety."

I lifted an eyebrow. "And?"

"And," he sighed. "Give me time to cut back on smoking."

REAPER

"How's it look from up there?"

Gunner blinked, his irises returning to focus on me. "About what you'd expect," he sighed. "A mass exodus."

I could only imagine. I didn't need a bird's-eye view to know that a long trail of vehicles stretched out behind me. Some stayed on bikes, but much of the club piled into their trucks and RVs to haul their families and belongings. We had to stick together, so we'd be making one hell of a caravan once we hit the road.

Fluttering in the wind, the Steel Demons flag slowly lowered down the flagpole at our front gate. That was the moment it hit me, like a sucker punch to the gut. This place wasn't our home anymore. Someone meticulously folded the flag and held it out to Jandro for safekeeping. He took it carefully, to store it with his things.

One day, she'd fly again.

Mari walked up to me, securing her helmet with a frown, then settled onto my rear seat without a word.

"What is it?" I ran my fingertips up her thighs.

"Keep guys on Big G," she said. "Apparently he's done being on his best behavior. Tessa and the kids are riding with Andrea in Dallas's truck, and he's making a big stink over it."

"I'm on it." Gunner made a wide U-turn and headed toward the back of our long line of vehicles.

I squeezed Mari's knee, watching the sliver of her face visible through the helmet. "Ready, sugar?"

"No," she sighed. "I don't think I'll ever be ready to leave this place."

"We'll find our home." I leaned in and kissed the bridge of her nose. "Our permanent home."

"I know. It's just hard." She touched my arm. "Now or never, I guess."

I gave her knee a final squeeze before settling in front of her, revving up my bike for the long road ahead. My woman's arms came around me with natural ease. With one loud whistle, Hades zoomed ahead as a black blur. I kicked the bike into motion and, after taking a final look at my former home in the mirror, drove away from the gate for the last time.

The first day was uneventful. As Dyno had suggested, we took the long way around the Hopi reservation on our way to Four Corners. Stops were frequent, as expected with fidgety children and vehicles that had been sitting in driveways for a year or more. Jandro and Slick kept busy, running back and forth to check tire pressure, change oil, or add coolant for whoever needed it. By the time night fell, it seemed like we barely made any distance at all.

So much for our once-nomadic lifestyle. When the Steel Demons were just six to ten single guys—plus Noelle—making the open road our home was like second nature. Now, we'd gotten used to staying in one place, and it showed. It didn't bother me like I thought it would. Sure I felt nostalgic about the old times, but I wouldn't trade what I had now for anything.

By day two, most people had gotten into the swing of being on the road again. With the vehicles getting tuned up as needed the day before, we didn't have to stop as frequently. But just the fact that we were a grouping of roughly fifteen vehicles felt like we went at a snail's pace.

"How many members did the Sons have before?" I asked T-Bone during a pit stop.

"Oh, about twelve I'd say." He stroked his beard, the loss still clear in his eyes. "We were a small club, but mighty."

"Sometimes that's better. A small, tight-knit circle."

"You're pretty lucky though, Pres." He looked out over the span of people eating, talking, and children and animals chasing each other. "You've got a lot of people who will follow you anywhere. Not because you force them or they're scared of you, but you're just a natural leader."

"I get that a lot," I sighed. "Sometimes I see it, sometimes I don't."

"They trust you." He looked at me, the raven on his shoulder eyeing me as well. "The Sons cycled through a few presidents in our time, so I've seen all kinds. Bash was a rare breed." He went silent for a moment, staring out at nothing. "I see a lot of similarities in your leadership styles. He wasn't a perfect president, but he was a good one. As are you."

"We'll see."

Hades growled, his nose pointing behind us. A woman's shriek and some kind of commotion spurred us into turning around, hands on our holsters.

"The fuck is your big man doing?" T-Bone said.

"Fuck me with a fucking rusty spoon," I muttered under my breath "Not this shit *again*…"

With Hades at my side, I stormed over, aiming to head off Big G who was walking away from a screaming, distraught Tessa, who was following and yelling after him. He held an infant car seat in one hand, swinging it at his side as he walked. The baby was clearly distressed, if the wailing coming from inside the carrier was any indication.

Mari was quickly at Tessa's side, supporting the distraught mother as she stared venomously at Big G's back.

"G, stop!" Tessa sobbed. "*Please* give her back."

"I'm fucking tired of this shit!" Big G spun around, the baby carrier swinging dangerously fast in his hand. "You don't wanna be with me anymore, fine! But you can't have *our* fucking kids all to yourself!"

"You fucking Neanderthal, she's an *infant*!" Mari yelled. "She needs to stay with her mother!"

He jabbed a finger in my woman's face, looking seconds away from exploding. "And I'm tired of *you* sticking your nose where it don't belong, medic."

"Say another word to my wife, G," I kept my hand

over my gun, "And you'll lose that finger, plus whatever else I feel like shooting off."

He glanced over, noticing me for the first time. By that point, all the commotion had drawn the whole club's attention. Gunner and Shadow pushed their way through the crowd to back me up, while Jandro stepped between the women and Big G's outstretched finger.

"Let's all just calm the hell down." My VP stretched his hands out to his sides to put distance between the two parents. "Everyone," he made a shooing motion with his fingers, "mind your business. This doesn't concern you all."

Once people quit rubbernecking, I let my hand fall from my weapon. "G, you want to tell us what's going on?"

He turned to me with a huff. "Vivian is *my* daughter too. I've barely seen her since she was born. The boys are one thing, they can come and see me as they please. But it's not fair for my…*ex*," he spat the word out, "to keep my newborn away from me just because *she* decided to move out."

"Vivian is three weeks old," Mari shot back. "She needs to eat every two hours. This isn't about fairness, but your baby's survival!"

"I can feed her!"

"She's breastfed, you idiot!"

"Don't call me—"

He lunged forward but Jandro's palm collided with his chest.

"Stay back," the VP warned. I wasn't concerned. G was bigger than him in every dimension, but Jandro was a more skilled fighter. Not to mention, Gunner and I would let all hell break loose if he came within spitting distance of Mari.

I was just dumbfounded as to what his thought process was, if there was any processing going on in that big melon at all. What did he think snatching the baby would accomplish?

"I'll let you see her whenever you want," Tessa sniffed, pushing against Mari's arm. "Just please, *please* give her back." Big G doubled down, stepping away as he swung the car seat behind his back, making Tessa whimper. "Please stop doing that, she's not strapped in."

"I have rights to my own kids," he insisted.

"Big G." I stepped forward, Gunner and Shadow silently moving with me. "Give the baby back."

"She's *mine!*"

"That is an order from your president," I continued. "If you do not comply, you're out of the club."

His eyes nearly bulged out of his head, they went so wide. "You're not fucking serious!"

"Do I look like I'm joking? Look at you, swinging that thing around. You think that baby's safe with you?"

"Look, we'll find you guys a mediator," Jandro said in an attempt to de-escalate the situation. "So you can work out visitation, custody schedules, whatever. But this is not the right way to do it, G."

"Give the baby back to Tessa," I ordered. "I will not repeat myself."

Big G's hand clenched around the arm of the car seat, and everyone stiffened. The last thing we wanted was for this to turn violent, but we'd given him plenty of warning.

In the time it took to blink, Shadow went from his position at my back, to squarely in Big G's face. Now those two were much closer in size, with Shadow a few inches taller. He also had the benefit of being fucking intimidating, even to grown men.

"The president gave you an order," he said, inches in front of Big G's nose, hands resting on his belt where we all knew hidden knives sat at the ready.

With Big G distracted by Shadow sizing him up, Gunner snuck around and plucked the car seat from his hand.

"Hey!—"

"Don't," Shadow warned, his body eerily still, but ready to strike if needed.

Gunner went behind me to hand the baby back to Tessa, who let out a sob of relief.

"Escort them back." I nodded to Jandro and Gunner, who began walking away with the women immediately. "Stay with me a moment, Shadow."

"Yes, president." He resumed his post at my back, leaving me to face a raging Big G.

"This is not the first time your impulsiveness has landed you in hot water," I told him. "First you accuse Gunner of betraying us, now you're kidnapping—"

"She's *my* fucking kid too!"

"Yes, I heard you the first five times," I snapped. "And after what you just did, I don't see why Tessa *should* trust you with the kids."

"I'm their fucking father! I have the right to see them!"

"And what if that baby fell out and hit her head while you were swinging her around?" I barked.

He stared me down, jaw clenching, without an answer to my question, which just pissed me off even more. Hades stepped forward and growled, showing off his teeth.

It wasn't like me to get so involved with my men's relationships, but Big G was getting under my skin in a major way. Maybe I was getting a soft spot for kids, not only due to thoughts of starting a family with Mari, but because the Steel Demons future was so up in the air now. Children were the only small hope for a possibly better world.

And if it had been Mari, sobbing and distraught because someone took our baby away—well, that someone wouldn't be standing, nor in one piece. Big G was lucky. Maybe I'd allowed him to be too lucky.

My eyes slid to Hades, the answer immediate.

You will not reap. His life is not yours to take.

"This is your last warning, G," I said, turning to walk away. "You step even one toe out of line, that cut on your back is going up in flames."

MARIPOSA

I didn't know what to expect once we crossed the border into Four Corners, but a long, noisy stretch of construction zone was not it.

The smell of fresh asphalt hit my nose as our vehicles gradually slowed. To my left and right, men in hard hats poured concrete foundations, sawed through fresh lumber, and assembled that lumber into frames for buildings.

Some structures looked brand new, while others appeared to have stood before the Collapse and were being repaired. I watched one man power washing long window panes on the side of a tall building, three stories high. As we came around a gentle bend in the freshly-paved road, my chest tightened at the sight of the word HOSPITAL on the adjacent side of the building.

We came to a stop about a quarter mile later at a four-way intersection. A man held up a stop sign as he waved a group of children to cross in front of us. Some of them wore backpacks and held the hands of adults leading the way. Once they crossed safely, the man lowered the stop sign and waved us through.

I lowered my chin to Gunner's shoulder and pressed my lips to his ear. "Did you see that?"

"Yeah." He took one hand off of the handlebars and squeezed my fingers at his stomach. "It's surreal to see something so normal."

I recalled Reaper talking about wanting a family before we left, and a flutter of warmth spread throughout my chest. Maybe here, if we decided to stay, we'd be able to make it happen.

The ride to the governor's house was a few more miles, with more stops along the way for crossing traffic. The whole place was teeming with activity. If not working construction or crossing guard, people had food vendor booths set up along the road. I spotted a few food trucks, and one guy had even dug a pit in the ground and was roasting a whole pig.

When the head of the pack finally stopped, it was where the paved street abruptly became a dirt road and a barricade blocked our way. Ahead of us, T-Bone leaned over to speak to Reaper, his hands gesturing and pointing. At Reaper's nod, T-Bone signaled for everyone to turn right onto a narrow, older road that hadn't yet been paved.

A clearing was carved out on the side of this road and T-Bone led the way, parking his bike under the shade of an overhang.

"We go on foot from here," he explained, after everyone started pulling in and cutting their engines. "They're paving the road up to the governor's house today, so we're supposed to stay off of it. We can take a short walk up this hill, though."

"Gunner and Mari with us," Reaper called, swinging a leg over his bike. "Shadow and Slick, guard the bikes. Make sure no one wanders off or gets body-snatched."

Freyja wiggled out from her cocoon inside my jacket, then darted over to Shadow and hopped up into his empty bike seat. He smiled amusedly, reaching down to pet her.

T-Bone chuckled, wiping his mouth free of water after a sip from his canteen. "You saw those kids crossing the street, right, Pres? I assure you it's safe here."

"You can assure me all you fuckin' want. I'm still not taking any chances." Reaper cupped my nape, turned my head to plant a smoldering kiss on me, then released me and continued on. "Where the fuck are we supposed to stay here? I didn't see a single building that looked finished."

Gunner smirked at my side, then held my hand as we, Jandro, and the two other Sons followed T-Bone and Reaper up a gently sloping hill.

"There are housing developments going up on the side streets," T-Bone said, pointing further down the road we'd just parked on. "Houses with bigger plots of land for farming and raising animals are that way." He pointed in the opposite direction.

"Need one of those." Jandro came up to sandwich me between him and Gunner, grabbing my hand to kiss my palm. "Space for Foghorn and the girls."

Gunner puffed out his cheeks and began making soft

clucking noises, earning a smack on the back of the head from his VP.

"Is the hospital in use?" I called ahead, ignoring their shenanigans.

T-Bone looked over his shoulder at me, slowing his pace enough for me to catch up. "It's in rough shape, was raided during the Collapse, but it's slowly getting organized into working order. Four Corners has one doctor and a few medics working on-call for emergencies, but no full-time staff yet. They mostly treat construction accidents so far."

"Why *is* there so much construction?" Reaper wondered out loud.

"Governor Vance calls it 're-investing'," Dyno answered. "He poured his personal wealth into rebuilding people's homes and essential businesses after everything was looted. But if people wanted to stay here, they had to work for it."

"Every person coming into Four Corners must take on a job," T-Bone picked up. "Some kind of trade, skill, or service they can offer. The governor isn't picky about what that is, as long as it serves the community in a non-harmful way."

"What about people with physical disabilities, who can't do manual labor?" I piped up. "What about girls running away from those camps that brainwash them? Don't tell me the governor turns these people away."

T-Bone looked at me with an endearing smile. "There are many more job opportunities here than just physical labor. Someone could tutor or babysit children. They need cooks, cleaners, servers, couriers, all kinds of jobs. If someone has no discernible skills, they're sent to the library to enroll in courses and assess what their strengths are. If they're interested in a trade, but have no experience, they can become an apprentice. Everyone is given an opportunity to succeed here."

I listened with rapt attention as he explained, trying to keep my excitement in check. This place seemed to have all the markings of a good, fair community being built from the ground up.

"You're really selling this place hard, despite not living here." Reaper did not sound as optimistic.

"Ah, you know how it is, Pres!" T-Bone laughed. "Guys like us can't be contained by a quiet, normal life. We need adventure and freedom. And sometimes, we like to play more than work."

"We probably *will* be staying here for the foreseeable future, though," Dyno chimed in. "Until we start doing some rebuilding ourselves."

The humor drained out of T-Bone's face, sadness and guilt replacing it. Losing his club and someone he loved weighed heavily on him. He reminded me of Reaper in that sense.

Dyno stroked an affectionate hand up his sergeant's back and T-Bone leaned into him, winding his fingers almost absently into the other man's ponytail. Their affection was brief and, on the surface, hardly more intimate than two brothers or friends. If I didn't have my gut feeling, and T-Bone hadn't explicitly told me he liked men, I never would have assumed anything about the touch.

Gradually, the hill we climbed flattened out to a

grassy field. Two long rows of soldiers in desert camouflage uniforms marched to our left, their faces solemn as their drill sergeant shouted orders.

"Vance's general is highly organized," T-Bone commented, noticing our gawking. "We'll probably meet him later. Four Corners is a target for other governors looking to increase their wealth and infrastructure, so General Bray is tough on his militia to defend the borders. But the soldiers are compensated well and have support systems in place, so morale remains high."

"They'll need the absolute best army they can put together," Gunner said next to me. "I guaran-fuckin'-tee you General Tash has already set his sights on this place. He has the two biggest territories bordering to the east."

T-Bone's shoulders went rigid at the mention of General Tash's name. "You may want to sit in on some meetings between Vance and Bray, Youngblood."

"Highly doubtful," Gunner retorted. "I'm just a road pirate looking for a place to lay my head down at night."

"Um, did you forget about right here?" Jandro reached over and groped my breast that was closest to Gunner.

"Get your mitts off me." I slapped his hand away. "We're about to meet a *governor*."

"I didn't, but you're always hogging 'em," my blond demon laughed. "I'm more of an ass man when it comes to pillows though."

"I'm done with you two," I huffed, breaking away from between them and walking up to squeeze between Reaper and T-Bone.

"Oh, you want to walk with the adults now?" my smirking president chuckled, drawing me into his side with an arm around my shoulders.

"It's been a long couple of days," I sighed, leaning my head on him.

I was not in the mood for my men being overgrown children. Gunner and Jandro's playful antics didn't normally bother me, but on top of being sore, dusty, and exhausted, we were about to meet a powerful man. Governor Vance would decide whether we stayed here for the time being or hit the road again early tomorrow morning.

"I know, sugar." Reaper brushed a kiss along my forehead. "This really couldn't have waited, huh?" The question was directed at T-Bone.

"If y'all were some small-fry club of nobodies? Maybe," he grinned. "But everyone here has seen, or at least heard of, those patches on your cuts. Vance probably already knows you're here, and the longer you stay without any clarity on whether you're friend or foe will make the citizens uneasy."

"At least that's what General Bray told us," Dyno added, "when he ordered us to bring any supposed allies directly to the governor if we returned to Four Corners."

"So you're protecting your own necks, first and foremost," Reaper concluded. "Following orders even though you're not citizens, so you can keep your cushy escort and protection contracts with the governor."

"Yeah, and?" T-Bone's eyes heated, his jaw jutting out in challenge to Reaper's statement. "What else are we supposed to do? Our friends and family are gone. We don't have a home, and now you don't either. We're not taking you to a prison cell for fuck's sake, we're just being transparent about who we're bringing into the territory."

"I would appreciate more transparency with *me*," Reaper returned with an eerie calm. "I'm trusting my whole club with you, following you here."

"I haven't kept anything from you. Are you not familiar with the idea of self-preservation? Do I have to tell you my personal motivations for everything I do? No, president."

"Guys, cool it." T-Bone and Reaper had started to lean into each other, and I forcefully pushed their shoulders away from the other man. "Let's just meet the governor and get this over with so we can get some fucking rest."

The two men gave each other stink-eyes, but otherwise quit arguing and continued walking in silence. Once at the edge of the grass field, a gravel road took us through some kind of orchard. The trees were young saplings, with some people walking through the neatly planted rows to adjust stakes or prune leaves.

"Apple trees." Dyno answered the question on my mind before I could voice it.

T-Bone cleared his throat. "The governor's house is just on the other side of the orchard."

Surprise washed over me at the sight of the oversized cabin beyond the orchard. It was big and luxurious, no doubt, but a fraction of the size of Reaper's mansion back in Sheol. Dark wood paneling gave the home a rustic feel. Porches wrapped around the ground floor and upper level, and a stone chimney jutted straight up against a slanted roof. It was a nice house, but the furthest possible image from where I expected a governor to live.

The only indication that a politician lived here at all was the two armed soldiers guarding the front porch leading up to the door. There wasn't even a gate around the house.

T-Bone raised his hand in greeting to the guards and received a sharp nod in return. "Wait here," he muttered, and walked up to speak to the guards alone.

It was a short conversation. Only a few seconds passed before the guards shifted into at-ease positions and T-Bone nodded back at us to follow.

Our small group walked up the porch steps to stand in front of two heavy wooden doors inlaid with glass. The doors pulled open from the inside and a young man wearing glasses and a suit smiled at us across the threshold.

"Come in, come in! I was hoping to see Sons of Odin faces again, good to see you, T-Bone!" He clasped hands with the large sergeant at arms and shook enthusiastically.

"Josh, we have some guests with us." T-Bone turned toward us with an arm outstretched. "This is Reaper, president of the Steel Demons MC, his old lady, Mariposa, vice president. Jandro, and captain of the guard, Gunner."

"A pleasure." The suited man nodded at each of us, sandy blond hair flopping into his eyes. "I'm Josh

Lemon, Governor Vance's secretary and chief of staff."

"Nice to meet you," I offered with an elbow jab to Reaper's ribs when none of my men said anything.

A couple of wordless grunts came out of them following my greeting. Overgrown children, the lot of them.

"Where's the rest of your crew, at the B&B?" Josh turned to face T-Bone.

"No, uh—"

"We have," Dyno cut in with a hand on T-Bone's shoulder, "a lot to update the governor about. Can we see him right away? It's been a long ride and we'd all like to rest."

Josh sighed and pushed his glasses up the bridge of his nose. "The governor is eager to see you as well, and also has lots to update you on. He has a job for you, and I'm afraid he won't let you rest for long."

"Fair enough. We're happy to stay busy after a bit of proper R&R."

The secretary shook his head. "This is a personal matter to Governor Vance. He would let Four Corners crumble before delaying this any further. You *must* take this job, and it must be carried out immediately."

"What the fuck's so important?" T-Bone demanded with a cross of his arms.

Josh glanced at us with a nervous clench of his jaw before answering the question. "His daughter's been kidnapped."

MARIPOSA

The whole second floor of the cabin was essentially an open loft, I realized, as Josh led our party from the foyer up the stairs. A collection of antlers and taxidermy animals like coyotes and elk decorated the sloping walls. I even spotted a jackalope perched on a shelf.

Our group was tense after hearing Josh's news regarding the governor's daughter. "I really hope we don't get roped into this shit," Reaper grumbled into my ear.

I pinched his side, urging him to be quiet, as we walked over a Navajo-style rug toward the far end of the second floor. A bay of windows looked out over more construction sites and people going about their work. In front of the windows, a disheveled middle-aged man sat at a heavy wooden desk, looking distraught.

Josh cleared his throat politely. "Governor, the Sons of Odin have returned. And they've brought guests with them who…may be able to assist with this matter."

Reaper made a noise of disagreement and I jabbed him with my elbow.

The man at the desk lifted his face from his hands, his eyes bloodshot and features looking haggard and exhausted. He clearly hadn't slept or eaten well in the past few days.

"T-Bone, Dyno," the governor rasped, a weary smile lighting up his face. "And even you, Grudge. It's great to see you all. Thank God you're here."

"We're sorry to hear about Kyrie, Governor," T-Bone said in response. "You've been good to us over the past few years and we're happy to help in any way we can."

Reaper thankfully bit his tongue that time, but I didn't miss the hiss of breath and his jaw clenching.

Governor Vance's watery eyes fell to us. "Who are your friends?"

"Governor, it's my pleasure to introduce the Steel Demons MC." T-Bone pointed us out and gave our names, just as he did with Josh. "They're looking for a new place to settle and have a club of around 25 at the bottom of the hill."

Reaper cleared his throat. "If you would allow it, governor, we'd like to stay temporarily to see if Four Corners is a good fit for us. My club has excellent mechanics, cooks, carpenters." He nodded at me. "My wife here is a skilled medic. I'm sure we can contribute to the development of your territory in exchange for a temporary stay."

I took a moment to bask in his praise and him calling me his wife before stepping forward.

"We are very sorry to hear about your daughter, governor. All of us will pray that she's found soon, safe and unharmed. We're extremely grateful for your generous hospitality in the meantime. Please let us know if there's anything we can do." Returning to Reaper's side, I felt him fuming and caught Gunner trying to hide a grin.

"I know you." Vance tilted his head as he peered at Reaper. "You're the one who rides with a hellhound at your side."

"You mean this one?" Reaper leaned down to pat Hades' head, the dark four-legged guardian never making a sound. "He's no hellhound, just a hell of a runner."

"And you." Vance's gaze fell upon Horus perched on Gunner's shoulder. "You're some kind of shaman with that bird. I've heard stories that you turn into a bird yourself."

My golden demon huffed out a chuckle, his smile wide and relaxed. "Just tall tales, governor. I'm a trained falconer, nothing more to it."

"People have said the same things about our ravens," T-Bone added with a shrug. "Now regarding the matter at hand, the Sons of Odin are yours, governor, but—"

"I need *them.*"

Vance lifted a weary hand from the desk, finger pointing shakily at us. I only then noticed the empty liquor bottle on the corner.

"They...they use some kind of witchcraft. Some Indian Great Spirit magic. They can find my daughter, bring her back to me safely."

"Um, sir?" Josh cut in nervously. "I understand your worry, but you've been up for several days. Perhaps you should rest."

"I can't! Not until she's home! Oh God, to think of what they're doing to her…"

"Sir, if I may remind you." Josh rounded the desk, placing a comforting hand on the governor's shoulder. "We know who she's with, and that she hasn't been harmed."

"Well, fuck," Reaper muttered under his breath. "What the hell do you need us for?"

"They sent a picture, but how do we know she's really okay? Jesus, my poor baby…"

"Sir, if you don't mind," Josh reached across the desk and hit a button that made a brief buzzing sound, "I'll brief T-Bone and our guests on the situation while you take a shower and maybe sleep for a few hours, okay?"

Three women in simple, matching dark-blue uniforms politely slid past us to attend the governor. House staff, by the looks of it.

"If you could please wash him up, see that he eats soup or something, and make sure he sleeps for a bit." Josh pinched his brow, just above his glasses, as the women surrounded Vance and gently eased him out of his chair. "Give him a sleeping pill if you have to. Thanks, ladies."

We all stepped aside to allow them down the stairs, when Vance twisted in their grip to look back at us.

"Save my daughter, Steel Demons," he begged, weakly fighting against the women practically dragging him down the steps. "Save her and Four Corners is yours. A home, a place of refuge. An army…"

With that final word, his body slumped against his caretakers who buckled under his weight. The governor's lips continued to move as they dragged him across the first floor, mumbling what appeared to be his daughter's name, at my best guess.

"I am terribly sorry about all that," Josh huffed. "She's his only child and her mother passed away, so he's been all out of sorts since she was taken."

"Nothing to be sorry for. His reaction is understandable." T-Bone swallowed, his jaw tight, and I watched his expression with curiosity. He'd never mentioned having children, but appeared to be the one in the room who empathized most with the governor.

"You are welcome to sit down. Um, I apologize for not having enough seats." Josh looked around the room awkwardly, with only a loveseat and a couple of armchairs in the office area.

"That's all right. We ought to head out and find somewhere to crash for the night." Reaper started to turn, gently guiding me in the same direction with a hand on my back, but I resisted.

"Wait. I want to hear this."

"Sugar." He narrowed his eyes, but didn't seem angry, just tired. "Why?"

"We might be able to help. I can, at least, if she has any medical needs."

Josh cleared his throat, which became a cough at the glare from Reaper. "I would suggest you stay for this, just to listen. The governor did ask you specifically."

"And I'm *politely* refusing to be part of this," my husband growled. "The governor's all bent out of shape, anyway."

"Reaper," I chastised.

"I have my own people to take care of. I ain't gonna ride all over fuckin' kingdom come just for some girl."

"A few minutes," I pleaded. "I just want to listen."

He blew out a long breath. "Fine." He wasn't even in the mood to say, *but you owe me,* in that teasing smirk, so I knew his patience would only hold out for so long.

When I turned back around, the Sons of Odin were already squished up into the loveseat adjacent to the desk. Dyno was practically sprawled across T-Bone and Grudge's laps.

"You know where she is, you said?" T-Bone began.

"We know who she's with, not necessarily the location," Josh corrected. "There's a newer territory north of here, Blakeworth, and their governor's family has been trying to kiss Vance's ass ever since they established power, about three years ago. They've attended nearly every diplomatic event here, bringing lavish gifts for Vance, Kyrie, and staff. "

Careful to avoid colliding with antlers or taxidermy heads, I leaned against the wall to listen.

"For the past year or so, the governor's been not-so-subtly trying to arrange a marriage between his son and Vance's daughter, Kyrie."

A scoff puffed out behind me. "What is this, the Middle Ages?" Gunner muttered.

"How old is Kyrie?" I asked.

"Nineteen this year," Josh replied. "Governor Blake's

son, Malcolm, is twenty-four." Josh's eyes nervously darted around the room. "Just between us, I think Kyrie might have gone willingly."

"Hardly a fuckin' kidnapping then, is it?" Reaper spat. "She's a fucking adult."

"Reaper," I growled. Jesus, he really did not have anything resembling a filter today.

"We have reason to believe she was manipulated into leaving," Josh continued. "She's an adult, yes, but young and impressionable. She's also had a rebellious streak, as young women with protective single fathers tend to have."

"What makes you think these people have nefarious plans with her?" Dyno asked. "What if they're just two rebellious youngsters who genuinely want to be together?"

Josh's lips tightened into a thin line. "Ever since the Blake family came into power, we've had an increasing number of refugees coming in from the north. A big part of Blake's talks with Vance include deals for repatriation. They also want to contract labor from us, because so few people are willing to stay in his territory."

"What do the refugees say?" Jandro's tone sounded odd when he was so serious.

"About what you'd expect," Josh sighed. "Long hours of unsafe working conditions for little pay, or no pay at all. Food rations are barely enough to keep people healthy. Armed police patrol the streets and beat people for the slightest infraction. Very little is being done in the ways of education, housing, and general safety."

"Let me guess," I ventured. "No reliable medical services, or very poor ones at that."

Papers crinkled and shuffled as Josh's fingers tightened around the documents on the governor's desk.

"Birth control is outlawed," he confessed with a grim expression. "Blake says it's a temporary measure to help boost their population, but…"

A heavy scratching cut into his words, and all heads turned to see Grudge scrawling on a notepad. T-Bone rested his chin on the silent man's shoulder to read the message, then looked up at Josh.

"How is Blake justifying the working conditions? What excuse does he give for people leaving?" he read aloud, while Grudge looked on expectantly for the answer, lips pursed slightly in determination.

"From what I've overheard," Josh rubbed his forehead, "Blakeworth is a hot spot for oil and natural gas, which is what most of the workforce revolves around."

"It's tough work," I said with a nod. "I grew up in an oil-rich area in Texas."

"Right, so Blake kept saying that his people are soft and they're not used to hard work. That they're just lazy, entitled, and need to be corrected."

"Hence why he wants labor from Four Corners," Jandro realized. "He sees all the progress going on here and wants it for himself."

"Motherfucker sounds like Hitler," Gunner breathed. "I wouldn't be surprised if he was running labor camps and shit."

The whole room nodded their silent agreement

while Josh rifled through more documents on the governor's desk.

"So it's reasonable to assume Kyrie is *not* in good hands," the secretary muttered, pulling out a folder and opening the top cover. "But a messenger delivered this three days ago, and that's what really sealed it for us."

He passed the folder to T-Bone, whose eyebrows shot up the moment he saw its contents. Dyno and Grudge peered over eagerly to see, their faces morphing into knitted brows and narrowed eyes.

Once all three finished looking, T-Bone glanced at us, then at Josh as he held the folder limply in his lap. "Can they see this?"

"Of course."

T-Bone crossed the room, holding the folder out to Reaper and I with a grim face.

"Oh my…" My hand flew to my mouth.

"Jesus," Reaper bit out.

Jandro and Gunner looked over from next to and behind me, letting out similar curses.

A photograph of a young, willowy blonde woman was paper-clipped to a letter that appeared to have written on a typewriter. In the photo, the woman sat barefoot on a filthy concrete floor with her knees to her chest. Her arms, pale with distinct purple bruises from rough fingers, wrapped around her knees, her head buried under her arms with only one eye peeking at the camera.

Underneath the photo, the letter said:

.   .   .

DEAREST GOVERNOR VANCE,

IT HAS BEEN *a pleasure getting to know you and your darling daughter over the past couple of years. It's easy to see why you dote on her, why you're so reluctant to let your little bird fly from the nest. Unfortunately, birds with under-developed wings most often fall prey to predators who will eat them without a second thought.*

Don't worry, Vance. Kyrie has merely been transferred from one cage to another. She has not yet been eaten, in any sense of the word. Her current cage may not be as gilded as yours, but in time, she will learn to appreciate it and forget all about the glossy veneer of her former prison.

Especially if she finds a reason to stay. Such as, if she finds herself with child, and as a result, must agree to marriage if she does not wish to end up as trash in the gutter. These events will happen regardless, dear Governor, but if you would prefer to have more input on the timeline, and thus, extended time with your daughter, you will agree to lend Blakeworth two-hundred contracted soldiers, and one-hundred contracted laborers.

The contract length and terms shall be decided by my father and I, with no input from Four Corners. Any attempt to renegotiate these terms will be considered a refusal, and you may find yourself grandfather to the heir of Blakeworth before your next birthday.

Either way, congratulations are in order. We look forward to your response in one week's time. Any delay in receiving an answer will also be considered a refusal.

YOUR HUMBLE SERVANT,

Malcolm of Blakeworth

. . .

"WHO IN THE fuck does this chode think he is?" The disgust was clear in Jandro's voice.

"The crowned prince of Doucheville," Gunner scoffed. "He writes like he actually believes the sun shines out of his asshole."

"Vance has been a wreck ever since seeing this," Josh said tiredly. "He does not want to give in to their demands, naturally. Losing two-hundred soldiers and a hundred laborers will devastate us here. And if we agree…"

"You don't expect to get those citizens back," Reaper filled in.

"If Blake sets the terms of the contract and does not allow any negotiation," Josh shook his head. "They'll be trapped there as indentured servants, most likely. Escape will mean risking death. We can't sacrifice three-hundred people like that. It'll be sending them to slaughter."

T-Bone leaned his head back with a groan, rubbing a hand over his shaved crown. "How far's the border from here?"

"About five-hundred and fifty miles."

"So at least a day's ride, probably two if we want to be stealthy."

"Then we still gotta find out where she is," Dyno said. "We'll have to do some interrogation, send Munin out. But even if we get her location relatively quickly…"

"We'll have to ride out early tomorrow at the latest," T-Bone concluded. "Before that sick bastard fuckin'—"

He shook his head, unable to complete his thought when he looked over at us, chin lifted. "What do ya think, Demons? Feel like riding in and being fucking heroes?"

"No."

Reaper answered before any one of us could voice an opinion, ignoring my bewildered stare at the side of his face.

"I wish you all the best in getting the girl back, but I've got too much on my plate. If Governor Vance doesn't want us sticking around, I respect that. We'll rest up, and then keep moving. We'll be sure not to overstay our welcome."

"Reaper!" I hissed.

He ignored me and turned to leave, heading down the stairs.

GUNNER

Mari was pissed. And not in the cute, adorable way.

"Reaper, stop." She marched after him, breaking into a jog to keep up with his storming out of the governor's house.

Jandro reached for her shoulder. "*Bonita*—"

"Not now, Jandro."

He lifted both hands away and looked at me with a shrug, walking a few steps back to trudge alongside me a few paces behind the arguing married couple.

"What do you think?" he asked.

"That I need a drink," I sighed. "And a night in a real fucking bed." I reached up and tapped my hand on Horus's talons. "Go."

He spread his wings and launched himself off of my shoulder. Once he got high enough he'd be able to see the club where we left them.

"Agreed on those points. What about *this*?" Jandro

gestured ahead to where Mari kept after Reaper, demanding that he talk to her.

"I can see both sides," I admitted. "This isn't our business to get involved in, and we do have our own people to look after. Refusing to help doesn't make us look good to the governor, though. And we might need him in the future."

"And it pisses our woman off that we're not stepping up to help someone," he added.

"That, too."

We caught up to Mari and Reaper on our way down the hill, catching their heated back-and-forth conversation.

"I don't understand," she was saying. "We have plenty of capable people who can do something to help. Why are you refusing this?"

"I'm not sending any of our people to some fascist territory where they'll be beaten to death if caught." Reaper turned abruptly, holding his index finger up in Mari's face. "I'm done with this conversation."

"No, you're not." She batted his hand away, not even flinching. I couldn't help the swell of pride inside me. She really was becoming fearless. "What about the girl who's already there, already a hostage? She's alone and scared. What if that was me?"

"It's *not* you, so it doesn't matter," he growled. "It's an awful situation, but I can't save every girl in trouble."

"You can save *this* one!"

"She means nothing to me, so why should I?!"

"Okay, okay." Jandro wedged his way between the two of them, who looked moments away from literally tearing into each other. "Let's all take a breath. Reap, you need to chill."

"I *would* chill if people would get the fuck off my back."

"She means something to someone," Mari muttered, still glaring daggers at him. "She's a human being. That should be reason enough."

"Okay, sugar, that's fair. But I can only be stretched so thin."

"It doesn't have to be you. You have an entire club—"

"Who I am still responsible for. It's on *me* if something happens to them. Jesus, fuck, I don't want to go in circles like this."

"Come here." I wrapped a hug around Mari from behind, partially to comfort her, partially to hold her back from lunging at Reaper, which she still looked eager to do.

"If I can say something..." Jandro looked between the two of them, still poised in the middle. "Gunner mentioned we might need the governor in the future, Reap. Refusing to do this doesn't swing anything in our favor."

"He also mentioned his army," I reminded them. "Which we'll need if we're taking on Tash directly."

"Who knows if he'll stick to that?" Reaper argued. "Politicians lie. He's a delirious old man offering up whatever he can think of. But once we do our part, who's to say he'll do his?"

"Rescuing his daughter will give us leverage," I reminded him. "He'll owe us. When it comes down to brass tacks, I'll remind him of that. I'm sure there's more we can bring to the table once we get a better lay of the land."

"Fuck." Reaper turned and started back down the hill to the rest of our people at the bottom.

"Talk, Reap." Jandro moved to his side while Mari and I followed, my arms still around her. "What's on your mind?"

"What's on my mind is that we're basically homeless, with no defenses, and the most vulnerable we've ever been," the president growled with a glance over his shoulder at Mari. "We have more to lose now than ever before. I just think we should take care of ourselves now, before others."

"I hear you," Jandro nodded at his side.

Gripping my forearms wrapped around her chest, Mari leaned her head back on my shoulder. "What do you think? We can't ignore the fact that this girl needs help, right?"

"I don't like it, but I get what Reaper's saying." I took a nip at her earlobe at her disappointed groan. "Go easy on him, baby girl. He's not being heartless. It's a hard decision for him, even if it doesn't look like it. He's choosing what's most important to him."

Mari grumbled, her anger now at a more adorable level, all the way to where our vehicles and people waited for us.

"Meeting go well?" Slick asked with a jovial grin, which quickly faded at a closer look at Reaper and Mari's faces.

"Let's find some place to fuckin' eat and spend the

night," Reaper said in a non-answer. "No one goes alone, pairs or groups only. They probably can't accommodate all of us in one place, so we'll have to split up. Prospect!"

Larkan straightened up, but his hand clamped tighter around Noelle's waist. "Yes, president?"

"Come with us. When we've found a place, go around and tell everyone where we are in case someone needs us."

I closed my eyelids, slipping into Horus for a brief moment. He was perched on a tree with a clear view of us and half the town. He'd be able to track everyone, plus our vehicles, until it got dark. Then we'd need someone with better night vision to take over.

Something bumped my shin. Freyja. The black cat seemed to read my mind as she wound herself around my boots with a calming ease.

You're safe here, I thought I heard her say.

"Shadow." Jandro nodded at his tall, silent friend. "Come with us."

With that, club members began splitting off into the town on foot. Reaper and Jandro led our small group, followed by Mari and me, Noelle and Larkan, and Shadow bringing up the rear.

Exploring on foot proved to be the wisest option, despite wishing I could roll through on my bike. Streets and sidewalks were narrow, with tons of blocked areas for construction zones, even off of the main roads.

"They're really rebuilding from the ground up," Mari observed as a crane slowly lowered some kind of pipe into a hole in the street.

"Makes you wonder how badly this place got fucked over," I said.

Her hand found mine, slim fingers lacing through. "Makes you admire how resilient people are."

I kissed her forehead as we walked past the construction zone, squeezing my arms tighter around her. That was my girl, always seeing the best outcome in every situation.

We came upon a bed-and-breakfast and piled into the small lobby. The plump old woman behind the front desk looked frozen in terror at the leather clad bikers in her establishment, until Mari and Noelle pushed their way to the front.

"Hi, do you have three rooms available? With one big enough for four people?"

After a few surprised blinks, the owner breathed a sigh of relief and began to explain her options to the women. Looking around, the place was charming, clean, and smelled freshly painted. I peered out the window to the vegetable garden alongside the building.

"That's what I want." Jandro pointed over my shoulder to the chicken coop against the back fence. "Only mine's gonna be even more dope than that."

"If we stick around, I bet you can sell your extras to this lady."

"Extra eggs? Or you mean…?"

"Chickens themselves. I heard you have quite a virile cock there, buddy."

"Shut up." He smacked my shoulder. "But that's a good idea. That way I can keep my population under control without upsetting," his eyes darted to the side, "you know."

"We got rooms," Mari announced. She eyed me and Jandro turning innocently away from the window. "And Mrs. Potts here says there's a bar with an open grill down the road. We can barter for food there or bring our own."

"Thank fuck." Reaper was the first to storm out of the place. "Let's go."

———

AFTER THE REST of our club squeezed into the bar an hour later, followed by the Sons of Odin, I had a hunch there weren't yet many fun places to go in Four Corners.

"Reaper!" T-Bone walked in with a grin on his face, arms spread wide, with his guys flanking him on either side. "You owe me big time now, Pres. I just saved your reputation in the Four Corners territory."

"I don't need you to save dick." Reaper's arm lifted, gesturing the Sons to our table. "But if you bring a full bottle over, I might be willing to hear you out."

While T-Bone went to the bar, Dyno and Grudge grabbed chairs and dragged them to us, the latter pulling up beside Shadow. The scarred man nodded at him in greeting and leaned over to say something over the din of the bar.

"Whoa," I muttered to myself. "Shadow's making friends."

"It's great, isn't it?" Mari watched for a moment over her cocktail.

The two men's communication consisted of Shadow speaking and Grudge writing on the notepad he always carried around.

"Yeah, good for him," I agreed.

T-Bone seated himself next to Reaper at the head of our table, holding a bottle out for our president to examine. "Heard you like the good stuff, Reap."

Reaper gave the bottle an approving nod and gestured for the man to pour. "I'm listening."

A hush came over our group as we all leaned in to hear what T-Bone had to say.

"Dyno, Grudge, and I are riding out in the morning to save the girl—"

"Thank you," Mari cut in smugly, with a scathing look at Reaper.

"—and we convinced Josh and Vance to give you the benefit of the doubt. Josh seemed convinced the governor would've ordered the army to march your asses out of the territory if you didn't lend a hand in this rescue."

Jandro and I exchanged an *I told you so* look from across the table, but Reaper didn't seem fazed by that news.

"Fine by me. We can ride on tomorrow morning."

"You better not." T-Bone sucked his teeth following a long swallow of whiskey. "Because I told them we'd work together on this rescue."

Reaper looked moments away from punching him in his face. "That's what you told them, but what's it really mean?"

T-Bone threw back another shot. "We've got this

handled, but I need one man from you. Two at the most. Can you swing that?" When Reaper didn't answer, he pressed, "We'll sing your praises and give you all the credit when we get back. The governor will host you, and your officers, at a dinner and give you everything you need to fight Tash. I'm giving you vengeance on a silver platter here, Pres, and you'd be a fool to refuse it."

"Why?" Reaper wasn't threatened by T-Bone, but still didn't fully trust him. His body language said it all—arms open and draped carelessly over his chair, but eyes narrowed in suspicion. "Why would you do that for us?"

"Because you have the manpower, brains, and resources to strike Tash where it hurts." T-Bone's voice wavered with emotion. "You can topple the king looking down at us from his tower, but *we* can't. Our goal is the same, but we've already been wiped out. If my whole club was here to back us, I wouldn't be asking you for shit. But they're gone. *You* still have a chance."

Reaper kept silent, but the suspicion lifted away from his eyes. His whole expression softened as he took in the weight of what T-Bone was saying. Before he could respond, Larkan abruptly stood.

"I'll go, president."

"Sit your ass down, prospect," Reaper growled.

"Yeah," Noelle hissed through her teeth at her boy toy. "What the fuck are you doing?"

"No, I should do this," Larkan insisted. "I'm not even a Demon, so you're not sacrificing anyone important by sending me." The prospect shrugged his shoulders. "If I don't come back, it's no skin off your nose,

Pres. If I do?" He leveled his gaze at Reaper. "Maybe then I'll be worthy of a patch."

"He's got a point," Jandro weighed in, slouching low in his seat.

It took Reaper only one dram of whiskey to make up his mind. "Fine. Shadow, you're going too." He fumbled for his cigarettes and a light. "Because whatever happens, I know for a fact you'll come back and tell me accurately what happened."

"Yes, president." Shadow didn't seem to feel one way or the other about the situation. He did his job without question, and was therefore the perfect pick.

With a jovial grin, T-Bone clapped Reaper on the shoulder. "Thank you, Reap. We can't fucking lose with two Demon riders with us. We'll be in and out with the girl in no time."

The matter seemed settled until Mari spoke up. "I'm going too."

"*No!*"

The three of us were loud enough that the whole bar fell silent. Lookie-loos at other tables craned their necks to see what got our hackles raised.

"Hey, all y'all mind your own business!" I snapped. When the peering eyeballs were gone and the background noise resumed, I grabbed Mari's chin to make her look at me. "Baby girl, I love you, but are you out of your fucking mind?"

She pulled my hand away with an icy glare. "No, I'm not. But the girl might need medical services that shouldn't wait for a two-day ride." She looked at the Sons over the table. "Do any of you know CPR? First aid? How to set a broken bone or treat an infection? If so, then fine, you don't need me." Her gaze swept over Shadow and Larkan. Her questions only met with blank stares, she looked back at me. "I'm going."

"Like *fuck* you are," Reaper roared.

"I'll be fine. The guys won't let anyone come within a mile of me. Especially with Shadow there."

It was hard to tell with all his hair hanging in front of his face, but I swore the big dude blushed and tried to hide a smile.

T-Bone cleared his throat. "If I may add something to the little lady's defense?"

"No, you fucking may not!" Reaper stared at him, incredulous.

"Go ahead, T-Bone," Mari implored him with a loud slurp on her straw.

"The governor's daughter will likely feel better about coming with us if she sees another woman in our company." He gave his beard a thoughtful stroke. "I mean, we'll tie her up and throw her on a bike if it comes to that, but we'd get out a lot easier if we didn't have to. 'Til we get her home, she'd just feel like she was being kidnapped again."

"Excellent point!" Mari was getting louder the more she drank. "I'll make the girl feel safe. The whole thing will go a lot more smoothly if I'm there."

"Sugar?" Reaper leaned as far across the table as he could without standing up. "Be quiet. You're not going."

"We've got the majority of the club here, right?" Mari looked around. "Let's put it to a vote."

"This isn't church," Reaper hissed. "We aren't voting on shit."

"Who thinks I should go on the rescue?" Mari bellowed.

Everyone at the table, save for the men currently sleeping with her, raised a hand.

Jandro grabbed Dyno's arm and brought it down to the table. "Y'all don't get to vote on our business. Neither do you, Prospect, or Noelle!"

Reaper's sister just shrugged and lifted her arm higher. "I want Mari watching out for my man. But I draw the line at her kissing his boo-boos."

"Don't worry, Nellie. Even if I wanted to, I bet Shadow would snitch on me."

"What?" Shadow looked confused for a moment, until Mari tossed him a smirk that almost seemed flirtatious.

"Don't fuckin' matter anyway," T-Bone laughed, leaning his chair back. "Y'all are outvoted. Your woman is ours for at least two days."

MARIPOSA

I fell into bed with the room spinning slightly. The guys shoved the two queen beds together to make one gigantic bed in the middle of our room. I was tired enough to fall asleep almost immediately, but it became clear Reaper wouldn't let that happen.

Smack!

"Oww!" I rolled away, clutching the side of my butt he'd spanked harder than ever before. "What the hell?"

"I oughta tan your hide for that stunt you pulled." He sat in a chair and kicked off his boots, then slid his cut from his shoulders, but otherwise didn't undress for bed. "At least one of us should be with you at all times. What the hell are you thinking volunteering to go off with men that aren't yours?"

"Is that what you're mad about?" I asked, still rubbing my stinging cheek.

"One of us can still go with her," Jandro cut in from where he lay on the other side of me. He could lie comfortably on his back now, and looked delicious in that position with his fingers laced behind his head. Too bad Reaper was ruining the moment by looking for a fight.

"You all need to be here," I told him. Reaper *was* right about that, at least. "You two need to lead the club and keep order, and Gunner needs to keep an eye on things with Horus." I turned my gaze back to Reaper, anger burning in my chest. "I don't like what you're insinuating by me going off with other men. What exactly are you worried about?"

My husband sighed, scrubbing a hand down his face. "That's not what I'm saying. I trust the men, and I trust you. What pisses me off is you undermining me. I'm still president, sugar. You cannot call a vote on club business. In fucking public, no less."

The anger withered down to guilt. He was right, I'd stampeded over him when I shouldn't have. At the time, it felt lighthearted and fun. Everyone was drinking and laughing. We had compromised on the mission and came to a solution. Now, with him sitting there looking all disappointed in me, it sank in how seriously he took it.

"I'm sorry." I reached over the edge of the bed for him. "I didn't mean anything by it. I just saw an opportunity to help and went for it."

He looked at my outstretched hand, then back to my face, face stony and unreadable.

My hand dropped over the side of the bed as I rolled onto my back, letting my shirt ride up my torso. "Can I do anything to make it up to you?"

A beat of silence passed before he rose from the

chair, standing over me as his gaze drifted over my body. I was only in panties and a T-shirt, my breaths already shallowing with deep rises and falls of my chest as I waited for him to do something.

Make-up sex with him was always intense, rough, and passionate. I hated when we got into arguments, but those animalistic sessions afterward were on another level. We kept it only between us though. I wasn't sure how he'd respond with Jandro and Gunner in the room.

"I have to punish you," he bit out finally. "On your belly."

I rolled to my stomach, core and thighs clenching in anticipation of what was coming next. Reaper reached out, fingers trailing gently over the backs of my thighs. When the spank came down on my other cheek, I was ready. My fists curled around the sheets as I bit down my whimper.

He smacked the other side, heat cracking on already tender flesh. Alternating sides, his palm switched between soothing and cruel, rubbing over my sore bottom before slapping down hard again. When I couldn't hold in my cries anymore, he stopped.

"Gunner." He nodded at my blond demon across the room, but I didn't know what he was ordering. "Jandro."

The VP slid across the bed to me, remaining stretched out on his back. "Straddle me, *Mariposita*."

I lifted up and slid my weak knee to the other side of Jandro's torso. He pulled me down for a kiss, sweet relief after Reaper's punishment. Much gentler hands roamed inside my shirt and down my sides, bringing sighs of contentment to my ragged breaths.

"Take her shirt and panties off," came the harsh order.

Jandro obeyed, pulling my top over my head to discard in a corner of the room. I brought my legs together briefly so he could hook his fingers in my underwear, dragging them down to my knees. I shimmied them down the rest of the way and kicked them off when they reached my ankles.

Once naked, I straddled Jandro again and looked up at Reaper, still fully dressed and sitting next to the bed.

"Come here." I reached for him again, my lips parted and already longing to taste him.

"No." His expression was aloof, smug, even cruel.

My hand lowered slowly, the shock slicing through me with a sharp pain. He didn't want me?

I willed my lip not to tremble. "Why not?"

"Because that's your real punishment, sugar." He cupped my chin with just his thumb and forefinger, not allowing any more touch. "You can't have me until you come back."

"What?" I cried. "I'm not gonna see you for two, maybe three, days!"

He shrugged. "Should've thought about that before being so eager to go."

"Reaper, please!" I looked down at the man under me, then Gunner standing on the opposite side of the bed, hiding something behind his back. "Guys, come on!"

"Sorry, baby girl." Gunner walked slowly around the

bed until he stood behind me. He was shirtless, jeans unbuttoned and hanging low on his hips. "We follow our president. In the bedroom, he's your first man and sets the rules for the rest of us."

Traitor. I glared at him. After all the time he spent resisting our whole dynamic, now he decided to just fall in line?

"Don't worry, though." Gunner's playful grin returned, his arms giving nothing away to what hid behind his back. "We have a surprise for you."

"What—ow! Hm!"

Jandro pulled me down with a fist in my hair, silencing me with a rough kiss. His hips moved underneath me, his length, hot and thick, rubbing through his boxers against my lower belly.

I jumped with a shriek when something cold touched my pussy, and whipped my head around at the sound of Gunner's amused chuckle.

"Relax, baby girl." He sat at the edge of the bed, rubbing the cold thing against my soaked core, and pressed a kiss to my lower back. "It is a punishment, but you'll still enjoy this."

"What is it?"

I breathed out a soft gasp as he pushed it inside me. It felt heavy and quickly warmed up with my body temperature. Gunner's eyes heated, breaths coming out in soft puffs as he gently fucked me with the toy. Then he pulled it out and showed me with a triumphant grin.

A silver, metallic butt plug.

Crack!

"Ah!"

Reaper's punishing spank came out of nowhere, but neither of the guys seemed surprised. They must have planned this, in some way or another.

"Give that to me and play with her, but do not let her come until I say so."

Gunner handed Reaper the plug without another word. My eyes locked onto those predatory green eyes as Reaper stuck it in his mouth. His cheeks hollowed out as he sucked my juices off the metal toy like it was an ice cream cone. Our stares remained locked, even as Jandro moved me up and down over his length, and Gunner's thumb massaged circles around my ass.

My pussy closed around nothing and it bordered on painful. It felt completely unfair that he got to taste me, without even touching me himself, and I wouldn't feel any part of him for days.

And it hurt the worst, knowing that was the whole point of this.

Reaper pulled the toy from his mouth, the metallic surface now shiny with his saliva. He reached with it, circling the pointed end slowly around my nipple.

"If you were any other woman," he said softly, dragging the wet, heated metal across my breast. "If you were just some club bitch that didn't matter to me, do you know what I'd do to you for undermining me?"

The heat and wetness from the toy on my skin didn't hurt, but the lack of touch from him was painful. He brought it back to his mouth, wetted it again, and continued his torturous path to my other nipple. It could almost feel like a tongue, but wasn't soft enough, wasn't *him* enough.

"I bet you'd actually fuck me," I ground out at him. "If I was just some whore that mouthed off."

He laughed lightly, dragging the plug along my sternum now. "No. I'd use my belt on you, for one. Not just my hand." Pulling the toy away, he reached behind me and dipped it into my pussy again a few times, then returned it to his mouth. "Mm," he moaned around my taste. "And I wouldn't wait to punish you privately in a bedroom. I'd tan your ass raw, out there for everyone to see."

Jandro sucked in heavy breaths beneath me, his shaft pressing hard on my clit as he kept rolling me back and forth on him. I bit the inside of my cheek to fight the building pleasure, knowing Reaper would punish me further if I came without his permission. Behind me, Gunner squirted a generous amount of lube onto his fingers, then returned to playing with my ass.

"Fuck!" I gasped as he pressed through the tight ring of muscles.

It was a completely different sensation, a stretch with a bit of a burn, but not altogether unpleasant. Gunner's finger worked through gently, his thumb still massaging around in a circle to relax me. I was relieved he was the one back there, the perfect person to work with me through something new and uncomfortable.

"You're safe, baby girl," he reminded me in a whispered kiss on my back.

It didn't feel bad, but my pussy was the one aching for attention, needing to be filled. I had soaked Jandro, who shoved his boxers down and slid me up and down his length with ease now. His clenched jaw and grip on my hips told me he was barely hanging on to his own control.

"If you were any other woman," Reaper continued, my skin trembling under the heat of the plug now, "after I was done spanking your ass, I'd make you crawl naked across the room, in front of the whole club. Ass in the air, on hands and knees, all the way over to me, while I sit and watch like this." He sat in the chair and leaned back, knees open and inviting. "And like a good girl, you'd suck me dry for everyone to see."

My lips parted, mouth watering at the sight of the bulge pressing through his jeans. I wanted to be right there, as he described it. On my hands and knees, between the long muscles of his thighs. Worshiping or controlling him, the power dynamic didn't matter as long as I could touch him. My fingers curled into Jandro's chest, his touch was soothing, but I still ached for the man who was punishing me.

"You're really not going to touch me until I come back?"

A muscle feathered in his jaw, the only shift in his demeanor. Just as quickly as it happened, he reeled the control back in. "I might give you a goodbye kiss tomorrow."

"Reaper," Jandro groaned beneath me, sliding me off of his shaft so I sat on his legs. His dick pulsed and his balls were tight and snug up against his base. He was already close.

"Take a break, but do not make her come," Reaper snapped. "Here." He handed the plug back to Gunner, who dragged the now-cooled metal through my sex again.

Jandro slid out from under me to lean against the headboard while Gunner played me—one hand in my ass, the other stroking my greedy pussy with a toy that didn't hold a candle to what I wanted. I needed my men, all of them. I wanted fresh memories of their touch and warmth while I had to be away from them. Reaper *knew* how badly I wanted him and used that information to fuck with my mind.

"Please…" There were no words for what I was begging for. I needed someone inside me, but I would've cried with joy if Reaper would just touch my face. Just gave me a kiss. Just told me I was being good.

"Come here, *bonita*." Jandro beckoned me forward and I crawled eagerly up the bed to him, just as Reaper had described .

Warm, hazel eyes drank me in as he cupped the sides of my neck, looking at me with adoration before he kissed me, passionate and languid.

"Beautiful," he murmured with another luscious tug of my lips. "You're a pain in the ass sometimes, but you're ours and we love you."

"I'm gonna miss you." I nudged my nose against his, angling for more of those pillowy lips.

"We'll miss you too. *All* of us," he said pointedly, hands caressing down my chest. "Someone's just more upset and worried about you leaving."

I knew that, but hearing him say it was comforting. Reaper, the most protective and dominant of them, was frustrated—both sexually, and with the helplessness of being unable to protect me for a few days.

Jandro's soothing touch reached my breasts, rolling over my nipples as he kept sucking luscious kisses from my mouth. I became painfully aware of nothing in my pussy or ass now, and arched my back with a wiggle of my hips, hoping Gunner would do something about that. Instead, I got two more punishing spanks from Reaper's palms.

He's making sure you'll feel him, all right, I realized as Gunner's hands smoothed over the stinging flesh. *You'll feel him on every bump and piece of gravel on the road tomorrow while you're on someone else's bike.*

Pressure returned to the tight ring of muscles around my ass, and I knew it wasn't a finger this time. More lube aided the plug in sliding through the entrance, filling me deeper and wider than before.

"Good, baby girl?" Gunner's hands and lips caressed up my back.

"I want you there," I whimpered, twisting around for a kiss.

"Not yet." He nuzzled my neck, wrapping his arms around my middle. "You're not ready. We'll get there, though."

Gunner slid around from behind me to kneel next to Jandro, who still reclined against the headboard. My breath was stolen for a moment at how gorgeous they looked next to each other. Jandro's dark tan and beefy muscles contrasted with Gunner's leanness and fairer complexion. I grabbed Gunner's waist, holding him for balance as I scooted up Jandro's legs to rest on his dick again.

I was so wet, my body so needy for affection and touch. And this was just the beginning of Reaper's mind game—his punishment for undermining him and for leaving him.

Jandro looked at him, still sitting to the side of the bed, fully dressed. The cool, collected puppet master of this scenario. I'd do anything he wanted just for the hope of him touching me.

"Go ahead." Reaper lit a cigarette and crossed his arms. "You can only make her come once though, so make it count."

I leaned forward, angling my hips as Jandro grabbed the base of his dick. He slid into me in one deep thrust, our mutual moans reaching the rafters in the ceiling. Everyone staying at the B&B would probably hear us, but I didn't care at that point.

Bracing one hand on Jandro's chest, I turned Gunner's hip toward me for easier reach. I found a rhythm with my hips first, grinding back and forth on my Latin lover, before leaning to the side to take Gunner in my mouth.

"Oh, baby girl," he groaned, fingers digging into my hair as he slid over my tongue, long and heavy.

I let out a satisfied hum, taking my two thick cocks deeper with every swallow and rock of my body. The plug in my ass added a new sensation, like Jandro filled my pussy even more with the added pressure. I leaned into it, rolling down to take him deeper and pressing the end of the plug between my body and his.

"Don't let her come," Reaper growled from the other side.

I lifted my hand from Jandro's chest to flip him off, earning a laugh from the man underneath me. To my disappointment, he lifted my hips up to reduce my friction.

"Boss's orders, Mariposita," Jandro groaned beneath me.

"Fuck him," I growled, lips resting on Gunner's pulsing crown while I took a minute to stroke him.

"That's not allowed either," my golden man chuckled above me. He stroked my cheek tenderly, turning my gaze up to his hooded blue eyes. "Can't say I'm mad about it, though, when I have you like this."

I leaned against his hip, resting my head there while my fist slid up and down the long, beautiful cock jutting out from his body. His breaths were loud, echoing around the room with the furious pulsing of my heartbeat.

Jandro took control beneath me, his strong grip on my waist as he drove up inside me. He filled me deep with long strokes, feeling even thicker with the plug's fullness in my ass. I teetered on the edge of release, but tried to steady my breath and whimpers. Maybe I could get away with more than one if I controlled my reactions.

Reaper's gaze was heavy over my shoulder. He loved seeing me pleased no matter what, so not touching me wasn't as bad for *him*, as long as my other two did their jobs. But only letting me come once? That had to be some kind of punishment for himself, too.

"Baby…"

Gunner couldn't even finish saying my pet name as my lips sucked a trail from his hip bone to his balls. He stiffened like concrete in my hand, his fingers tightening against my scalp as I licked and sucked the most tender parts of his body. A sharp inhale, that I knew didn't belong to him, reached my ears. My chest swelled with satisfaction as I ignored the surly president watching the show. Two could play at this game, and I wanted him to know what he was missing.

"Not gonna last if you keep that up," Gunner rasped in a rush of breath.

The confession just encouraged me even more, keeping one hand on his balls as my lips returned to his crown, tongue flicking the sensitive underside. Jandro's thrusts into me continued relentlessly, my clit crashing into his body with every impact.

Forgetting everything else but the sensations of my men filling me and pleasing me, I moaned around Gunner's dick as I pressed down against Jandro, matching him thrust for thrust. There was no stopping my release now, and I wanted their pleasure as much as my own.

My orgasm closed around Jandro like a vice, aided by the weight and pressure of the plug in my ass. He gasped with the rush of his own release, fingers curled into my flesh as he stiffened beneath me. Gunner's salty taste filled my mouth a moment later, his moans dragging heavily out of his chest as he flexed and twitched between my lips.

We untangled into a slick, sweaty pile. Gunner carefully removed the toy, but it wasn't him who came over to gently clean me with a damp washcloth.

Reaper shut off the lights before I could react, leaving the guys to fumble blindly for their sleeping spots in the bed. His shadowy form made the bed dip under his weight. The calloused touch of his palm opening my legs made me shiver with aftershocks. Cool softness pressed to the heat at my core, making me gasp.

"You're touching me," I panted.

"I know," he said, all anger and bite gone from his voice.

He dragged the washcloth all around my tender pussy first, before moving to my ass and wiping up any excess lube. When he stood and went into the small, adjoining bathroom, I wasn't sure whether to expect him to return to bed or not.

I turned on my side, facing away as I snuggled up to Gunner. Already half-asleep, he rained kisses down on my cheeks and forehead. The water faucet in the bathroom ran as I settled my head on Gunner's shoulder, my leg draped over his.

Clothes rustled behind me, and then the bed dipped again as bodies shuffled and moved around. I didn't turn around to see who'd snuggle up to my back, as much as I wanted to.

The broad arm wrapping around my waist felt like a shield, protective while sometimes unyielding. Cloves and whiskey filled my senses, and I melted with relief into the broad chest at my back.

"Sleep well, sugar," Reaper murmured in my ear. "You've got a long day tomorrow."

FIFTEEN

SHADOW

I need to get laid.

The thought wasn't one that came to me often, but with the sounds of Mariposa and her men through one wall, plus Larkan and Noelle from the other, it didn't leave room for much else to think about.

I popped a sleeping pill and chugged down a glass of water. While waiting for the pill to kick in, I double-checked my weapons. My shortest knives were under the pillow I was sleeping on, handgun under the other pillow. My daggers were under the bed, carefully placed with the handles out so I could reach them at a moment's notice. And my favorite rifle was tucked between the mattress and the headboard.

Anyone who broke into my room and searched for weapons wouldn't be able to find them without waking me first. Such was my standard procedure for sleeping anywhere that was unfamiliar.

When all weapons were checked and I had nothing else to do, I shucked off my shirt and kicked off my boots to the sounds of sex through the walls around me. Once undressed for bed, I reclined on the mattress, propping my pillow up against the headboard.

Someone mentioned there was a brothel in this territory. I briefly toyed with the idea of paying for some company, but quickly dismissed it. None of the service girls I'd slept with had ever really done anything for me. They were just there, convenient.

And the one person I actually wanted to spend time with was already busy next door.

You'll have her company for the next two days, though. Without *her men.*

The thought sent a flutter of nerves through me, and not for the first time that night. It sounded like a dangerous rescue mission, nothing I couldn't handle, but I was usually focused to the point of being robotic for these kinds of missions. Now I couldn't stop thinking of everything *but* the objective, my thoughts bouncing around like tennis balls.

I wondered if Mariposa and I would get the chance to talk over coffee, like friends. Like she suggested before the move. Would there be an opportunity to hug her again? Would she want to ride on the back of my bike?

That last thought sent a rush of heat to my dick so abruptly I groaned, my hand moving down my torso toward that annoying organ. I never exposed my back to anyone. It was why I always rode in the rear, why I always faced the door when inside a room. And I sure as fuck never had a woman ride with me.

I wanted to, though.

As long as it was her.

Even just as friends, I could trust her at my back. I wanted to take that chance. I wanted to know what it felt like.

I closed my eyes and my fist at the same time, willing my thoughts to stop bouncing all over the place, my cock to calm down, and to go the hell to sleep. But her soft voice continued to murmur through the walls, with deeper voices responding. I knew I should dig through my bags for my earplugs, but I couldn't stop listening.

I couldn't stop wishing she was here with me.

It was purely selfish. It wasn't like I could give her anything. I couldn't please and satisfy her like her three men did on a daily basis. I'd probably make a fucking fool of myself if we ever ended up in a physical situation again. *Not that we ever would, but…*

I might've been rock hard for her, but I couldn't help that response. All I really wanted was for her to be here next to me.

Lost in my own fantasies, the small, dark blur completely startled me when it jumped on my bed. The knife under my pillow was in my hand and pointed at the thing in the blink of an eye. Freyja just lowered herself into a seat as she stared at me from across the blanket.

"What are you doing here?" My gaze moved to the locked bedroom door. "How'd you get in?"

I can't tell you all my secrets now, a feminine voice that definitely wasn't my own floated softly through my mind. *I have a reputation to protect. Cat-like reflexes will mean nothing to humans if you learn my ways, Shadow.*

My hand with the knife lowered slowly to the mattress. "You can speak too. Like…like…"

Like Horus, yes. And Hades. Although those two are particular about who they speak to. Hades is not yet concerned with you, though I see Horus has taken you under his wing. The cat's green eyes dilated, her gaze growing darker. *He's touched you, and I can see why. You poor, lonely creature.*

"What…do you want?"

This didn't at all seem like the animal who purred endlessly, who rubbed herself all over me, and allowed me to pet her. No, there was something unsettling and…*human* in the way this cat looked at me. Her mouth didn't move, but the voice could only be hers. I heard with my ears and from a place deep inside me.

I'm here to give you permission, since you won't give it to yourself.

"Permission?"

To think of her. Lust after her. Talk to her and touch her if you feel the urge. Hell, even touch yourself at the thought of her.

"What?" Heat and shame filled me, my hands jerking away from my own body as though I couldn't trust myself. "I don't want to—why would I—"

You do *want to, son. And that's all right.* The cat walked across the bed toward me, a loud purr starting up from the small animal. *No one polices your thoughts, your wants, and desires. You're not hurting her or anyone else. So do not feel guilt or shame for feeling the way you do.*

Her head bumped against my hand, the side of her small, furry body following to press along my side. The contact made the panic in me subside just slightly. Freyja had a similar calming effect to Mariposa.

"What do I do?" I whispered to whatever wisdom inhabited the animal. "I can't stop thinking about her. I want to touch her every chance I get, but I—"

You're terrified, I know. But you must take some risks, son. Take a leap of faith. She is a gentle woman. If you fall, she won't drop you painfully.

"But I don't want anyone else," I said. "It feels like I'll never find anyone like her if I fail, but I feel like a fucking idiot for even thinking I have a chance."

That is the poison you've heard all your life, dear one. You know in your heart it isn't true. What did she herself tell you? These men you ride with, what do they tell you?

The cat stared at me expectantly, like she really wanted an answer.

"That I'm good at what I do. My loyalty is unwavering. I'm an asset to the club, and I'm, um, a good tattoo artist."

Yes, what else?

I looked down at my hands, remembering Mariposa's fingers wrapped around them just a few days ago.

"She told me I'm already good enough as I am. That I'm already a better man than many out there, better than others she's known."

And does that sound like someone who considers you beneath her?

"No, she's nothing like—like them."

My chest tightened as I fought memories of my past, feeling like cold blades trying to cut their way to the forefront of my mind. Mariposa said I'd have to confront them one day to truly beat them. But I was perfectly fine with keeping them locked away for as long as I lived.

You won't grow as a human unless you face what terrifies you.

I stared at the cat, unsure if she was reading my mind or referring to taking a chance with Mariposa.

Try something tomorrow. Share a part of yourself. She wants to know more about who you are.

"She does?" My heart leaped. "She told you that?"

The rhythm of Freyja's purr changed abruptly, sounding almost like a laugh, but the cat said no more. She jumped off my bed and disappeared.

I laid back against my pillow and closed my eyes, my body heavy with the sleep medication now settling into my limbs. They were either finished next door or I was already too far under to hear. But I returned to that feeling, the one that made my thoughts bounce around knowing I'd spend at least two full days with her.

I think this means I'm excited, was my last thought before drifting off.

THE SKY WAS STILL DARK when I woke up, the coldness of right before dawn settling into my room. I pushed back the covers and rose from bed, already wide awake and eager to start the day.

Walking around my bed on bare feet, I was unsurprised to find I was alone—no cat trapped in here with me, despite never opening the door last night. I splashed cold water on my face and wondered if Freyja's pep talk last night was some kind of hallucination from my sleeping pills.

You know it wasn't. Your own brain would have never encouraged you like that. Plus, it wasn't the first time. At this point, it was hardly unusual for anyone in the SDMC to hear voices.

I dropped down to the floor and started a quick workout routine, hoping it would calm my nerves. Since joining the SDMC, I'd never spent extended time away from the majority of my brothers, and that gave me a mixture of excitement and nervousness.

Jandro taught me how to function in the real world, and I leaned on him heavily in the first few years of my freedom. Lately, I'd started to wonder if I was outgrowing the routine we established. I could talk to people without him prodding me now. I might even be able to talk to a woman besides Mariposa, if a situation called for it.

I held myself up at the top of a push-up, clenching my jaw as I slowly lowered down. Jandro almost felt overbearing lately. Not that I wasn't grateful for his help in getting by, but with each passing day, I was starting to feel like I didn't need him for that anymore.

Whenever we found a permanent place to settle, I might even like to try having my own home.

The sun just started to rise as I finished my workout and took a quick shower. After packing a few necessities in my saddle bags, I left my room to enter a still quiet common area of the bed-and-breakfast. Everyone's doors were closed and I couldn't detect any movement —none except for the man already at the coffee pot.

"*Buenos dias.*" Jandro seated himself at a table with a full cup. "You're up early, man."

"Yeah." I'd forgotten he was such an early riser. "Wanted to make sure I was prepared for today."

"Mm-hm."

I felt him watch me as I headed for the pot myself and filled a clean cup, then meandered to the same table and sat across from him.

"What are you up to today?" I brought the steaming, dark liquid to my lips.

"Exploring Four Corners, probably." He leaned back and stretched, lacing his hands behind his head. "Try to keep my mind off missing the hell out of my woman while she's gone."

"Mm." I nodded with a swallow of coffee, like I understood how that felt. If it was anything like the ache I felt whenever Mariposa wasn't around, I knew it well. "I'll make sure nothing happens to her. You have my word."

"I know I do." He didn't seem relieved, but continued to peer at me from across the table. "You think it's gonna be…difficult for you?"

I nearly choked on my next swallow. "Difficult how?"

"You know."

I placed my mug down on the table. "I don't, Jandro."

"You've slept with her before. Now you're going to be in close proximity again, without any of *us* there for days."

The hard, familiar clamp of anxiety tightened

around my chest, as it always did when someone insinuated that I did something wrong. But I felt more in control this time. Now, I felt confident that I might not actually screw up like I was expected to.

"You know I wouldn't do anything behind your back, Jandro. And I'd never put Mariposa in a situation where she'd be frightened like that again. We've both gained a lot of trust in each other."

His eyebrows lifted. That wasn't the answer he was expecting. While Jandro meant well, I realized he was used to ordering me around. Both because he was vice president, and also because I was once meek, scared of my own shadow, and didn't know any better.

"Not behind my back," he repeated slowly, weighing each of the words. "Do you really mean to say…"

"It's Mariposa's decision too," I said, which made his mouth drop open. "I don't know if she wants…anything with me, or just to be friends. But I'm grateful to her and value her in my life, regardless."

Jandro rocked forward in his chair, placing his palms down on the table. "Shadow, dude. We've talked about this before—"

"You told me I'm inexperienced, which is true. But I'm not dumb, and I'm not a bad man."

"I never said—"

"No, but you think I'm not good enough for her." I sucked in a breath that was almost painful to take in. My chest felt like it was going to explode, but I had to finish saying my piece. "Which is fair enough, Jandro. But that's ultimately not your decision. It's hers."

His mouth abruptly closed and opened again with surprise, before stroking his chin with his hand.

"I suppose you're right." His expression turned a bit embarrassed. "I just want the best for her, you know. But she's her own woman, and I do love that about her." He looked toward his bedroom door, still closed, with silence behind it. "One of my best friends is already with her. I suppose it's not too weird if another one joins us."

"I just want you to know that," my grip returned to the coffee mug, "I appreciate everything you've taught me about the world. And now I'm at a point where I think I'll be okay managing on my own."

He nodded sagely at that. "I respect that, Shadow. Hell, I might've held your hand on some things for too long. But I'm glad you're feeling more confident now. It's a good look on you, bro."

"Thanks." I hid my heated face behind another large swallow of coffee.

"I trust you out there, in every respect," he said. "And while I'm gonna be counting the seconds til she comes back, I trust Mari too. So, if you still get those moments where you feel…skittish, let's say, just know that you can trust her too." My oldest friend gave me a solemn look across the table. "Remember that, man. She'd never hurt you."

"I know." I set my now-empty coffee cup down on the table. "But thanks for the reminder."

SIXTEEN

MARIPOSA

"All set, little lady?"

T-Bone was in a cheery mood, whistling a tune as he approached me with a cup of coffee in his hand.

"Almost," I assured him, rummaging through my supplies.

"Yeah, yeah. Take your time, get your goodbye smooches."

Chuckling to myself, I double-checked my medic bag, securing all the side pockets but left the main compartment open for Freyja to jump in. She was getting goodbye pets from the guys on the front porch of the B&B.

I made my way over to them, sliding my arms through the straps. My heart skipped a beat when Reaper's green gaze leveled on me. I woke up this morning with tender, bruised butt cheeks, and felt every square inch of fabric as I pulled my pants on.

"Sore?" His lips quirked amusedly.

"A little," I replied in a snippy tone. "You still mad at me?"

He sighed, staring at me longingly from head to toe. "I'm gonna miss you too much to be mad."

We moved toward each other at the exact same time, closing the short distance with enough momentum to crash into each other. We collided, the force strong enough to knock me back if he hadn't grabbed my bag straps to hold me in place. The kiss came down with equal force, his tongue invading my mouth like he'd never get to taste me again.

Coffee, leather, and clove cigarette filled my senses. It was early morning and I knew he hadn't drank yet, but I picked up that hint of whiskey on his tongue, too. I clung to his shirt, sucking on his lower lip as though my life depended on holding on to every one of my husband's flavors.

The kiss came to a slow, gentle ending, but our mouths never fully separated and our hands continued to hold the other person.

"I'm gonna miss you too," I breathed against his mouth. "And I'm sorry about yesterday."

Reaper released my straps, his hands gliding down my sides to hug around my waist. "It's forgiven, sugar. I think you were adequately punished last night." With a wicked grin, his palms slid down to cup my ass.

I winced, shifting in his grip, much to his amusement, as he kneaded my sore flesh. I was definitely going to be feeling every single pebble and pothole throughout the ride. And yet despite it, I craved his hands on me and his cock filling me up. This romantic goodbye felt wholly unfair since he deprived me of him last night.

"No time for a gentle quickie?"

"Nope," he chuckled. "Nice try though." His touch slid back up the front of my body, shamelessly running over my breasts before he cupped the sides of my neck. "I love you, sugar," he breathed, nose nudging mine. "And it's gonna be so fucking good when my wife comes back home to me."

Another rough, biting kiss felt like the fresh hit of a drug high before he tore himself away.

"Be safe, old lady." His forehead nuzzled mine. "Don't let these dickwads get themselves killed, either."

"We'll be back before you know it." I stood on tiptoes to steal one last kiss from him. "And I love you too, old man."

Reaper stepped back with an amused smile, making room for Gunner and Jandro to come up to me.

"*Oh, Mariposita,*" Jandro sighed, pulling me into him to wrap me in a bone-crushing embrace. "I don't like this at all. Frankly, I'm scared to death," he whispered into my neck.

"Shadow won't let anything happen." I wrapped my arms around his neck. "Just don't jump in front of any explosions until I get back."

The VP groaned his displeasure, squeezing around me tighter as he peppered kisses to my neck and cheek.

"You can fight and shoot now, baby girl," Gunner reminded me, with a kiss on the back of my head. "You'll be fine."

I spun in Jandro's arms to face my golden man. "Finally, a vote of confidence."

He grinned, cupping my chin with a gentle hand as he lowered an incredibly hot, languid kiss to my mouth. Our chemistry buzzed through the contact of our lips, but he didn't deepen or speed it up. It was Jandro who pushed my hair aside and sucked at my nape, leaving me gasping and writhing between them.

"You two are evil together," I whined.

"Hurry back, then." Gunner moved his lips to my ear. "So all three of us can fill our woman when she gets home."

Right then was the moment I almost decided to stay. But I swallowed the hungry need to feel all my men at the same time, and looked out toward the packed, revving bikes, ready to go. I was about to see a new territory, spend time with new friends, without my men hovering. And Reaper was right—it would be so much sweeter after some time away.

The Steel Demons president had the Sons of Odin, Larkan, and Shadow in some kind of group huddle. I couldn't hear him over the bikes, but it sounded like he was barking instructions. Or threats. Probably both.

T-Bone caught me watching and winked over Reaper's shoulder. When the group broke up, Reaper turned with his back ramrod straight and chin high. I smirked as he approached and grabbed me around the waist for a final, *final* kiss.

"What did you tell them?"

"That I'll skin every one of them alive and let Hades

feast on their organs if you get so much as a scratch on you."

"Figured it was something like that." I pressed my hands to the sides of his face. "I *will* come back to you. My place is at your side, love."

"I know you will." His palms squeezed around my shoulders. "I need you with me, sugar."

We parted slowly, our hands the last to disconnect. As I walked up to the men waiting by their bikes, Larkan came over to me with his chest puffed out.

"Mrs. President," he declared. "It would be my honor if you rode with me at the start of our trip."

I smiled, catching the glances of the other guys. T-Bone and the Sons were trying, and failing, to hold in their laughter. Shadow glanced over quickly but looked away, preoccupied with tying something down on his bike. I had intended to ask if I could ride with him, but Larkan beat me to the punch, and he looked so hopeful.

"Larkan, the honor is mine." I accepted his outstretched hand.

"Fuck," Dyno spat. "I owe you a beer, Grudge."

His silent, long-haired comrade grinned smugly as he snapped dark goggles over his eyes.

Freyja jumped into my backpack just as I got my helmet on and settled into Larkan's seat. With a final look back at everyone as we took off, I realized this was the second time I rode off on a man's bike to somewhere unknown.

Hopefully it would turn out just as successful as the first time.

———

THE LANDSCAPE BECAME GREENER, lush with dense trees and rolling hills as we rode north. Instead of desert heat and sand blasting my face, cool, damp air made my skin dewy.

The Sons of Odin led the way, followed by Larkan and I, then Shadow bringing up the rear. I stared at him shamelessly in Larkan's mirrors, now that I couldn't be caught.

It baffled me that Shadow had no idea how hot he was. He always hid part of his face, but now the wind whipping his hair back showed a strong jaw and prominent cheekbones. The scar cut through his eyebrow and part of the beard on his left cheek, and the presence of it only made me want to touch his face and kiss him there. Freyja's words echoed in my mind. *He has wounds only love can heal.*

At this rate, Shadow would be confident enough to talk to any woman soon. Maybe he would find love in Four Corners, or wherever we ended up.

The closer and friendlier we became, the more I wanted that person to be me.

A few hours into the ride, the road took us from smooth asphalt to potholes and gravel. Every bounce of Larkan's tires felt like Reaper's hands on my sore ass all over again.

Thanks a lot, Reap. Your spanking did what you intended.

I gritted my teeth and didn't realize I was clutching harder around Larkan's waist until he tapped my fingers.

Reaper. My protective, ruthless husband. How

would he feel about something developing between me and Shadow? I was also surprised Jandro hadn't said anything to me yet, considering how close the two of them were. He got an eyeful of Shadow doing my second tattoo, and had to know we were closer than before.

We stopped twice briefly for piss breaks during the day, then made our final stop for the night once the sun began dipping over the trees. Larkan, Shadow, and I all found our own spots to put our things down, but the Sons worked together as a single unit, like they'd done this hundreds of times before.

Grudge dug out a fire pit and began setting up logs and kindling. Dyno set up their bedrolls and shared tent, and T-Bone checked all his weapons.

"What do y'all Demons want for dinner?" the sergeant asked with a grin. "Bet I can take down a buck before it gets dark."

"No, get something light." Dyno shook out a blanket. "We'll be in and out tomorrow, right? Don't need to carry half a buck along with a girl."

"On that note," I leaned against my pack, stretching out on my own blanket with Freyja at my side, "is there a plan for tomorrow? Josh mentioned not knowing where she actually is."

T-Bone nodded, his smile faltering. "I have some ideas, but let's eat and relax first." He checked a rifle before cocking it and leaning the barrel over his shoulder. "Settle in and I'll find us something *light*." He gave Dyno an affectionate shove before walking off toward a densely wooded area.

A half-hour later, Grudge had a cozy fire going and the two Sons cuddled up while waiting for their third to return. A pang of longing hit me at the sight of them, knowing I wouldn't be sandwiched between my own men tonight.

Larkan caught me staring wistfully and nodded in my direction with a smile. "Yeah, I'm missing my favorite snuggle partner too."

I returned his smile. "For what it's worth, I really hope Reap patches you in soon. You deserve it, and you and Noelle are already official in every way but the title."

"Yeah," he sighed, tilting his gaze up toward the stars. "It's cheesy as hell, but the Demons, her—it feels like my destiny, you know? Even though I thought I was gonna fucking die when I ran into all of you."

"I thought the same thing when Shadow tied me up and put me on Reaper's bike." I laughed, tossing a glance over to the man in question. "Remember that?"

"Yes," Shadow huffed with air of amusement. "And I was just following orders." He poured something from a flask into two mugs, then squeezed lime wedges over the drinks before dropping the fruit in. "Vodka tonics?"

"Sure, if you're offering." My insides fluttered as he handed one mug to me, the other to Larkan.

"Sorry I don't have ice, and it's not the same as that tequila you like."

He remembers, I realized. *And pays attention.*

"It's tasty," I assured him, smacking my lips at the lime's tartness and bubbles of the tonic water. "You can sit closer to us if you want."

Shadow eyed Larkan and my tents set up right next to each other, while his bedroll and bike were several paces away.

"Um, if you're sure."

"Man, if anything, I should be the one on the outskirts," Larkan said. "I don't have a patch or nothin'. Hell, I should be the one getting food and making drinks too."

"Normally you would be," Dyno called from across the fire. "But we're leading this mission and luckily, you're not our prospect."

"Consider yourself on vacation." I elbowed Larkan playfully. "My guys aren't here to boss you around."

"Yeah, but is their old lady gonna tell on me?" He grinned.

"My lips are sealed."

While we bantered, Shadow dragged his stuff closer to us and settled down on my other side. Now I was sandwiched between two men again—neither of which were mine, and only one I was entertaining the idea with.

Freyja couldn't be more pleased at Shadow setting up next to us. She rose up from my blanket and crossed over directly to his, climbing up his torso to rub her head directly under his jaw.

"Hello again, kitten," he chuckled, stroking a hand down her spine. "I guess you're not really kitten-sized anymore. You're getting bigger."

Larkan choked on his drink. "Dude, a cat is one thing, but never tell a woman that."

"Why not?"

"It's just not what they ever want to hear." He poked me in the arm. "Help me out here."

"Not all women are the same, Lark." I poked him back. "But generally speaking, yes. Most women aren't happy to hear it if they're gaining weight."

"I used to be rail-thin, much thinner than Gunner." Shadow scratched Freyja's cheeks with both hands. "But I gained weight quickly and got a lot stronger as a result. I was happy to get bigger."

I almost couldn't believe what I was hearing. Not that I couldn't believe Shadow was ever thin, but the fact that he was sharing something about himself, unprompted. I wanted to curl up on his chest like the cat and listen to anything and everything he had to say.

"Yeah, same here," Larkan nodded, oblivious to the fact that there was anything groundbreaking about this conversation. "Lifting did wonders for my confidence. I think getting bigger is a different mindset for us guys, though."

T-Bone emerged from the brush a short while later, holding up three dead pheasants like they were trophies. "Dinner time!"

Each person had plenty to eat with half a bird. Grudge set up a spit and turned them over the fire with careful precision, while T-Bone informed us of his plan for tomorrow.

"We should leave the bikes hidden just outside the territory border and go in on foot. Ah, thanks, man." He accepted a drink from Shadow. "Their big thing is cheap or free labor, so one of us should pose as a foreman and the rest as laborers."

"You mean an overseer with slaves?" I asked.

"If you want to be technical, yes." He looked over at Shadow. "You could play the role well. All those scars, avoiding eye contact while staying observant. It'll keep people from messing with us."

"I don't know." I wrinkled my nose, feeling defensive for him. Shadow had been exploited enough. "This feels…gross."

"It's fine," Shadow shrugged. "I'll do it if it helps the plan."

"Right, thanks." T-Bone nodded appreciatively. "So we know the area roughly, but none of us have actually been *in* the territory. We're just going off what Josh told us. We have to get the lay of the land. Find the right people to talk to."

"How likely are we to really do this in one day?" I asked. "They're probably not keeping her out in the open, right? And how big is this territory?"

"Right now, the bulk of the action is in the one big city right on the border." Dyno unfolded a map and laid it out on a rock. "They're in the process of making it into a shiny metropolis. The rest of it is open land for drilling oil. If we go through the heart of the city, act like we're looking for work, we should be able to see where the governor and his family hang out. If we can capture him, the son, or someone close to them, we might be able to find out where the girl is. If we're *really* lucky," he looked up at all of us, "she'll be out in the open with them. But that's only if it's public knowledge that she and the governor's son are betrothed."

"According to Josh, the governor takes daily strolls

through his square," T-Bone picked up in a mocking, posh accent. "To survey the blood, sweat, and beatings that build the foundation of his great territory."

"Sounds like a piece of fuckin' work," Larkan observed. "But potentially easy to grab, which is good for us."

"Mari, as a woman," T-Bone looked at me apologetically, "your role to play should be someone's whore or wife. I'll let you pick, but it's essentially the same—"

"Don't speak unless spoken to, and do so quietly. Smile sweetly. Dress modestly, but not in a way that hides my femininity. Don't invite ogling from men. Don't try to act smarter than men." I rolled my eyes while rattling off the list.

"I guess you'd know it better than any of us," Dyno said sheepishly.

"We got pamphlets handed to us constantly while I was in nursing school," I explained. "The new governors had been working on getting women out of medicine for years, telling us what our roles should be instead. They couldn't even be original. It was all straight out of the 1950s."

All the guys, except for Shadow, gave me guilty looks. He appeared curious, if even confused.

"Sorry," T-Bone offered. "If you're not comfortable—"

"It's fine, I'll do it," I said with a wave of my hand. "It's all about getting the girl out. And you're right, we should play convincing roles to not bring suspicion. It's a good plan."

Grudge stood up to check on the cooking food while

T-Bone scrubbed a hand over his beard. "If no one has any objections to this, then eat up and sleep well. We ride out early for another couple hours before we reach the border."

Shadow and I returned to our spots with bowls of roasted pheasant and rice, while Larkan remained chatting with the Sons across the fire.

"I didn't know that, about how they tried to control women back then," he muttered, digging into his food. "It's not in any of the history books I've read."

I washed a mouthful down with more of his deliciously bubbly vodka tonic. "It wouldn't surprise me if they cut it out of the books published in the last decade or so. They burned and deleted all the ones about feminism itself. Wouldn't want to give modern women any ideas."

"How did you learn about it?"

"My parents told me," I said. "They told me about their grandparents. How women couldn't even vote almost two-hundred years ago, back when we could actually choose our leaders. They couldn't get divorced, get paid the same wage, or control their own money for a long time, either. It was like that and worse going back hundreds, even thousands of years."

"That...explains a lot of my upbringing." He drank deeply from his own mug. "The anger toward me and other men. I never knew the true reason for it. Now I have an idea."

I gripped my mug and food bowl painfully tight so as to not drop them. He seemed relaxed, completely at ease to be talking about himself with me. His long legs stretched out in front of him, crossed at the ankles and his back propped up on his saddle bags. Of course the picture wouldn't be complete without Freyja at his side, eyeing his bowl of pheasant.

He was opening up by his own choice, and not while under any distress. After how withdrawn he was when I first met him, did he have any idea how groundbreaking this was?

"Nothing justifies what was done to you," I said. "Hurting you, keeping you isolated—no one with a normal amount of anger does that to another person. It's completely wrong, and I'm sorry you were a target of that."

Shadow didn't answer for a few moments, but just ate his food quietly. Once finished, he set his bowl aside and turned toward me, making my heart jump.

"Thank you for saying that, Mariposa." He reached into a saddlebag pocket and pulled out the orange bottle of sleeping pills. "Hope you sleep well," he added, shaking one into his palm.

"You too," I answered, lowering my back onto the ground. I glued my eyes to the starry sky, because if I looked at him it would feel too much like we were lying next to each other. "Good night, Shadow."

SEVENTEEN

SHADOW

I wanted to stay alert on the road, so I only took half of a sleeping pill. The fire died down not long after Mariposa went into her tent for the night. Like me, the guys preferred sleeping under the stars. Unlike me, the world around them went dark at night, and they kept solar lanterns on low power nearby so they could still have some sight if needed.

I dozed off for a couple of hours, waking up with a start and my heart pounding. Looking around quickly, my surroundings told me whether or not I went "ape-shit" in my sleep again, as Jandro put it.

Much to my relief, everything was in place and the others were still in their bedrolls. Even after Mariposa started me on the pills, I'd wake up paranoid that I'd destroyed my room again, or worse, hurt someone. So far it hadn't happened, but overnight rides like this made me nervous about it. That was why I also made drinks before bed, to knock out my subconscious a little more.

Anything to keep the monster at bay.

Mariposa alluded that I needed to confront the source of my nightmares in order to be truly free from them. That I should talk to a brain doctor when I was ready. The thing was, I wasn't sure if I, or a doctor, would survive the full brunt of what lurked inside me.

Taking a pill, having a few drinks. That was an easy solution I felt comfortable with.

I went to the fire pit and knelt down to blow on some embers. Just enough heat to make some coffee would suffice. Carefully disassembling Grudge's meat spit, I replaced it with a grate and a metal percolator.

Something caught my eye just past our camp as I waited for my coffee to heat up. Several bright white things, roughly shaped like stars, stood out against the muted tones of the landscape. I squinted over the fire, my hand drifting to my holster as I saw more of them emerge slowly out of apparently nothing. They seemed to cluster on rocks or tree trunks, dozens of them in one place.

A memory struck me like a fist to the chest, one buried under years of loss, loneliness, and so much blood.

But this one didn't hurt. This one didn't send me spiraling into darkness and fear. The memory surfaced like a seedling breaking through the soil. It was from *that* time, but I was still here. I was okay, and witnessing something I never thought I'd have the chance to see again.

"…Shadow, is that you?"

I turned to see Mariposa halfway out of her tent, rubbing her eyes.

"I'm sorry. Did I wake you?"

"No, I'm just a light sleeper out here, and woke up smelling coffee this time." She grinned sleepily, making my chest ache. I wanted to hug her to me again, to feel her head resting over my heart. "What are you doing up?"

"I only took half a pill because I wanted to be alert. It'll be dawn in a few hours anyway." I took the percolator and began pouring the coffee. "Would you like some? Or are you going back to sleep?"

"Oh, I don't think I'll be getting any sleeping done." Wrapped in a blanket, she came over and plopped down next to me, her knee brushing my leg. "Thank you."

We sat quietly, with only crickets and the crackling of embers filling the silence between us. I kept my eyes on the white star things hovering in the distance, growing brighter by the minute. I was just about to take a closer look when Mariposa woke up, but I didn't want to leave her by the fire alone.

Freyja's crackling purr floated up from my opposite side, her head rubbing along my thigh before looking up at me with those knowing eyes. She didn't need to say anything this time. The voice in my head was my own.

Take a risk. A leap of faith. The worst she can do is say no.

I spoke the words before I lost the courage to do so. "Would it be all right if I showed you something?"

Mariposa's gaze flicked over to me in surprise, the fire embers lighting up her irises.

"Sure."

She said it with no fear, no apprehension, and my body soared with lightness.

"It's just on the other side of the camp. I can see it from here."

I rose to my feet first, waiting for her to follow. She looked up at me, sitting cross-legged on the ground with a tiny smile pulling at her lips. After a final swig of coffee, she set the mug down and raised a hand toward me.

"Help me up?"

I wondered if she could hear my pulse. It thundered in my ears as my hand reached to clasp around hers, pulling her to her feet.

"Thanks." She left her blanket on my bedroll, and removed her hand from mine to dust herself off. "Lead the way."

I turned, walking past the sleeping Sons of Odin and toward the bright white things. If I was right, it could be a nice moment to share with her. That was assuming she didn't think this was dumb or—

"Shadow, wait!" Mariposa called from a few paces behind me. "I can't see anything. I didn't bring my flashlight."

"Oh, sorry." I went back to her side, shame burning my face. "I forgot."

"It's okay," she laughed lightly, wrapping a hand around my bicep. "You can be my night-vision. Just tell me if I'm about to trip over something?"

"Of course. I won't let you hurt yourself."

We began again, side by side. She squeezed gently around my arm, leaning on me slightly as I told her to step over various rocks and branches in front of her feet.

"Is this okay?" she asked at one point. "Me holding on to you like this?"

"Yes, it's okay." *More than okay.*

My other hand itched with the desire to cover her fingers, to feel what it would be like if they laced through mine, like I saw her do with her men. I kept that arm stiffly at my side.

"What are those?" She could see the white things now, bright as star-shaped diamonds clustered on boulders. "Is that what you're showing me?"

"Yes." My heart pounded with recollection, the familiarity of those shapes and their brightness back when I knew nothing but darkness. "They're flowers."

The blooms attached to scrambling vines that covered the boulder in a complex net-like structure. It was a cactus plant, the vines covered in spines, and looked altogether unremarkable, if even ugly without the blooms.

But the flowers, they were breathtaking.

"Oh my god!" Mariposa leaned forward, pulling me with her hand still around my arm. She looked back at me, the white flowers practically casting a glow on her face. "These were in your sketchbook, that pencil drawing."

"Yes," I admitted, cringing at the memory.

I didn't know she'd come over, and had left my sketchbook open. She asked about it, and I slammed the book shut while telling her it was nothing. I had drawn the flower that morning in a half-asleep daze, the memory murky and fleeting. Not crystal clear as it was now.

"It's beautiful." Mariposa turned back to gaze at the long, thin petals, the spines circling the base of the flower like a crown. Some of them rivaled the size of sunflowers, nearly as big as her face. "What does this flower mean to you, Shadow?"

"It's called, um..."

My voice threatened to leave, to retreat into silence where I risked nothing, shared nothing, and closed myself off. But I didn't want to do that anymore, not with her. I forced myself to speak.

"It's called Night-blooming Cereus," I said. "It blooms once a year, and only at night."

"Amazing," she breathed, eyes moving all around the various blooms. "So this is a rare opportunity, huh?"

"Yes." Her observation was correct, but I could only bring myself to look at her instead of the flowers. Even wide-eyed and bedheaded, I never saw a more beautiful woman in my life.

Her gaze turned to me, a smile curving at her lips as her hand slid from my bicep, fingers trailing down my arm, to my palm.

"Thank you for showing me," she said. "This is really special."

"I..." I cleared my throat, still fighting past my instinct to retreat. "I thought you might like to see them."

"So you've seen them before." She said it as a statement, not a question.

"Yes." Her fingers skimmed over mine, and I

allowed my hand to close around hers. "A long time ago. It's one of my few good memories of um, before joining the club and everything."

"Will you tell me about it?"

Some of the flowers had already begun to close, their blooms incredibly short-lived, but nothing diminished the radiance of the woman standing next to me.

"I...met a man." The memories were desperate to pour out of me now, but I held back on the grisly details. None of that deserved to be heard. "When I was a boy, maybe eight or ten years old. He was a plant scientist, a uh..."

"A botanist?"

"Yes, that. The only thing he had on him was a small book of his field notes. He showed me what he'd been researching when he, um, was placed with me."

If Mari was confused or annoyed by my vague details, her face gave no indication. She just held my hand, circling her thumb inside my palm.

"He was researching these types of flowers?" she asked.

"Um, yes. He said it was strange for them to be growing this far north. They're native to Mexico and Central America. So to see them in Arizona, either they had adapted to the drier climate, or the climate itself changed to become more habitable for them."

I was rambling now, my nerves getting the best of me. Here was where the memory started turning dark, where the horror that followed didn't deserve the light of day.

"You saw these blooms with him?" Mari moved

closer to me, standing directly between my feet. The side of her body started to lean against mine with soft warmth and pressure. A light touch skimmed across my back, resting on the far side of my waist. "That must have been magical to see, especially as a kid."

"It was." I lifted my arm to rest it on her shoulders, spreading my fingers on the opposite hand to allow them to twine with hers. She kept me in the good part of the memory, and I was grateful for that. "He woke me up one night and told me to look out our, um, window. It was at a weird angle and I couldn't see well in the dark then, but I saw something white and thought it was a ghost. Or a fallen star."

Mari chuckled, resting her head on my shoulder as her arm tightened around my back. Her fingers laced through mine and gently squeezed as she watched the quickly-fading blooms.

"He was so excited," I went on. "He'd been wanting to see one of them bloom for months. Their growth cycle was all different up here and he kept missing them when going out in the field."

"And he got to share something meaningful with you." Mari turned in toward me, her chest now against mine, and her cheek resting on my heart. "That must have been nice."

"It was."

The blooms had completely faded, but the last thing I wanted to do was move from this spot. Her body pressed against me, my forearm around her upper back, and our hands entwined at our sides. I just wanted to keep this feeling, both the physical sensations of her, and what surged through the deepest parts of me. But I should have known it was foolish to even think about keeping this.

Mari pulled away slowly, her cheek that had been pressed to my chest more flushed than the other.

"Thank you so much for telling me that, for showing me this." Her arm slid away from my back. "We should probably head back."

"Yes," I grunted, already longing for the warmth and softness of her again. "Of course."

She continued holding on to my hand as we walked back, her other hand wrapping around my forearm as I led us back to camp.

"What happened to him?" she asked quietly when we were almost there. "The botanist."

My throat closed up when I heard the question, the dark emptiness wanting to drag me under until I was alone and cold again. It was familiar, a twisted type of comforting when faced with an uncomfortable question.

But talking to her, giving her small bits and pieces of me, felt good, even if doing it was strange and scared me to death. I liked the warmth better than the coldness, and I wanted to hold onto that.

"He died the next day."

"I'm sorry." She squeezed around my arm, hugging her body to it with her temple on my shoulder.

"Thank you. Me too."

One day, a long time from now, I might be able to tell her the rest of it. That I heard his screams until his throat gave out, and his blood rained on me through the cracks in my cage.

EIGHTEEN

MARIPOSA

Shadow and I stayed up talking over coffee when we got back, about small, innocuous things. I learned his favorite color was orange. Not because he liked to wear it, but because it reminded him of sunsets. He seemed very curious about why I was passionate about helping people, even total strangers. I found it difficult to articulate a reason, aside from feeling like I was meant to do it.

A few hours later, the others roused and the sun was just emerging from behind the trees. Larkan took a long look at me and my blanket sitting on Shadow's bedroll, but thankfully didn't comment.

"Mind if I ride with you?" I murmured quickly to Shadow before Larkan could swoop in.

Freyja meowed and wrapped herself around his ankles, looking up with a pleading kitten stare, as if she was backing me up.

He rolled up his bedroll and turned to his bike to

secure it, but he couldn't hide the pink flush creeping up his face.

"Sure, if you'd like to," he muttered.

After a quick breakfast and packing everything up, we hit the road. I couldn't even see over Shadow's shoulder without lifting my butt from the seat. My hold around his waist was light, casual, just like with Larkan. But with this driver, I had to seriously restrain myself from squeezing around him and nuzzling my face into his back. He was like a brick wall I was desperate to turn into a soft, pliant place to cuddle.

I saw a glimpse of that side of him last night, and with every touch or hug it felt like we were disassembling this wall together, brick by brick. But I wanted him to feel safe in this process. He could still be strong without a wall built around him.

This ride was much shorter, and the landscape quickly changed again. Trees and lush greenery gave way to felled logs and barren ground. Pumpjacks in the distance moved in their slow, methodical rhythm, positioned over oil wells underground. And just beyond them…skyscrapers?

By my estimate, we were in what was once known as Wyoming, maybe roughly in the northern Colorado-western Nebraska area. But the shiny glass and metal buildings in the distance looked reminiscent of New York City or Los Angeles, both of which had been evacuated and then leveled to nothing decades ago.

T-Bone led us down a barely marked side road just as we passed the oil wells. He came to a rusted, barely-standing barn when he cut his engine and turned to us.

"We'll leave the bikes in here," he said. "No one will tamper with them."

"Are you sure?" I looked at the structure skeptically.

"Trust me, little lady." He grinned as the sound of wings fluttered, his raven temporarily blocking the sun before landing on his shoulder with a *caw!* "Your men ain't the only ones who got their connections. Our things will be safe here. But once we're in the city limits," he nodded at the buildings, "I make no guarantees about our safety."

"Just another day in an MC then," I sighed.

Dyno laughed. "She gets it, T."

We filed into the barn, parking side by side along one wall. Shadow got off as I unsnapped my helmet and shook my hair out. When I swung my leg over to follow, he took me completely by surprise when he placed both hands on my waist and lifted me off of the bike.

"Why thank you, sir," I laughed when my feet touched the ground, my insides bursting in a mass of flutters.

For a moment, he looked utterly terrified. "Was that okay to do?" he whispered. "I'm sorry if I—"

"It's completely fine," I assured him, clasping his arms just above his elbows. I wondered if his heart was racing like mine. "Just unexpected, that's all."

"I wasn't thinking. It just came to me and I—"

"Do it again next time." I patted his arm before turning to secure my helmet to his handlebars. "That was fun."

"Oh. Okay."

He, Larkan, and I came into a group huddle to

decide who would be playing what roles when we entered the city. After taking a look at the changes of clothes everyone brought, it was decided Larkan would play the foreman looking for a contract, and I would be his wife. Everyone else would be laborers.

The guys were polite enough to turn around while I changed into the one dress I brought as a just-in-case measure.

"Feels fuckin' weird to not wear a cut," T-Bone complained, rubbing at his shoulders.

"Okay, I'm good," I announced, smoothing my hands down the skirt in hopes that it would hide my motorcycle boots.

They all turned slowly, and it was Dyno who let out a long whistle.

"I am so fucking glad Reaper isn't here," he chuckled. "We would all be dead just for looking at you."

"Oh, stop," I grumbled.

It was a simple black maxi dress, which thankfully wasn't cut into a halter top like most of my clothes. My back was covered, which meant my SDMC tattoo was hidden. But the Rod of Asclepius on my arm wasn't.

"Is this gonna be a problem?" I asked, pointing to the tattoo.

"Maybe just keep that arm facing me," Larkan suggested. He had brought a white collared shirt and looked the cleanest, most upper-class out of all the guys. "You should be on my arm pretty much the whole time, anyway."

"Alright, are we good?" T-Bone's eyes darted over all of us. "Any questions?" When no one answered, his raven cawed and flew toward the open barn doors. "Stay close to each other. Eyes and ears open."

———

WE HAILED a cab just outside the border, instructing the driver to drop us off downtown. My stomach churned immediately upon entering the city limits. The streets were shiny and pristine, without a speck of dirt in sight. The skyscrapers looked like sculptures of glass and metal that defied gravity. The few trees and plants were perfectly-manicured topiaries, without a leaf or flower out of place. It felt like stepping into the future, but also wrong somehow. Like this glittering, beautiful city was just a mask for something much uglier.

The people walking on the main street alongside us looked like extensions of the city. They wore expensive clothes with crisp, precise tailoring. Women wore heavy makeup, most looked like they had plastic surgery, and each hairstyle and color was more extravagant than the last. The road didn't have many vehicles, but the few that did pass us were sleek sports cars in flashy colors. By all accounts, these people and their lifestyles looked like perfect images to envy. But my whole body screamed with warning and distrust.

"This whole place," Larkan leaned close to my ear, pretending to be an affectionate husband whispering sweet nothings, "it feels fucking fake."

My thoughts exactly.

"Look down the alleys," T-Bone muttered behind us. "That's where the real people are."

I plastered on a smile, holding tightly to Larkan's arm while my head swiveled around like I was sightseeing. But I made sure to peer down the narrow walkways and side streets branching off the main road.

Hidden in those dark corners, people crouched low, watching the passersby warily. Some sat on the ground, others leaned against the walls of the building. More sat on trash cans and dumpsters. I spotted what looked like children, teens, adults, and even elderly people sitting out of sight. Everyone was thin, dirty, and silent. None of them dared to step foot onto the glossy main road.

"How many people do you think," Dyno kept his voice low, "came here because it was supposed to be this wealthy, beautiful place? Next thing you know, you're eating out of a dumpster."

"Look at the servants." I pressed a smile to Larkan's cheek, playing up the part of the doting wife. "The ones following the rich people."

Across the street, a wealthy couple walked arm-in-arm, while a more simply-dressed man walked behind them, eyes down and arms full of shopping bags. They passed by a restaurant, where patrons sitting on the patio loudly berated a waitress with dark circles under her eyes. She flinched as one of the men pawed at her arm.

"Fuck this place," Larkan muttered under his breath. "I bet all these rich fucks are related to the governor somehow, or are in his favor for some shady shit. People like this don't want anyone outside their circles getting a piece of the pie."

"Focus," T-Bone growled at him. "Look, there's City

Hall. Let's see about getting a contract or a permit or whatever the fuck we need."

Our small group approached an intersection and waited for a small cluster of vintage Lamborghinis to pass before crossing. In that time, the couple with the servant behind them had crossed and were coming toward us.

"Can I spit on that bitch?" Dyno mumbled.

"No," the remainder of us told him in unison.

"Damn, I really want to ruin her makeup."

The woman, her eyes an unnatural turquoise color under lashes as long as my pinky finger, took no notice of Dyno or the other Sons, but seemed very interested in Shadow.

"Now that's an exquisite specimen," she purred, reaching out to run a hand along his arm.

"Don't touch him," I snapped without thinking.

She pulled her hand back, her filler-injected lips parting in a soft gasp. "I apologize, I didn't realize he was yours. Excellent taste, I must say. A build like this comes with good breeding. Shame about all the scars. I imagine you got him at a discount?"

She looked at me expectantly with those fake crazy eyes, and I realized she expected an actual answer. The urge to spit on her as Dyno had suggested was incredibly tempting. I even felt the saliva begin gathering in my mouth, but reminded myself I had a role to play here.

"He's worth every penny," I told her smugly, wrapping tighter around Larkan's arm. "Perfect the way he is."

"Well, aren't you a charitable one." I imagined she

would have wrinkled her nose if it weren't for all the Botox in her face. "Do I know you? I don't believe I recognize you."

"We're new to the territory," Larkan cut in, casting a glance my way. "Looking for some labor contracts. You'll have to forgive my wife, she's a bit possessive of our erm, specimens."

"Ah, welcome to Blakeworth!" The woman's male companion spoke up for the first time, a forced smile on his face.

The woman didn't even bother hiding her displeasure. "Contracts are in high demand here," she said in the snobbiest voice I'd heard since high school. "You're better off renting your muscle to those of us who are already...established in the territory." Her unnatural gaze slid appreciatively over Shadow once again, who looked unnerved by the attention.

"I'm sure we'll find the most profitable methods for our needs," Larkan turned us back in the direction we intended to cross. "Good day to you."

"Good job in keeping your cool," I told him, taking a final look back at the couple and their poor servant struggling to carry all their belongings. "I was this close to spitting on her, like Dyno said."

"Me too," Larkan sighed. "At the Sandia outpost, I guarded tons of rich, pompous assholes. Guess I learned to emulate them."

"You're playing the part of a rich asshole very well." I patted his arm.

"Thanks," he smirked before glancing at our "laborers". "One of you, get the door for me and my wife," he requested loudly.

"Bitch," T-Bone snorted, jogging around and ahead of us to grab the frosted-glass front door of the city hall building. "Sir, Madam." The sergeant-at-arms did a dramatic, sweeping bow as he held the door open for us. Everyone was fighting to hold in laughter.

Thankfully, the person at the clerk's desk looked relatively normal, and not like a rich asshole. Although it made sense that a member of the territory's elite class wouldn't be working a desk job dealing with the public.

"Can I help you?" they asked, peering through thick-rimmed glasses.

"Yes, please." Larkan smiled charmingly as he approached the desk, and I released his arm. "I understand the territory is in need of labor for the oil fields, and my team here is looking for work. Can you walk me through the process?"

The other guys hung back while Larkan chatted with the clerk, and I did my best to look like I was meandering through the lobby out of boredom. Clasping my hands loosely in front of me, I looked down demurely at the pattern of tiles under my feet.

They were polished to a high shine and a little slippery, like this place didn't get enough foot traffic to build traction into the floor. That, or they were excessively cleaned by the territory's biggest asset—human labor.

The echoey sound of footsteps scuffling away brought my gaze up. I looked just in time to see three people disappear through a door, dragging mops and buckets behind them. Blakeworth's elite seemed adamant that their working class remain unseen and unheard.

I wandered toward a long window that stretched to the multiple floors above. The view showed more of the city below, indicating we were at the top of a hill or valley. More skyscrapers stretched so tall from the district below, it was hard to get a sense of the natural landscape.

One building, though, drew my attention more than the rest.

There was nothing remarkable about it—just another glass and concrete monstrosity, but it felt like my gaze was pinned there. Distantly, I was aware of Freyja rubbing around my ankles.

A small black bird seemed to be circling the building, going multiple times around the same floor. My stomach dropped as I turned to look at the guys, and saw T-Bone supported between Dyno and Grudge. His eyes had rolled back in his head so only the whites were visible, and he was twitching. Smartly, they had turned him away from the clerk Larkan was still talking to.

Heart drumming in my chest, I made my way back to them, still trying to look calm and bored. When T-Bone's irises returned, they focused on me and he nodded.

"She's in there," he mouthed.

Dyno coughed once, an apparent signal to Larkan who leaned up from the front desk.

"Well, thanks for all your help. We're going to—"

"Oh, one last thing, sir. The best way to seize a governor-approved contract is to attend his mixer and introduce yourself in person. He gives the best work to people who make a good impression on him."

Larkan paused. "Mixer?"

"Yes, he hosts them in the public gardens every week," the clerk smiled. "The next one is tonight."

MARIPOSA

"Is this really necessary?"

"Yes. Now stop grumbling and hold still. Look away." I held Larkan's eyelid open and gently placed the contact lens over his eyeball, then released his lid. "Okay, now blink for me. Does that feel okay?"

"Yeah." He sat up, blinking several times with now fiery orange irises. "How do I look?"

"Almost exactly like these elitist assholes, but we're not done yet." I held up a black tube and Larkan's face paled.

"Is that…?"

"Mascara, yes. All the dudes here are almost as made-up as the women. Now hold still and let me paint those lashes."

"You better not *ever* tell Noelle. I mean it, Mari."

"How do you know she won't like it? Guyliner was hot back in the day, Lark."

He never stopped grumbling and the others couldn't

contain their snickering, but he allowed me to apply mascara, a bit of concealer, and some tinted lip balm.

We did a remarkable amount of work in the few precious hours before the governor's mixer. I traded some painkillers for a fancier dress, appropriate menswear, makeup, and colored contacts so Larkan and I could blend in at the mixer.

I sported some glittery, mossy green contacts myself, and piled on more makeup than I had ever worn in my lifetime. I looked and felt like a clown, but judging from the people we'd seen on the street, that was the whole point.

The other guys would stay hidden and scout the building for the best way to get Vance's daughter out. It turned out to be only five blocks from the public garden so they planned to run by if they got her and we'd make a speedy exit. Shadow was quickly taught the hand signals used by the Sons to communicate with Grudge, and we were golden.

"Goddamn, little lady." I couldn't tell if T-Bone was laughing at, or appreciating my new look. "You look some kind of fuckin', I dunno, tropical bird or something."

I quickly penciled in Larkan's brows as a finishing touch. "Should I say thanks, or shut the fuck up?"

He just laughed and turned to the others. "We all ready?"

They made affirmative sounds while Larkan and I straightened up, and I took his arm once again. "Ready as we'll ever be."

"Be safe," Shadow said, looking straight at me. "You won't see us, but we'll be nearby."

My stomach did that fluttering thing as our gazes locked. "You be safe too."

Larkan and I were the first to leave the massive department store dressing room where we'd holed up. The others would wait a few minutes before heading to their destination.

We held our chins high, walking arm-in-arm to the gilded glass elevator.

"Will you look at that," he muttered. "Now that we look like circus freaks, no one's paying attention to us."

"We're like chameleons," I said, giving his arm a playful squeeze.

The public gardens were across the street and we could see the mixer getting started. People dressed just as ridiculously as we were drank flutes of champagne and nibbled morsels of food set out on long tables. Service workers quickly grabbed empty glasses and discarded napkins before retreating out of sight.

"All of these people come to kiss the governor's ass, huh?" Larkan snagged two champagne flutes and handed one to me.

"That's what it seems like." Rather than drink it, I looked around for a place to toss my champagne without getting caught.

The grass felt spongy and plush under my feet. Exotic flowers and all their curious scents surrounded me—those that weren't drowned out by people's perfume, anyway. I wondered if the governor had a

Night-blooming Cereus in his collection, if he had the patience to appreciate such a bloom. Probably not.

"I'm Wren, and this is my wife, uh—"

"Butterfly!" I said with my most dazzling smile to the couple Larkan introduced us to.

"Ah. How…*creative*," the woman said snootily, with a sip of champagne.

"God, I hate these people," I muttered as we walked away, slyly pouring a bit of my drink out on the grass.

"Which one's the fucking governor?" Larkan growled in reply. "I can't tell any of these bedazzled fucks apart."

"There's gotta be something that sets him apart. Maybe he has a separate table? I dunno, keep looking."

We mingled and meandered for another fifteen minutes or so, when I spotted T-Bone walking quickly up the sidewalk across the garden.

"Lark!" I hissed in a whisper, tugging at his arm. "There he is! Let's go—"

T-Bone caught my eye and quickly shook his head, making a slicing motion at his neck.

"Oh fuck, something's wrong." Larkan squeezed my elbow. "Stay here."

I browsed by one of the food tables, trying not to look worried as Larkan got brought up to speed. He returned to me quickly, wearing the same grave expression as T-Bone.

"She's not there anymore," he whispered. "He thinks they probably move her every night."

"Well, shit! Now what do we do?"

"I dunno, but we need to come up with a new plan.

It's getting dark and his raven doesn't see well at night. Let's—"

"Excuse me. Have we met?"

Lark and I turned to face an older gentleman who had come up to greet us. He wasn't dressed as flashy as the rest of the guests, but his black suit still had a silky, expensive sheen to it.

"Governor Henry Blake," he said, offering a hand and a polite smile. "Welcome to Blakeworth."

"Butterfly, uh, Jones!" I returned, accepting his hand. "And this is my husband, Wren."

If the clumsy delivery of my fake name raised any alarm bells, the governor gave no indication. "The pleasure is mine, Butterfly." He lowered a kiss to the back of my palm, all while maintaining a creepy amount of eye contact. "I knew I hadn't seen a dazzling creature such as yourself in Blakeworth before. What brings you here?"

Larkan clamped onto my opposite arm, a silent reminder that we needed to go *now*. My mind went blank, scrambling for an excuse to tell the governor.

"We've come seeking an oil contract," I explained through a tight smile. "And we were so looking forward to meeting you at this mixer, sir! You have a beautiful territory."

"Ah, you're too kind. Although hard work has its rewards." He placed his champagne flute on the table, then snapped his fingers at a waiter to pick it up.

What a piece of shit.

"This is such rotten luck, but I'm afraid the drinks have given me a migraine." I pressed my fingers to my temple, furrowing my brow. "My husband should really get us back to our room. It was lovely to meet—"

"Oh dear, I'm so sorry! Please." Rather than give me space, the governor moved in and splayed his hand on my lower back. Larkan's eyes visibly widened at the move. "Have a seat with my family. Take a little pill and see if you feel better. I'd hate for us to miss a business opportunity due to a little headache."

"My wife suffers from migraines regularly, I'm afraid," Larkan stepped in. "It's really best for her to lie down and rest."

"Nonsense! You know how women exaggerate these things. Let's all have a seat. I'll make some introductions you do not want to miss, and if Butterfly here isn't feeling better in a bit, you can say your goodbyes."

The governor was smooth, persuasive. Lots of tiny signals flashed at me through his words and body language. He didn't take no for an answer, and seemed desperate for us to not leave. But there was one other tidbit I fixated on.

"Your family's here, sir?" I continued playing up the migraine, squinting my eyes as I rubbed my temples.

"Yes, my wife, son, and soon-to-be daughter-in-law are all under the gazebo there," he pointed across the gardens.

The gazebo was covered in dense vines, something elegant, like ivy. A warm light radiated from inside it, but it was impossible to tell who was inside from this angle. We never saw her. That was why we didn't know.

Larkan released my arm as I turned to look at him, trying to not give anything away in my face. Forcing a smile, I lightly pushed him away. "Wren, would you be a dear and fix me plate? I just might need something in my stomach."

He nodded tightly, looking between me and Blake. "Of course. I'll be right back."

"Ah, you must be one of those women who doesn't eat much to keep her figure." The governor pulled me tightly against him as he led me to the gazebo. "I know I speak for all men when I say we appreciate the sacrifice, but if only it didn't contribute to those pesky headaches of yours."

"Yes," I said through gritted teeth, following his lead. "It's an unfortunate side effect."

"Watch your step, dear. Don't trip."

It was only one step. I swallowed the desire to tell him to fuck off, but plastered on a smile for the curious glances from his family members.

"Everyone, this is Butterfly Jones. She and her husband are new to Blakeworth. Butterfly, this is my wife, Eva, my son, Malcolm, and Malcolm's fiancee, Kyrie."

"A pleasure to meet you all." I allowed my gaze to rest on governor Vance's daughter for a single extra moment. "Congratulations on your upcoming nuptials. I wish you both much happiness."

Kyrie's eyes shifted downward after a small, forced smile.

"Don't be rude," Malcolm chastised. "What do you say?"

Kyrie flinched, then said softly, "Thank you, ma'am. I'm very excited."

"She's from another territory," Malcolm huffed with an eye roll. "So you'll have to excuse her rudeness."

"Oh, it's all right." Remembering I was supposed to have a migraine, I quickly took a seat next to Kyrie, and groaned softly as I rubbed the side of my head. "I'm from a different territory too. It might be the, uh, elevation here that I'm not used to."

"Where are you from?" Blake's wife, Eva stared down the length of her nose at me.

"East Texas." I figured the simplest answer was an honest one. "Or, Texahoma as it's known now."

"Ah, so you are new to our heightened elevation." Blake had sat down next to his wife, but with some distance between them. He kept staring at my legs, like he wanted to be close enough to touch them. Ew. "Has General Tash gotten that shithole under control yet?"

The question didn't register until a few seconds after I heard it. "I'm sorry, what?"

"Ah, nevermind. I should have known women have no ideas of these things. Malcom, have you heard?"

"The general's moving west, not east," his son scoffed. "He's crushing the vermin way south of us first, in New Mexico and Arizona. Outlaw gangs on motorcycles are out of control."

While the men talked, I leaned back against the ivy-covered frame of the gazebo, looking outside for any sign of Larkan. There was no indication of him, or any of the guys, so I could only hope he was able to relay the new intel successfully. In the meantime, I had to let Kyrie know I was here to help, and that she could trust me.

"Guess your husband went off to chase some fresh tail," Malcolm taunted, watching me.

I glared at him, hoping it would pass off as headache-induced squinting. Poor Kyrie. This territory was full of Grade-A Assholes, from the top all the way down.

"So what else is new?" I quipped with a playful smirk.

"See there?" He swatted Kyrie's thigh, which could have been harmless, had she not jumped in her seat. "A woman who knows her place. Men have to spread their seed, you see. It's in our nature."

I wanted to hug her. To sit between her and him, anything to keep him from touching her. But I had to stall, had to just play along, until the guys figured something out.

I opened my clutch and dug through it, pretending to look through my makeup items when the soft pack of tissues gave me an idea. Twisting open the lipstick, I quickly wrote, *4C, here 2 help* on the tissue. Heart pounding, I folded up the tissue and flipped open my compact. While I pretended to check my face, my eyes darted around again in search of the guys.

Come on. Where the fuck are you all?

Clicking my compact shut, I slid it back into my bag and turned my palm over with the tissue still in my hand. Turning to Kyrie, I gave her my best friendly smile.

"That's a gorgeous engagement ring! May I?"

"Um, sure."

While the men dismissed us as empty-headed vessels

gawking at shiny objects, she allowed me to hold her hand for a closer look at her ring. I pressed the tissue into her palm as I inspected the rock, making a big show of admiring it. Without missing a beat, her thumb held the tissue in place, and my heart soared.

"That's um, a pretty ring you have too," she said, discreetly unfolding the tissue in her lap.

"Oh, it's all right." I tilted my hand with Reaper's ring on it, a pang in my chest from missing him. The shifting colored stone covered me from catching her eye as she read my note. "It's a starter ring, from before my husband had any money. He promised me an upgrade when he got his big oil contract."

"*If* he does," Blake corrected me from across the gazebo. "I'm very selective about who I offer contracts to."

"As you should be, governor."

"Your husband has not impressed me so far, and seems to have gotten lost," he sneered. "Lucky for him, I enjoy looking at his wife very much."

"I'm very flattered, sir." My fingers clenched in my lap, but I forced my posture not to change. Next to him, Eva threw back a full glass of champagne, and I didn't blame her. How could anyone stand to be around him sober?

"You should be. Do you know how many prospective contractors throw their wives at me? Nearly all of them. It's standard procedure at this point. But your man wanted to drag you away." His smug grin was infuriating. "Now, I couldn't have that."

"Isn't that so typical of men?" I blurted out before I could stop myself. "Wanting what they can't have."

Oh fuck. Talk about the wrong fucking thing to say.

Governor Blake narrowed his stare at me while my pulse skyrocketed. This was it. I was found out and I'd never see my guys again.

"Of course we do," Malcolm cut in with a snort and a tight grip on Kyrie's thigh. "When you're as rich and powerful as we are, everything comes so easily and life gets boring. But when you go after something forbidden," his hand dragged up to her hip, "it's much more exciting."

"How did you two meet, then?" As long as I was still breathing, I wanted to find out if the sick men in this family would come out and admit to kidnapping and imprisoning people like pets.

"Our families are acquainted," Malcolm deflected smoothly. "Ky's the daughter of a much poorer governor. We did him a favor by agreeing to the match, after all his begging. An act of charity, really, when I had much better prospects in the northeastern territories." He pinched her chin tightly. "Good thing she's nice to look at."

"Butterfly, do you object to men taking what they want?" Blake was still pinning me with a hard stare.

I stared back as aloofly as I could, not bothering to dart my eyes to the sudden motion going on outside the gazebo.

"Even if I had an opinion, it doesn't fucking matter to you, does it?"

His lip curled as he jumped to his feet. "What a foul-mouthed little—"

I stood up and moved in front of Kyrie, my hand now wrapped around the handle of Gunner's small dagger that he loaned me. The silver metal reflected the lamplight and I saw the first look of genuine fear in the governor's eyes.

"Who sent you?" he hissed.

"Doesn't matter." I waved the dagger in front of his chest. "But you're going to back away, right now."

"What do you want, land? Goods?" Blake stared at the weapon in my hand. "We can work something out."

"Dad!" Malcolm had finally caught on to the commotion outside the gazebo. "Something's happening!"

People were running and screaming in my peripheral vision, but I didn't dare take my eyes off of the governor. The guys must have created a diversion of some sort.

"Tell me what you want." Blake raised his hands. "Just don't hurt my family."

I could have laughed. Like he really cared about anyone but himself. He just needed family members for his image.

"Leave her." I jerked my head toward Kyrie. "The rest of you can go."

Blake's mouth tilted up into another smug smile and I realized my mistake. "You're with Four Corners then?"

"No fucking way!" Malcolm bellowed. "I *need* her!"

A loud boom sent all of us stumbling. The gardens were now covered in smoke as armed police filed through, their weapons readied. They didn't look to be pointing at anyone in particular, but that grenade had been meant for someone.

"We'll find you another bitch," Blake reached over and yanked his son up by his jacket. "Four Corners just declared war."

They stumbled out of the gazebo towards the cover of their police. Forgotten, Eva followed with a drunken wobble. I didn't have time to feel bad for her and grabbed Kyrie's wrist.

"You have to come with me!" I pulled her to her feet and started running.

"Is it true?" She hurried alongside me. "You're with my father?"

"Sort of." I whipped my head in all directions as I ran, searching for a familiar face. "We're taking you home. You'll be safe."

I hoped the police would just write us off as panicked women from the mixer running around aimlessly, but I should have known Blake wouldn't let us go that easily. A pair of armed men in matching black uniforms pointed and yelled at us to stop.

"Come on!" I grabbed Kyrie's arm and ran faster, my lungs already burning.

"Where are we going?" she cried, looking back over her shoulder.

"Don't know yet, I'm looking for my people."

A series of loud shots rang out and I dove to cover my head. The momentum sent me sprawling and I thought of Reaper, how I wouldn't be with him for a final time. Gunpowder filled my nose when I hit the ground, and a ringing screeched in my ears. Kyrie crashed-landed next to me and I threw an arm over her to shield her.

My trembling hand moved over her back in search of any blood or bullet wounds, but felt nothing. No more shots came through the ringing in my skull, so I dared to look behind us.

The cops lay dead in the grass.

"Let's go, come on!"

A masculine voice sounded far away, but the rough hand that tugged me to my feet was very close indeed. T-Bone had purple bruising forming around his eye, and a bloody lip. His hands pressed to my cheeks, pupils searching mine.

"Are you okay?"

I nodded, looking back to Kyrie, who was being helped to her feet by Grudge. "This is her. She knows we're the good guys."

"Good. Dyno and Lark are stealing a car. Let's get to the edge of the block—"

More shots rang out, followed by voices yelling. We took off toward the street, the guys pushing us in front so they could have our backs.

"Where's Shadow?" I looked around for him desperately.

"Don't know. He went stealth to pick off these cops." T-Bone ran backwards, he and Grudge returning fire to the cops that chased us.

We ran around trees and jumped over bushes, zig-zagging through the park. Once we reached the side-walk, I nearly tumbled straight into traffic with all my forward momentum. Following me, Kyrie did the same thing and I pulled her back.

"Watch out!" she shrieked, pointing behind me.

I whirled around to see a massive black Hummer drive up onto the sidewalk, heading straight for us. If it weren't for the driver sticking his head out of the window, I knew I'd have met my death under those massive tires.

"That's our ride," I told her, waving at Dyno in the driver's seat. "Let's go!"

He shoved open a door as we ran up, and I pushed Kyrie inside.

"Mari, get in!" Larkan yelled, firing his own weapon out of the window.

"We can't leave without Shadow!" I hid behind the open door, looking through the dark glass as T-Bone and Grudge made their way to the vehicle.

"I'm sorry, hon. We can't fuckin' wait around." T-Bone stood in front of me as a shield, helping return fire.

"There he is!" In a bold move, Larkan stuck his torso out of the passenger window and waved his arm. "Shadow, come on!"

Through the smoke and gunfire, I saw him. And then I didn't. Holy shit, he was fast. He made his way to us, taking cover from gunfire under the plants and patio furniture, swift and powerful like a black jaguar in the jungle.

"Don't return fire, we'll cover you!" Larkan yelled, aiming his weapon.

Shadow picked up speed, making a break for it as he

sprinted across the grassy lawn. My chest began to relax with relief. He was so close! Just a few more yards and he'd be right here.

"Bro, look out!" T-Bone screamed at the top of his lungs, waving his arms frantically. "Take cover!"

"What? What is it?" I demanded.

Shadow suddenly fell forward and I screamed. Fear and confusion rose in equal amounts. I didn't hear a shot, so why had he fallen?

He sprang to his feet quickly, so I thought he must have tripped. Then he fell again and I saw them— arrows sticking out of his back attached to long ropes. I followed the lines with my eyes to the top of the gazebo, where the shooters were hidden by dense tree covers.

I realized with horror they must have had some kind of crank or pulley system, because despite Shadow's fighting to move forward, they were pulling him back.

SHADOW

I bet this fucking hurts on normal people.

I fell to my knees again, bending over to keep my weight low and forward. If I stood up, they could pull me straight back off my feet and potentially embed the arrows deeper.

My hands swept over my hidden pockets, but all my knives were gone, embedded in various people's throats and hearts. It became too chaotic earlier to retrieve them. Bracing one hand on the ground, I reached back, feeling for an arrow shaft to snap, but just my luck, they were both out of my reach.

A harsh pull on the ropes sent my knees sliding backward on the ground. Fuck, this was bad. These arrows hit me deep, and were probably barbed in some way to stay embedded in my flesh. Sick fucks and their torture devices.

"Shadow!"

Something else hit me from the front, but this was

warm, soft, and had small hands wrapping around my neck.

"Mariposa?" What the fuck was she doing? I *saw* her get in the car. "You can't be out here, it's not safe!"

She ignored me, reaching over my shoulder for the arrows. I felt a weird pulling and jerking motion on my back. "Shit, I can't break them! They're too solid."

If I wasn't on my knees already, I would have fallen to them. She ran out here to save me. She was too good, too perfect, and she could *not* be captured by these people.

"Stop." I grabbed her arms and brought them back between us. "Run back to the car. Now."

"No." Her hands flew over her dress, searching herself. "Shit, I must have dropped my knife. You don't have any of yours?"

"No, I don't—ugh, fuck!"

The ropes pulled me back another foot.

"Shadow!" She was crying now, and panicked. Her fingers curled into my shirt, forearms braced against my chest. "I'm not letting them take you."

I wrapped both arms around her back, shielding her in case any one of these fuckers dared to take a shot. Using all my strength, I walked my knees forward to reclaim some ground. The ropes went taut, and while it didn't hurt, I swore I could feel my muscles tearing.

"Mari." I wasn't sure when exactly I started using the shortened version of her name, but it felt right now. "If they capture you, it's going to be a lot worse for you than it is for me."

"I don't care." Her fingers grazed my cheeks,

stroking over my scar. I felt her shaky breaths over my nose and lips. "I'm not leaving you behind."

"I'll be fine. They can't hurt me, remember?"

"That doesn't make it okay to leave you."

We slid back again a few inches, and she clutched onto me tightly with a whimper. Her forehead rested on mine, the salt of a wet tear falling to my mouth. I realized then I was holding on to her just as tightly. I didn't want to be taken. I didn't want to lose my club, my only friends. And I never wanted to let her go.

But their hooks were already in me, literally, and she deserved so much better than to be dragged into whatever awaited me.

I dared to do something I'd never done before—touch a woman's face. Cupping her soft cheek, I looked into her watery, red eyes. She was still wearing the fake eye-color lenses, but I still saw her underneath them.

"Thank you for everything you've done for me," I told her. "I'll never forget any of it. But you have to let me go."

"I won't." She shook her head defiantly, her forehead still brushing mine. "You're not alone anymore. I won't let you be."

My fingers curled into the fabric at her back, holding her tight with what remained of my fading strength for this last moment.

"Then I hope you forgive me for this."

I shoved her away as hard as I could.

Mari stumbled back several steps, arms windmilling for balance before she fell back. Her mouth still open in an O of shock, she jumped to her feet and started toward me again.

"Run!" I roared at her, no longer resisting the ropes pulling me back. "Get back to the car!"

Shots were already popping off and she bent low, covering her head. While ducking to protect my own head, I saw the massive black car driving through the garden. Dyno mowed down hedges, bushes, small trees, and crashed into toppled patio furniture to get to her.

Hurry. Hurry.

I barely noticed that my ropes went slack. I was heavy, so I figured the cops just took a break from their pulling. But then someone grabbed my arm with a hand much bigger and stronger than Mari's. I looked up to see Grudge's impatient expression, his mouth growling with wordless screams to *fucking move.*

I rose to my feet, following his lead with no time to question it, and bolted toward the car. I must have lost a lot of blood or something, because my body was going much slower than I was telling it to. Grudge kept pulling on my arm as we ran. The glint of something metallic in his other hand must have been what cut me free.

My vision was going blurry, unfocused. I felt like I was swimming through fog and getting nowhere.

More hands grabbed me, shoved me. I was in a dark place again, great. Oh no, this place had windows that were just tinted dark. And Mariposa was here. She touched my face and her mouth moved. My body felt like it was being tossed around, despite staying stationary. I couldn't figure out if I was sitting still or moving, and multiple voices were yelling.

Cool water touched my lips and I opened my mouth for more, just like when it rained over my dungeon and I drank only what I could catch on my tongue. But this water flowed freely, cool and satisfying to my parched throat.

I wasn't sure how much time had passed when Mari came into clear focus, her finger pulling up on my eyelid.

"Shadow?" Her makeup and contacts were gone. Now it was just her normal, beautiful face etched with concern. "Are you with us?"

"Um, yes."

The car was dark and silent, Dyno driving on a dirt road with the headlights on the lowest setting. Next to him sat Larkan. In the next aisle sat Grudge and T-Bone, sandwiching the small blond woman we came to rescue. Mari and I were alone in the backseat.

"You were in shock," Mari explained. "I think you still are, but at least you're lucid now."

"Where are we?" I peered out of the dark tinted windows at the endless, dense forest rushing past us. Not a single light of the city was to be seen. Good fucking riddance.

"Only about a hundred miles in the wrong direction," Dyno called up from the front seat. "We had to zig and zag all over kingdom come to lose the cops. We're damn lucky this beast had an extra full gas can, 'cause we'll need to loop back around to grab the bikes tomorrow."

"The plan is to camp tonight, head for the bikes early tomorrow, then hit the road hard, back to Four

Corners." T-Bone stretched his arm along the back of his seat, casting a glance down at the woman next to him. "Then deliver this little lady back to her father, safe and sound."

The woman didn't move or reply. I wondered if she felt as Mariposa did when we first took her, or if she already knew she wouldn't be harmed.

"I'll get these out of you tonight." Mari's hand glided over my back, and I realized just how closely she was sitting.

Her leg pressed against mine, with one hand on my arm and the other gently prodding the pierced area of my back. If I focused on how ragged and shitty my body felt, I could ignore her breast pressing against my arm.

Mari's mention of the arrows did succeed in drawing attention to how tight and seized up my back felt. Sleeping would be a bitch, if I managed to sleep at all.

"Grudge."

The man sitting in front of me turned and looked over his shoulder.

"Thank you, brother."

He nodded his chin down sharply. "Hm."

Dyno took the Hummer off the road for another hour before we finally stopped for the night. My legs felt stiff too, as we piled out of the car.

"Girls can sleep in the car," T-Bone said, walking around to the trunk. "We ain't got much else for shelter. I'll try to hunt us some dinner. Y'all get a fire going and watch your fucking backs. If *anything* moves that's not one of us, shoot it."

He took what he needed and headed out into the wilderness, while the others started up a fire. Mari led me to sit on a fallen log and had me turn away from the fire so she could see my back.

"I can't do much with limited supplies," she grumbled, rummaging through her bag. "But I can get those out and close you up until we get back."

"I trust you," I said, bracing my hands on my knees and staring into the dark woods. I could just make out T-Bone creeping low and silently.

"Thank you." Mari squeezed my arm and got to work. Her scissors snipped away at my shirt and I heard her soft laugh. "This is the second time I've had to cut your shirt off of you. Maybe you should just stop wearing them."

"You don't want that," I grunted, helping her pull the fabric away and down my shoulders. "I'm not much to look at."

She was quiet for a moment, then I heard gloves snapping and her rummaging through her items again.

"That's not true, Shadow."

I didn't know how to answer. Was this...*flirting?* If so, I was completely out of my element and better off not saying anything. I just sat still as she gently prodded around my wounds.

"These are definitely barbed and they've torn like hell through your muscle tissue already," she reported. "I'm going to have to make a few small incisions—"

My eye caught the glint of a metal blade, a sharp edge in her hand coming to slice me again.

"No!"

I jumped up from the log, spinning to face her as I backed away. What was I thinking? I never exposed my back to anyone. My heart drummed in my ears, while my chest and throat closed up. I was suffocating, sweaty, small, and weak. The floor was coated in my dried blood.

"Shadow! What's wrong?"

"Don't come near me!"

I backed up against a tree trunk. No, a cold brick wall. Mari's face looked concerned, and then morphed into the face of the woman who haunted me since my first memories formed. She was sitting right there, taunting me as she painted her face in my blood. She dragged one bloody finger into her mouth and moaned with her lips around it.

I shut my eyes, feet kicking out in front of me to scoot further away, but I was trapped. I was always trapped.

"No more cutting, please…" My head shook from side to side, as if that would make the grotesque vision go away. "Don't cut me anymore. I didn't do anything…"

"Shadow, listen to my voice." A pair of hands held the sides of my face, keeping my head still. "You're a member of the Steel Demons MC. You're among friends right now and you're not in any danger. No one is going to hurt you."

"Don't cut me." It was Mari's voice I heard, but I couldn't trust my eyes to open and show me it was really *her* there. "Don't cut me, please."

"I want to help you, Shadow. I want to make you better."

"Okay, just no blades. No cutting, please."

"Shadow, I need you to trust—"

"I do. I can't explain it, but I can't…just please don't cut into me. Don't cut my skin, don't make me bleed. Just, please…"

A weight pressed down into my lap, like someone laid a warm sandbag across my legs. When the vibrating started, I kept my eyes shut, but felt around with one hand. I felt soft fur and the nuzzling of Freyja's head on my palm. She dialed up the purring even more, until the soft rumbles reached all over my body. Slowly, my throat and chest relaxed. My pulse started to normalize, and I dared to open my eyes.

Mariposa sat between my legs, her face inches away, and her hands still holding my cheeks. Her palms were soft on my stubble and she blinked away water that had accumulated in her eyes.

"Are you with me now?" she whispered.

"Yes." I swallowed. "I'm sorry, I—"

"Don't apologize." She shook her head, thumbs caressing over my cheekbones. "Don't ever apologize for what someone else did to you."

"But I scared you."

"You worried me for a minute. But I'm glad you're back." She pulled in a deep, tired breath. "In regards to your back, I need to make incisions to extract the arrows with minimal damage. I could pull them straight out, but that will shred the hell out of your muscle and skin.

Your mobility is already affected, and I don't want to injure you worse."

"It's okay. I won't feel it."

"That's not what I'm worried about. They could still get infected. You'll have a longer recovery time while those tissues heal." Her hands lowered from my face, trailing for a brief moment over my collarbones until they rested on top of mine, on Freyja. "You believe that I would never want to hurt you, right?"

"Yes."

Her tongue darted out to wet her lips. "And you trust me to know what I'm doing in a medical sense?"

"I do."

She swallowed, her eyes cast down to our touching hands and the cat before looking back up at me. "And you know that I—I care about you. A lot. I don't like seeing you hurt. I would have been devastated if you were captured. You're not just my patient, but my friend. So everything I do is with your health and well-being in mind, okay?"

My pulse skyrocketed again, but for different reasons than before. I ached to find the words that echoed everything she said, with the same simple eloquence. But my words were gone, as they often were with flashbacks. And the poisonous part of me I fought so hard to keep buried, whispered to my brain for the first time in months.

She's lying, like all women do. She'll watch your blood spill and take pleasure in your suffering. And you'll let her, because you're a sad, submissive little animal in a cage. Doesn't matter how far you ride on that bike. You're always caged and you can never escape.

"Shadow?"

"Yes," I bit out, harsher than I intended. If only grinding my teeth could crush the voices and darkness I fought tooth and nail to silence. "Yes," I repeated—softer with a deep breath. "Thank you for being my friend."

Her brow furrowed, noticing my discomfort. She squeezed my hands. "If I keep talking to you, will you let me use my scalpel to get the arrows out?"

Trust.

A new voice stepped in to join the ensemble cast in my head.

Trust, it repeated. Warm, familiar, and feminine. *Love is not possible without trust.*

"Freyja," I realized.

You know what you have to do, son. The cat rubbed her head on my hand. *Step into your fear. Show it how brave you are. Show this woman that you trust her.*

"She's talking to you?" Mari scratched near the base of the cat's tail.

"You didn't hear her?"

Mari gave a small smile. "Not this time. Whatever she's saying must be only for you."

I removed the cat from my lap, grimacing at the stiffness taking over my arms already. If I didn't do something, I might not be able to drive my bike.

"Okay," I turned back to Mari. "You can make your, um, incisions. Whatever you need to do."

She searched my face. "You're sure?"

I took one of her hands, a gesture that seemed normal and comfortable between us now. Her fingers opened and I laced mine between them.

"Keep talking to me? So I know where I am, and… who you are. It's not that I don't trust *you*, I just…"

She squeezed my hand, leaning forward until her forehead touched mine again. Her other hand stroked lightly down the side of my neck. Such a simple touch felt too good to be real.

"I know, Shadow." Still holding my hand, she pulled away with a warm, gentle smile. "Come back to the fire."

I followed her lead, my hand never leaving hers until the last possible moment.

MARIPOSA

I woke up with my back aching in at least ten different places. My neck didn't fare much better. Stretching with a groan, I forgot that I slept in the back-seat of the Hummer until my fist hit the seat in front of me.

"Shit," I whispered, hoping I didn't startle Kyrie.

My worries were for nothing I realized, as I sat up and saw her poking the charred logs from last night's fire. With one shove of the heavy car door, I stepped out into the chilly morning.

"Trying to get it started?" I asked, pulling my arms close around me.

"Um, yeah. Seeing if there were any embers left." She gave me a sheepish look. "I've never been all that outdoorsy."

"That's all right. Here, let me show you."

I tip-toed over to Dyno, sleeping curled up with his back to us. All three Sons of Odin were cuddled into a puppy pile to stay warm for the night. Dyno's head never even twitched on T-Bone's chest as I carefully pulled the lighter from his pants pocket.

"The thing about traveling with bikers," I said to Kyrie, tossing the lighter once in the air, "they're always carrying gasoline in one form or another."

She helped gather pine needles and sticks for kindling, then I set up a triangle of fresh logs and lit them up.

"How are you holding up?" I asked her. "I was so exhausted after helping Shadow last night. I'm sorry I never checked on you."

"That's okay. I'm fine." She extended her palms to the growing flames. "Just can't believe this is really happening. I thought I'd never get out." She shook her head with a heavy sigh. "I thought I actually wanted to marry him. I'm so stupid."

"Hey, you're not," I insisted. "That whole family is a bunch of manipulative pricks. They took advantage of you."

Kyrie sucked her lip between her teeth, her hands wringing in front of her. "Do you really think they'll declare war on Four Corners?"

"I wouldn't put it past them. But we'll deal with that when it happens. Right now, our priority is getting you home safe."

She nodded, her worried expression relaxing slightly. "How did you end up with these guys? No offense, but you seem…a little less feral, I guess."

"None taken," I grinned. "It's a long story, and I certainly never thought I'd end up in a biker gang. Life has a funny way of dumping you right where you belong." I reached out and placed a hand on her fore-arm. "These are good guys, you can trust me on that. They're rough around the edges, but they don't use people like those pricks we took you from."

She looked over at the Sons, still wrapped up in their cuddle pile. "They actually look really sweet like that."

"They are sweethearts," I agreed. "Armed, danger-ous, and foul-mouthed sweethearts, but sweethearts nonetheless."

Kyrie's head swiveled across the fire, where Shadow and Larkan slept a few feet away from each other. "Are you one of their uh, old lady? Is that the right term?"

My chest squeezed with the aching memory of last night. Shadow's fear of my scalpel, his trauma rearing its ugly head. And then when he finally allowed me to remove the arrows. He trembled the whole time, but he *let* me. I couldn't even put into the words the amount of trust that must have taken.

And then afterward, when he laid down to sleep, it almost physically hurt me to leave his side. I wanted to stay near him the whole time, to soothe and reassure him. To show him I understood how difficult it was to face such a lifelong fear. That I was so proud and did not take his trust in me lightly.

"No," I answered Kyrie, watching Shadow's deep breaths. "Larkan, the smaller one, was posing as my husband, but he's kind of my brother-in-law. Shadow and I, we're," I swallowed, "we're friends. My men are actually all waiting for us in Four Corners."

"Men, plural?"

"Yeah," I smiled sheepishly at her. "I have three husbands."

"*Three?!* What?"

"My first husband, it's um, part of the culture he grew up in. For one woman to be with multiple men. It's normal for him. He introduced me to the idea, and his best friend was all for it. My third was a little more resistant, but he came around."

"That's, wow." Kyrie went back to staring at the fire. "I've never heard of anything like that."

"I didn't either before meeting them. It weirded me out too, at first." I grinned. "But it has its perks."

"I can imagine," she snickered.

We heard moving and rustling behind us, and turned to see the Sons untangling as they roused.

"Mornin', ladies," Dyno yawned. "Mari, I'll take my lighter back."

"Damn it. How'd you know?" I tossed it back and he caught it in midair.

"You're not the first person to lift my shit while I'm sleeping." He scrubbed his face. "Did y'all make any coffee?"

"No time." T-Bone's voice was gravelly as he sat up. "We gotta get movin'. Mari, can you wake up your guys?"

"On it."

As I walked toward Larkan and Shadow's sleeping spots, I heard T-Bone ask Kyrie, "You hungry, little lady?"

Larkan woke up with just a small shake to his shoulder. I went to rouse Shadow with more caution, remembering how Jandro had to lock him up at night because of his violent nightmares. I advised him not to take a sleeping pill last night, considering we had to be up in a few short hours.

Shadow looked peaceful, if a bit pale. His face was softer in sleep, without his perpetual glower. I stroked the back of my fingers against his cheek. He seemed to like it when I touched his face. If only he knew how many times I thought about touching him like this.

He stirred but didn't wake. His face turned, the soft bristles of his beard leaning into my hand. I lifted a finger to push his hair back, exposing the deep scar carving through his cheek, eyelid, and brow. He was fucking beautiful, and I couldn't stop staring.

"Shadow," I whispered, my thumb stroking over his cheekbone. "Time to get up."

He rolled to his side, my hand now trapped between his cheek and the ground. His arm reached out, coming close to resting on my thigh before it stopped and jerked back.

"Ugh," he grunted, eyes now blinking awake. "I'm stiff as a fucking board." His head lifted and I slipped my hand out.

"How do you feel, aside from that?" I watched him roll up to sitting, one of his hands skimming over the cheek I just touched, before he pulled his hair forward to cover it.

"Fine, I think."

"Can I see?"

He turned his back to me, allowing me to lift his clean shirt up to his shoulder blades to examine the wounds. I frowned and huffed out a breath. They didn't look good. The flesh puffed out and looked discolored between the stitches I made last night. Infection was setting in, but there wasn't much I could do until we got back to the bikes.

"Do you feel weird at all?" I fished my small bottle of alcohol from my kit and poured it over the wounds. "Nauseous? Too cold or too hot?"

"No, I don't think so. It itches a little back there, but I can't even reach them."

"Good." I pulled his shirt down, resisting the urge to skim my hands over the many scars on his back. "Don't rub up on anything to scratch them. They're infected, but I don't have antibiotics to give you until later."

"I'll be fine. Thank you, Mari."

I sighed and reached out to squeeze his shoulder. It was easy to fuss and fret over him, but when not staring down the face of his trauma, he was so stoically calm. "I know you will. And you know what?"

"Huh?"

"I like it when you call me Mari."

———

IT WAS ANOTHER THREE-HOUR, bumpy, off-road drive, going around the Blakeworth city before we reached the barn where the bikes were stored. I half expected them to be stolen, all our belongings looted, but everything was as we left it.

Shadow, however, continued to look worse.

He was pale and sweating, moving slowly as he

walked his bike out of the barn. I had agreed to ride back with Larkan, but now that feeling returned, the urgency to never leave the scarred man's side.

"Shadow?" I approached him warily. "Are you sure you can ride?"

"Don't have much of a choice, do I?" he grunted, struggling to get his cut over his elbows.

"Here, let me."

His arms stilled at his sides while I grabbed the soft leather, pulling it over one massive bicep to rest at his shoulder, and then the other.

"Thank you."

I took the opportunity to touch his face, his eyes half-closing at the contact. It would have been sweet, even intimate, if his skin didn't burn against my palms.

"Shadow," I gasped, pressing a hand to his forehead. "You have a fever. Let me—"

"There's no time." His palms were clammy as he removed my hands by the wrists. "Blake could still be looking for us."

"I'd feel a lot better if you weren't riding," I frowned, noticing how heavily he leaned against his bike. I wondered if he could even fully stand. "I know you've got manly pride or whatever, but can't you link up with one of the guys?"

"And leave my bike here? We have no way to haul it."

"Mari, we've got to go!" Larkan hollered over the revving of his machine.

Shadow flung a hand weakly in his direction. "Get

going. I'll be fine." He sounded like he was trying to convince himself more than me.

"Okay, well just take this." I grabbed my bottle of prescription-strength ibuprofen and handed him two tablets. "They should help with the fever and muscle stiffness."

"Thanks." He didn't smile, but his gaze was warm. "You can take care of me all you want when we're home."

"Oh, good. Because you don't have a choice in that matter." I squeezed his hand around the pills before backing away. "Please ride safe. I'll be watching you in the mirrors."

"I'll guard your back," he said softly. "Always."

I left his side with a sinking feeling in my gut. *We're not going to make it home,* my thoughts whispered. He really needed more rest and proper care, but we couldn't stay here. We had no other option but to ride hard to safety.

After securing Freyja in my backpack, I climbed on behind Larkan and immediately checked his mirrors. Shadow had none of his usual grace and confidence as he sat astride his bike. He moved slowly, painfully. Even if his brain couldn't feel it, his body was reacting to the damage he took. My stomach knotted even tighter as we took off.

We took a different route home, T-Bone leading the way through a mix of forests and open fields. Kyrie clung to his waist, her blonde hair streamed out behind her like a comet. The landscape was pretty, but I couldn't bring myself to enjoy it. My thoughts were only on the injured man riding in the rear.

Shadow seemed to be holding on fine, much to my surprise. I had to remind myself how strong and capable he was. He had already survived so much. As hours passed, I started to relax. We weren't stopping, so I couldn't physically check on him, but every mile he stayed on that bike was a good sign.

When late afternoon turned the landscape golden and striped with long shadows, my stomach was cramping from hunger. My thighs and butt ached like they did when I first started riding. T-Bone's bike began to slow, and buildings started popping up on either side of the road. I lifted the visor on my helmet and blinked several times, certain that it had to be a mirage.

"I know this place," Larkan yelled to me over his shoulder. "We're way off-course from Four Corners, but this town is Toquerville. It's neutral territory, so nobody owns it yet. We'll be safe to stop here."

T-Bone seemed to have the same idea as he slowly rolled through on the dirt road. He pointed out things to Kyrie, but I couldn't hear what he was saying. Hope soared within me when I saw an apothecary sign on one of the buildings. It was dusty and didn't seem to be open at the moment, but I might be able to treat Shadow's infection here.

My eyes slid back to Larkan's mirror. Now that we were moving slower and the bikes were closer together, I could see Shadow clearly. He was bent low and forward over his handlebars, pale as a ghost and grimacing. His hair was slick with sweat, clinging to his forehead, and his breathing looked labored.

Holy shit! How was he able to ride for the past eight

hours like that? Panic gripped my chest, but before I could say anything Larkan suddenly picked up speed, following T-Bone's acceleration through the town.

I patted Lark's shoulder. "Where are we going?"

"I dunno. Just following T's signal."

"We need to stop. Shadow looks really sick."

He turned a corner, following the bikes in front along a side street, and I lost sight of Shadow.

"Lark, slow down! He can't see us anymore."

Thankfully he slowed, and I twisted in my seat to look behind me.

The whole world seemed to slow down as Shadow came around the corner, his bike turning too sharply.

The motorcycle spun off in one direction, his body flying lifelessly the other way, and I screamed.

TWENTY-TWO

MARIPOSA

I hit the ground while Larkan's bike was still moving, and painful jolts shot up to my knees. He yelled something after me, but I ignored him. I ignored everything that wasn't the man lying motionless on the ground.

"Shadow!" I knelt at his side, feeling desperately for a pulse in his neck.

When the beat throbbed weakly under my fingers, it was a small relief. He could have a head injury or broken bones now, on top of his infected wounds.

"I need a hospital!" I cried out. People were standing around gawking on the street. Where the fuck were the Sons? "Hey!" I yelled in the faces of onlookers. "Where's the hospital?"

"We don't have one, miss. I'm sorry. A doctor comes through sometimes, but he left yesterday."

"A room with a bed, then!" I screamed. "He's hurt! He needs to rest. He needs—"

"Shh, Mari." Someone grabbed me by my shoulders, shaking me gently. "There's a service center at the end of this road. We'll get him there, okay?"

T-Bone's voice was calm, his eyes sharp. Seeing him quelled my panic slightly.

"He can't ride," I whispered. "He shouldn't go anywhere for several days, maybe even a week or more."

"That's okay. We'll figure something out. Grudge, can you help me get him up?"

The silent man slid his hands under Shadow's shoulders and lifted.

"Careful with his head." I reached out, supporting Shadow's neck to minimize movement.

After I determined that he hadn't broken any bones, the Sons and Larkan carried Shadow down the street to the service center. Some people still rubbernecked, but most lost interest in the spectacle after the crash. When the guys finally carried him to a room and laid him on a clean bed, I snapped into nurse mode.

"I need boiling hot water, alcohol, and clean towels. Can someone ride down to the apothecary and get bandages, syringes with needles, and any antibiotics that end in -cillin, -cin, or -cline."

"Can I do anything?" Kyrie piped up.

"You can ask the kitchen for soup, broth, and drinking water. He's probably going to be on a liquid diet for a few days."

"What about you?" Dyno looked at me sharply. "Mari, you need to rest, too. You look like you're about to fall over."

"Just get what I asked for. Now, please." I was already cutting away Shadow's shirt. Hunger pains could wait if he was dying. "I'll be fine."

Everyone filed out of the room, except for Grudge. He made a noise that sounded like a harsh "Huh!". I looked at him and he tilted his head toward Shadow, pointing at the unconscious man with his thumb and a wry grin.

"You saying I sound like him now?"

Grudge nodded, pleased that I understood.

"Guess that's why we get along so well," I sighed. "Help me turn him over?"

We carefully rolled Shadow onto his side so I could access his back.

"Fuck," I hissed after lifting his shirt. "Those look even worse. I've never seen infection set in this fast."

Grudge made a gagging noise and went to the window as I finished pulling Shadow's shirt off. I didn't blame him, the smell was worse than the stitches looked.

"I'm sorry, Shadow," I whispered, grabbing my scalpel and dousing it liberally with the rubbing alcohol I had left. "I have to cut you again."

The others started returning just as I cut the sutures free and began draining the pus from the wounds. T-Bone and Larkan retched, quickly joining Grudge at the window. Kyrie, surprisingly, had no reaction at all.

"Here's some soup you can just heat up when you're ready." She placed the containers by the bed. "And here's a cold sandwich for you. I didn't know what you liked, so I just had them put everything on it."

"Thank you." I didn't even look up from poking through Shadow's infected flesh.

"Please don't talk about food," T-Bone begged, swallowing another dry heave. "Dyno went to the apothecary. He should be back soon."

"Thanks. I know it stinks, you guys don't have to stick around."

Their footsteps were little more than background noise as I sterilized Shadow's wounds as best as I could. A friendly squeeze came down on my shoulder.

"We're all on this same floor if you need us," T-Bone said before leaving.

Only Grudge remained, and he seemed in no hurry to leave. I didn't mind that he stayed. He certainly wasn't in the way. Concern etched his face as he watched me work on Shadow.

"You and him have gotten close, huh?" I asked.

"Mm," he nodded, moving to sit at the opposite end of the bed from me.

Shadow wasn't bleeding badly, so I opted to not stitch him back up. Air flow was important to fighting the infection, and it could possibly fester under his skin if I closed him back up. So I covered his wounds with sterile gauze and rolled him onto his back.

"Help me prop him up a little?" I asked Grudge.

Together, we scooted him up toward the headboard and I stuck a pillow under his head, making sure there wasn't a lot of pressure on his upper back. Only then did I pause to just take a breath. Dyno came in to drop off the supplies I ordered and quickly left, his face turning green at the smell lingering in the room.

Grudge came around and patted my shoulder, then pointed to the container with my sandwich in it.

"Guess I might as well," I laughed. "Make sure you eat, too."

He nodded and pulled his notepad from inside his cut. *I'll be back. Will watch him w/you.*

"Thank you," I expressed sincerely. Having an extra pair of eyes on Shadow would honestly be huge for my peace of mind. "I'll be here."

He gave a thumbs up before heading out the door. I tore open my sandwich and wolfed it down, my eyes glued to the man in the bed.

They could be brothers, I realized. Shadow and Grudge had the same long black hair, glossy like raven feathers. The same dark eyes and quiet, observant demeanor. Since the Sons first came to us, those two seemed to gravitate toward each other.

My sandwich gone far too soon, I washed my hands thoroughly, then dug out my thermometer. I ran the sensor across Shadow's forehead, and my heart sank when his temperature read 103.

"You poor thing," I murmured, running the back of my hands over his cheeks.

I opened the window, the evening air quickly chilling the room, then wet a washcloth to run over his face and neck. His skin erupted in goosebumps despite being drenched in sweat, and he finally, finally opened his eyes.

"M-mari…"

"It's okay, you're safe." I clasped one of his hands, the other continuing to drag the wet washcloth over his neck and the top of his chest.

"I'm c-cold…"

"I know, love. We need to bring your fever down." The pet name I usually reserved for my men slipped out, but it didn't faze me. He needed this care. He needed to feel loved.

Shadow dragged a hand along his taut stomach, following the lines of scars there. "Think I'm gonna be sick."

I found a trashcan just in time, and he heaved his guts over the side of the bed. He hadn't eaten all day, so it was mostly dry heaves.

"Try drinking some water for me." I held the glass out for him to take a few weak sips. He threw that up not a minute later.

"I'm s-sorry…"

"Stop." I ran the washcloth down his back. "You have nothing to be sorry for."

"I feel like shit," he moaned. "Like I got run over by a truck."

"Well, you did fall off your bike."

He coughed and spit into the trash can, then allowed me to wipe his mouth. "I'm no Steel Demon if I can't even sit on a bike."

"Stop. I don't want to hear that shit. Are you done?" At his weak nod, I pulled his shoulder back to help him recline in bed again. "You're hurt. Your wounds are infected. I'm amazed you lasted on the bike as long as you did."

"This has…" he took rapid shallow breaths, as if he'd been running for miles, "…never happened to me before."

"Well, thank fuck for your strong immune system. But I wonder if those arrows were covered in something. Some kind of bacteria or poison. Infection set in awfully fast."

As I filed through the list of antibiotics in my head, Shadow leaned over the bed again to dry heave into the trash can. I discarded the towel and asked Grudge for a new one. As Shadow's back heaved with ragged breaths, I mopped the towel over his feverish skin. The jagged map of scar tissue stretched with each breath he took. He looked completely exhausted by the time he sat up again.

"Please try to drink something." I ran the cloth over his forehead and neck. "I'd give you IV fluids, but I don't have the right supplies."

"Can't...keep anything down."

"I know it's hard, but please try for me."

He accepted a few small sips of water when I held the glass out to him. A full minute passed and he made no move to vomit.

"Good." I forced a tight smile.

"Why...are you taking care of me?" His eyes followed my every movement, still sharp as a falcon's despite the weakness in his body.

"You know why." I dug out my stethoscope and wiped the ends with alcohol.

"Tell me." His gaze rested on my face as I placed the dial over the dark tattoo on his chest. "I want to hear you say it."

"Stop talking and just breathe normally, please." His heart was beating rapidly, way too fast for a resting heartbeat. But his lungs sounded clear, which was a positive sign. "I'm taking care of you because of this." I pressed a finger to the grinning skull on his chest, the tattoo we shared, that he put on me with his own hands. "We both have a duty to the SDMC. Yours is to be an assassin. Mine is to be a medic."

I put the towel aside and scooted closer to him, my hip nudging against the outside of his thigh. He didn't move away like I expected, maybe out of weakness, or maybe the fear of touching me really was gone.

"But you're also my friend." My hand closed around his. "And I don't like seeing you unwell. I'm taking care of you because I want *my* Shadow back."

I didn't intend for the possessiveness to slip out, but didn't panic when it did. A calm settled over me instead. This man and I shared something unique, we had all but said it to each other in those exact words. Still, this was the first time I dared to speak aloud, claiming him as mine. In saying it, I realized I was ready to. This time, I wouldn't worry about being unfair to Reaper, Jandro and Gun. I knew what I wanted, and what I was able to give.

If Shadow realized the implication of what I was saying, his sickness didn't allow for him to dwell on the thought. He hugged himself, broad arms wrapping around his chest. "C-can't stop…shivering. I feel like… like I'm falling in and out of sleep."

"Lay down and rest." I got up from his side, moving toward the far end of the bed. What was between us didn't matter right now, anyway. He needed to get better first. "I can't give you a blanket, I'm sorry. You're already too hot. We need your temperature to come down."

He scooted down from the headboard and didn't object when I started unlacing his boots. I pulled them off his feet and placed them next to the door. Returning to his side, my eyes lingered on the silver button at the front of his jeans.

"Shadow? Are you okay with me taking your pants off for bed?"

He didn't answer right away, and I thought he'd fallen asleep. Then the weakly whispered, "Yes," floating up to me made my heart pound.

I unsnapped the button and pulled down his zipper, working to be as clinical as possible as I pulled the denim down his muscular thighs. I jerked my gaze away from the deep V-lines in his hips, the snug, black boxers outlining a thick bulge. *He's sick. He's my patient right now,* I reminded myself.

Something else caught my eye and I found myself looking out of sheer curiosity. A tattoo was on his upper right thigh, the ink blurred by scar tissue and faded to a bluish gray color. It was a band of symbols, small pictographs of some kind, stretching about five inches across and no more than an inch tall.

He never mentioned having other tattoos, although I didn't really ask. I did recall him saying that the scar tissue made it difficult for ink to keep over time. Why did those symbols look so familiar, though?

I kept thinking about it as I tidied up the room. Grudge came back a half hour later with more food and some books. Shadow tossed fitfully in and out of sleep. I kept sponging cool towels over him, and finally relented when he asked to cover himself with a sheet.

His fever kept bouncing between 101 and 103. I kept going through his symptoms in my head, looking at his back wounds, and re-reading the labels on the antibiotic bottles. His symptoms were generic enough that it could literally be any kind of bacteria, but the medicine would only work on certain strains. To give him the wrong one could mean bad side effects and wasted time as his infection worsened.

I explained all this to Grudge, who listened with attentive, curious eyes. Neither one one of us seemed eager to sleep, so he just watched over Shadow while I paced around the room.

"Hieroglyphics!" I blurted out after an exhausting, silent few hours.

"Hm?"

"The tattoo on his thigh," I said. "I undressed him for bed and saw symbols inked there. They looked familiar, but I didn't know from where. Now I remember seeing them in an ancient history class in high school, years ago."

Grudge smiled wolfishly. He didn't have to gesture or write anything down for me to know what he was thinking.

"I was *not* getting up to anything!" I told him. "He needed to rest and still had pants and shoes on."

The silent man chuckled and held his hands up in a defensive posture.

"I like you guys," I blurted out next. I was so exhausted, but not allowing myself to sleep made my mouth seem to disconnect from my brain like I was drunk. "The Sons are good allies. You saved us out there, and you guys have never steered the Steel Demons wrong. So, thank you."

Grudge glanced down at the floor, a smile still on his lips. He pulled out his notepad and quickly scribbled out, *Feeling's mutual. Feel bad S got hurt, though.*

"Nobody could have seen those fucking harpoon arrows coming," I told him. "And you cut him free. So, thank you for that. I'll make sure Reaper knows you saved one of us."

It's what friends do.

I gave his arm a friendly squeeze and went back to my worried pacing.

Freyja climbed in through the window at some point during the night and curled up in the bed next to Shadow. Her presence seemed to calm his fitful tossing, turning, and mumbling, but his fever never came down past 100.

I can help you put him under the shower, Grudge told me as dawn started creeping through the windows.

"Maybe, but," I rubbed my forehead, well past exhausted at this point, "it's not super high anymore so it's not life-threatening. The fever serves a purpose, it's trying to fight the infection in his body. If we keep bringing it down, the infection could run rampant. My instinct is to let it run, but…"

Something else nagged at me. My gut was trying to tell me something, I just didn't know what.

Shadow rolled to his side, seeking a cool spot on the sweat-soaked sheets. Taking a seat on the bed, I looked at his back for the hundredth time that night, noting the purple bruise-like discoloration spreading out from his wounds.

"I'm sorry, love." The endearment slipped out again while I touched his shoulder, and I seriously considered brushing a kiss along the scar running under my hand. "I don't know what to give you to help you."

It's sepsis.

That word clicked into the knowledge in my head like a puzzle piece. Freyja stared at me from the other side of him, but I couldn't be sure that was her voice. It felt like my own, but I was too tired to pay attention.

Even so, I knew what to do now.

I headed for the door and went out into the hallway. Picking the door on my left at random, I knocked with a heavy fist.

"Hold on!" T-Bone's gravelly voice called from the other side.

I pounded again. There was no time to wait. I heard the latch unlock, and pushed the door open just as he zipped himself into a pair of jeans. A blond service girl in the bed covered her chest with a sheet. Next to her, a naked Dyno slammed a pillow over his lap.

"Uh. Morning, Mari." He smoothed his hands over the pillow in an attempt to look casual.

I lifted an eyebrow at T-Bone in question.

"What?" he responded. "We like variety sometimes."

I shrugged. I thought women weren't their type, but it was none of my business. The girl didn't look mistreated, at least. On the contrary, she was panting slightly with dreamy, dilated eyes. Apparently, they'd been in the middle of something.

"How far is Four Corners from here?" I asked.

"Um." T-Bone scrubbed a hand down his face, shifting his thinking to the correct head. "Five-hour ride. Maybe four if we push it."

"I need you guys to ride back and bring some supplies here for me. I'll give you a list. My guys will know where my stuff is and what's what."

T-Bone shook his head. "We're not leaving without you. If Reaper doesn't have eyes on you, I'm as good as dead."

"Shadow isn't fit to travel and I'm not leaving him." I crossed my arms to show that I wasn't budging. "The bacteria has infected his bloodstream. He's getting worse, and I need specific equipment as soon as possible."

T-Bone sighed, casting an apologetic glance to the couple in his bed. "Well, we're not *all* leaving, then. You shouldn't be alone here."

"Grudge can stay," I said. "And Larkan. Reaper will want one of our own with me. But you and Dyno need to get Kyrie back and tell my guys what I need. Then at least one of you needs to come back here with my stuff as soon as possible."

"All right." He nodded, running a hand over his shaved head. "All right, we'll just, uh, finish getting dressed. Make me that list."

"On it."

I went back to my—or was it Shadow's?—room to find him thrashing around in bed, with Grudge struggling to restrain him. The silent man looked up at me with confusion etched in his eyes, but thankfully this wasn't a violent nightmare. Now that I knew the cause of his illness, the symptoms of disorientation and confusion weren't too alarming.

"Shadow, it's Mari." I pushed back the dark hair over his face and placed my hands on his cheeks. "You're safe, love. You're going to be okay."

"Mari?" His eyes were barely open, just slits, while his head moved around as though in search of me.

"Yes, I'm right here." I stroked his cheekbones with my thumbs and pressed a kiss to his clammy forehead. "I'm always here."

He stopped struggling, sinking limply into the mattress. I nodded at Grudge to let him know it was okay, and he climbed off the bed.

"Mari..." Shadow's hands stretched out in search of me. I held one in mine and let his other hand rest in my lap. "Why...why are you always here?"

"Because I'm taking care of you, silly." *And you're mine.*

"No, I mean..." he twisted in the bed as if trying to get comfortable. "Why are you always *here*?" His chin lifted, his feverish gaze pointed toward the ceiling. "In my head? I can't...I can't get you out. You're always there."

My heart drumming wildly, I brought his hand to my lips and kissed the lines of scars over his fingers and knuckles. This beautiful, battered man had been hurt so much and never encountered love a day in his life. Even just the slightest glimpses of it, he didn't know what to do with.

But I would show him. I'd give him what he didn't even know he hungered for, and never make him want for it again.

"Probably the same reasons why I can't get you out of mine," I answered.

TWENTY-THREE

REAPER

"Hey." Jandro smacked me with his bag of chicken feed. "Gun's coming back."

I sat up so abruptly, the cigarette nearly fell out of my mouth. Looking toward the hill where Governor Vance's house sat, I saw Gunner barreling down the narrow street on his bike, hair streaming out behind him. Jandro and I went out to the front porch of the B&B to greet him, both as eager as kids on Christmas for any news.

My heart sank at the sight of Gunner's grim expression when he pulled up.

"What happened?" I demanded.

"Don't know. They're still about two miles out." He climbed off of the bike and released a heavy breath. "It's just two riders—T-Bone and Dyno. With a blond girl I assume to be Vance's daughter."

"What?!"

Jandro and I rushed at him at the same time. I

couldn't speak for my VP, but my blood was already simmering. We fired questions rapidly.

"That's it? Are you absolutely *sure* it was just them?"

"You didn't see Mari at all? Or Shadow? Maybe he was riding further back?"

"Hey, back the fuck up!" Gunner shoved both of us out of his face. "I'm just the messenger, all right? I know what I saw, and I did not miss shit. It's just those three and no one else."

"They better have a good fucking explanation," Jandro glowered.

"Well, they'll be here in a minute and then we'll find out."

"There is no explanation," I seethed. "There is no fucking excuse to leave our woman—and two of our men—behind on a fucking rescue mission in some fucking slave labor territory—"

"Reap, calm down."

"Fuck you!"

I wanted blood. I didn't care if the Sons had a direct hand in leaving Mari and my guys behind, or they had to make a tough choice in rescuing the girl, none of it. All my people being left behind was the worst possible scenario I could imagine. Oh fuck, what if they had to trade hostages? I'd happily watch T-Bone's bald head turn red as a tomato, then purple while I fucking throttled him—

You will not reap.

My head snapped down and to the side, where Hades sat calmly next to my leg. His head tilted up, dark gaze meeting mine as his nose brushed the side of my hip.

"Well, aren't you full of useful advice," I glowered at him.

Their lives are not yours to take. You will not reap the Sons of Odin.

"We'll see about that, dog." I stepped off of the porch and headed into the street to meet the Sons at the edge of town.

Jandro quickly caught up to me. "What did Hades say?"

"I'm not allowed to kill T-Bone and Dyno," I grumbled. "So let's just hope that means Mari and the guys are okay. 'Cause if they're fuckin' not, I don't give two shits about defying an ancient god."

My eyes slid down to Hades trotting calmly at my side, seeing if he'd have any more commentary. But except for the soft panting from his mouth, he kept silent.

The Sons were just cresting the hill when we made it to the base. Dyno veered off toward the governor's house, the young blond woman clinging tightly to his back. T-Bone continued down the gentle slope to the bottom where we waited.

"Where are they?" I demanded before he even came to a complete stop on his bike.

"Safe and unharmed." He tried to sound reassuring as he cut his engine.

"That's not what I fucking asked."

"Reap." Jandro went to touch my shoulder, but I shook him off.

"Don't fucking touch me. I'm not gonna repeat myself, T-Bone."

"They're in Toquerville. A neutral town about five hours from here."

"Why?"

"Shadow took a bad hit and fell off his bike. Mari's fine, but Shadow can't ride and she won't leave his side. Grudge and Larkan are watching over them."

"Wait, what?" Jandro spoke up. "You're saying Shadow took a hit? *Our* Shadow?"

T-Bone nodded. "Arrows with ropes attached. He got hit in the back."

"Jesus," Gunner blanched. "They fucking harpooned the guy."

"Mari said something about an infection. She needs stuff from her medical kit and gave me a list." T-Bone looked at each of us. "And she needs someone to bring it back to her. Said it was urgent."

"I'll go," the three of us said in unison, like a bunch of stooges.

"It should be me," Jandro said. "Reap, the club needs their president. Gun, we need you and Horus to keep eyes out. I'll bring her stuff to her."

"Probably for the best, as much I want to go," Gunner said. "You know Shadow the best, anyway. If he's that sick, he'll probably feel better with you around."

"Reap?"

"Yeah, fine. You go," I muttered. "T-Bone, sorry for almost biting your head off."

"It's nothing, Pres. I completely understand."

"No, I wasn't finished." I stepped closer to him, getting into his personal space. "If you come back a second time without my people, I won't give you such a warm welcome."

"Understood, president." He didn't swallow or shrink back, which I had to give him credit for. He knew his place with me, but wasn't a pussy.

"You got that list?" Jandro broke in.

T-Bone fished a folded piece of paper from his cut pocket and handed it over.

"Chill out for an hour or so while I put this together." Jandro smirked at him. "Hope your *cajones* can handle another long ride in the saddle today."

"Nothing to worry about, VP," T-Bone chuckled, caressing a hand over his bike seat. "My baby knows exactly how to handle my goods."

"All right, then. I'll see you in a bit."

"What does she need?" The question came from Gunner, but we both looked over Jandro's shoulders as he unfolded the list.

"IV bags, sterile tubing, tape, needles," Jandro muttered, going down the list as we walked back toward the B&B. His head lifted as he refolded the paper and shoved it in his pocket. "While I got you guys, I should mention something about Shadow."

"Isn't there always something with him?" Gunner chuckled.

"I'm pretty sure he has a thing for Mari. And I think it's reciprocated."

"Wait, what?" Gunner grabbed his shoulder. "You serious?"

"Inside." I jerked my chin toward the B&B's front door just up ahead. "Let's talk in private while you get Mari's stuff together."

Hades led us up the front porch, earning head scratches from Mrs. Potts, the B&B's owner who was sweeping across the patio.

"Such a sweet dog you have," she beamed at me.

"Thank you, ma'am," I muttered as we made our way inside.

Our room had been tidied and cleaned. Thankfully, my cigarettes remained untouched on the side table. I avoided looking at the bed, well, beds pushed together, as I sat in the armchair and lit up. The nights had been too fucking long. Too fucking lonely without her in it.

Gunner leaned against the windowsill while Jandro grabbed Mari's assorted bags and started laying her medical items out on the bed.

"All right, talk. Mari and Shadow, really?" Gun crossed his arms, looking more agitated by the minute. It didn't entirely surprise me. He was the new guy to our arrangement.

"Yes, really." Jandro pulled out the list and laid it next to the items on the bed. "You can't tell me you've missed all the time they've spent together. He pretty much admitted to splitting up her tattoo sessions so he could see her more."

"What makes you think *she* likes him?"

"She hasn't really said anything about it, but it's not like she's avoiding his attention either."

"She was bringing him into the conversation the night before they all left," I pointed out. "Not quite flirting, but getting there. They're more comfortable with each other than they ever have been."

Gunner turned to me, his brow pinched. "What do you think of this?"

"What do *you* think?" I countered. "You're part of this too, Gun. What are your instincts telling you about them being together? I don't mean your knee jerk reaction, like when you first thought about sharing her. I'm talking deep, gut instinct."

He paused, stroking his chin as he thought about it. "I'm not against it, *per se*. I just have a lot of questions. Basically, why him? What does she see in him? I mean I like the guy, of course, he's a Demon through and through. But he *is* different. Is he going to be good for her?"

"Those are good questions to have," I nodded at him. "It's our responsibility to look out for her. Sometimes women see things through rose-colored glasses and miss red flags. It's up to us to see those clearly." I looked to Jandro. "You know him best. Your thoughts?"

He had been placing Mari's needed items in a small pile at the foot of the bed, and paused when I addressed him.

"I was worried at first," he admitted. "Like, I love the guy. He's my brother, and he's done so much better since she's been around. But I could tell he was still really attracted to her, and spending more time with her after, *you know.*"

Of course we knew. That time they fucked, early on in our relationship. Shadow had misread the situation, and Mari felt a whole storm of confusing things. What she made abundantly clear from that situation though, was her loyalty to me. Once she was calm and reassured, that incident was able to show her that sexual fidelity was not a requirement of mine. She even admitted to enjoying it with him, despite acting only out of self-preservation at first.

"I was worried about his lack of life experience, mainly," Jandro continued. "He doesn't know what to do with a woman besides stick his dick in her when it's offered. I'm damn certain he's never been in love before, probably never even had a crush before Mari."

"I think that's what's bugging me," Gunner said. "He doesn't know how to treat her. Or the subtleties of giving and taking in a relationship. Is he gonna act like us at sixteen years old and just expect to get his dick sucked all the time?"

"See, that's what I thought." Jandro pointed across the bed at him. "But is that really true? He's been through shit the three of us could probably never fathom. When he's not working out or drawing, he's reading history and psychology shit constantly. He's desperate to understand people, and he's fully aware that he's different. He doesn't act entitled or immature in any other way, so why assume he's gonna be that way with her?"

"Mari makes him feel normal," I pointed out. "Because she treats him like anyone else."

"Okay, but how does he make *her* feel?" Gunner argued. "What is *she* getting out of this, is what I want to know. And furthermore, what's she lacking with us that she's seeking out with him?"

"Careful with that line of thinking," I warned him. "You'll go in a downward spiral real quick."

"So explain it to me, then. Since you're the expert."

"Mari hasn't come to me about this yet, so I don't know what's going on in her head. But all people are different. Everyone has *something* that isn't present in others, at least not in the same way. Shadow has something that attracts her, which doesn't mean she's unhappy with us."

Gunner blew out a long breath, shoving his hair back. "I guess that makes sense. I just figured three dudes would be enough, you know?"

"She's meant to have four of us." I let my hand fall off the armrest, stroking down Hades' back.

"How do you know?"

"I just do."

"All right, well," Gunner sighed. "What are the boundaries to this? Do you think they're fucking?"

"She wouldn't do that." Jandro was now sweeping up Mari's personal items from the bed and putting them back in her duffel bag. He paused with a sigh, holding a lacy black thong in his fist. "Damn, I miss her."

"Says the fucker who gets to see her in a few hours," I growled, before addressing Gunner's concern. "No, she wouldn't fuck him without our explicit approval. He's probably too fucking sick anyway. But they've probably gotten closer, emotionally."

Gunner let out a pained sound. "I don't know if that's better or worse."

"It's better," I assured him. "She doesn't have sex clouding her judgment."

Jandro came around the bed and patted him on the shoulder. "Don't get yourself twisted in knots over it. She might be attracted to him, but she loves *us*. She won't jeopardize that, especially not after you got her all worked up with that toy in her ass."

The blond demon gave a wolfish smirk. "I think it was Reap that did the working up."

"What I do best." I ashed my cigarette. "Don't forget that Shadow is loyal to us too, in every way. He's probably the Demon I'm most proud of and trust the most, aside from you two."

"That's true," Jandro agreed. "Shadow is almost hyper-aware of his behavior because he doesn't want to fuck anything up. He won't do something that he feels wrongs us, or jeopardizes the club."

"So, what do you think?" Gunner returned his gaze to me. "You're just good with this?"

"I never said that," I shot back. "I'm a little surprised, but like 'Dro mentioned, the signs were there. They're getting closer, but for all we know, it may just be as friends. We still don't know how Mari feels about everything, and this is ultimately about her. As far as bringing Shadow into our fold, I'm cautiously optimistic. It's not who I would expect, but Mari could certainly choose worse."

"On that note." Jandro smoothed out the bedspread after packing Mari's supplies. "You had eyes on Big G lately?"

"Always," Gunner answered. "He's staying away from Tessa for now. Andrea and Noelle are helping to be a buffer between them."

"Good." Jandro pocketed Mari's list and shouldered the pack with her supplies. "I'm packing a lunch and heading out, *chingados*."

"Kiss her for me," Gunner sighed wistfully. "Fuck, I can't wait til she's back."

"Smack her ass for me," I pitched in. "See if she still feels anything from two nights ago."

"Sure thing, you domineering fuck." Jandro rolled his eyes as he headed for the door. "Don't worry, guys. I'm not coming back without our girl."

MARIPOSA

"You found some, Grudge?"

The silent man nodded, producing a small flask from his cut pocket. He held it out for me to inspect. I unscrewed the cap and took a whiff, the unmistakable burn of rubbing alcohol hitting my nose.

"Perfect, thank you." I ran out of my small stash, and only had one needle and set of tubing until someone came with the rest of my stuff, hopefully tonight.

Grudge held his pad of paper out to me. *What are you going to do?*

"The infection is in Shadow's bloodstream," I explained. "And I don't want to give him the wrong antibiotic, or a useless one, against the strain he has. We have no way of knowing what he has without a lab to test it. So the next best thing is bleeding him out."

His dark eyebrows pinched together as he listened.

"We drain the infected blood out of his body," I said.

"Which will prompt his body to speed up the process of creating new, fresh blood cells to fight the infection."

Won't losing blood make him weaker?

"I won't drain him too much." I looked at the bed, where Shadow continued to toss around restlessly.

Sometimes he slept for an hour or so, but kept waking up disoriented and confused. He could only eat and drink in small amounts before becoming nauseous. Touching and talking to him seemed to soothe him the most.

"Sepsis can go bad very quickly," I said to Grudge. "The best I can do for him right now is to literally get that infected blood out of his body."

What about a blood transfusion? If you drained him and he got fresh blood from another source.

"That might work, once someone gets here with my supplies and we find a blood type match," I sighed. "But Shadow's blood type is rare. Partial matches are okay, but a perfect match is ideal. And since he's AB+—"

Grudge's eyes suddenly widened as he sucked in a sharp breath. He tapped his chest repeatedly.

"You?"

"Hm!" He nodded emphatically, continuing to point at himself.

It took me a few seconds, but finally clicked into place. "*You're* AB+?"

He nodded again, a grin pulling at his lips.

I shoved a hand through my hair, which had to resemble a tumbleweed at this point. "Well, damn. We still have to wait for someone to get here, but that… makes things a lot easier for us."

Grudge chuckled on his way to Shadow's bedside. As he grabbed Shadow's shoulder in an affectionate way, I took a moment to look at the two men more closely. Same dark hair. Same quiet, observant demeanor. Grudge wasn't nearly as broad or tall as Shadow, but their builds were similar. It was hard to tell from his much longer beard, but I'd bet money on them having similar facial structures too. And the two of them having the same rare blood type? That felt like too many coincidences.

"I think you two are brothers." My exhaustion still had me blurting my thoughts out like a drunken sorority girl.

Grudge looked at me, unfazed by my observation. He pulled out his notepad and wrote a slow, thought-out response.

I think we are too. It explains our similarities, and also how we're both different from other people. He paused in thought before writing more. *There's a lot we know about each other that only the two of us understand, that we've never breathed a word of to others. T & D don't even know everything about me.*

"Did you both grow up in the same type of environment?"

He nodded, elaborating on his notepad. *Different locations, but yes. The same abusive cult of women.*

"I'm sorry, for what you both went through."

Not your fault, M. You're one of the good ones. He's lucky.

"I'm sure he doesn't feel like it right now." I ran a hand over Shadow's forehead and cheeks again. He was warm, but not burning up at the moment. I estimated his temperature to be somewhere between 99 and 100. "We should drain him a bit now."

Just tell me what to do, Grudge quickly scrawled out.

For now, he had to do little more than hold a bowl to catch Shadow's blood when I pricked him. I wrapped a strip of gauze around Shadow's arm below his bicep and tied it off tightly to find a vein.

"Please don't thrash on me, love." I leaned over him, brushing a kiss across his forehead. "I'm trying to make you better."

He mumbled wordlessly, moving his head back and forth a bit, but otherwise didn't resist.

"Ready, Grudge?"

"Hm," he nodded.

I inserted the needle and watched the dark blood wind through the tube to empty into the bowl in Grudge's hands. The coppery smell filled the air and I imagined the infection flushing out of Shadow's system into that bowl. It didn't work like that, but aside from this, positive thinking was all I had left at the moment.

"Okay, that's about a half pint," I said. "Let's stop there for now."

I removed the needle from Shadow's arm and bandaged the insertion spot while Grudge went to throw the contaminated blood away. When I went to sit down at the edge of the bed, it was Grudge gently shaking my shoulder that made me realize I dozed off.

"Jesus, sorry…"

"Mm-mm." He shook his head, lips pressed into a thin line, and pointed to the other side of the bed where Freyja sat curled up.

"I'm fine, really. We should wake him and see if he eats—"

"Hmm!" Grudge wrapped a hand around my shoulder and gently pushed me toward the empty side of the bed. Then he released me and made a shooing motion.

"Okay, fine." My eyelids were already drooping again, and that pillow did look super comfortable. "I'll rest just for a few minutes. Can you make sure Shadow eats and drinks something?"

"Mm-hm." He was already pulling an extra blanket down from the closet to cover me with.

"Thank you…"

I surrendered to the fatigue and let it pull me under.

———

THE ROOM WAS dark when I woke up, with only a dim lamp on the bedside table providing light. I was warm. Hot, even. Almost too warm, until I realized where I was. The pillow under my head had been replaced by Shadow's chest.

Somehow I migrated across the king-sized bed in my sleep, and found myself nestled into his side. His arm draped over my back, hand settled in the dip of my waist. His sleeping face was calm, his breaths deep with the steady rise and fall of his chest. I had abandoned my blanket and the sheets were a twisted mess at the foot of the bed, likely kicked away in his thrashing.

I lifted my cheek from his warm skin to just marvel at the long stretches of scars and muscles on him. Sure,

I'd touched him, seen him before, but not like this. He was like a map of an unknown continent I couldn't help but want to explore.

Not wanting to startle him, I skimmed a light touch with my fingertips to his waist. Deeply asleep, he didn't respond. I slid my hand with a slow drag across his stomach, his abs flexing with each breath. His skin was surprisingly soft, the scars little more than light texture on my palms. My hand inched up the solid planes of muscle to his chest, coming to rest over the Steel Demons tattoo a few inches away from my face.

His heartbeat was still too fast for my liking, but his fever didn't feel any higher. And at least he was resting.

"Hey, *Mariposita*."

The voice coming from the armchair in the dark corner of the room made me jump. I instinctively searched for my knife before my brain caught up.

"Jandro!"

I crawled to the bottom of the bed and ran around Shadow to attack-hug my man, who'd been watching silently.

"Fuck, babe." He squeezed me tightly to his chest, face buried in my neck as I wrapped my arms around his shoulders. "Fuck, I missed you."

"When did you get in?" I pulled back just enough to smack a kiss on those plush lips I missed so much. "Why didn't you wake me?"

"A couple hours ago." He held the back of my neck to kiss me deeper. "And you looked comfortable," he chuckled against my lips.

Our kisses were full of relief and longing. Every sip

and tongue flick was passionate and savoring, dragging out the moments we didn't get to have over the past few days.

"How is he?" Jandro dragged the question with a kiss along my temple, loosening his hold on me, but never letting go.

I rested my head on his shoulder, my gaze returning to Shadow. "Better, but still not great. Did you get everything?"

"Yeah, it's all there." He nodded toward a duffle bag on the floor against the wall. I waited for him to make a comment about me cuddling up to Shadow, but it never came.

"Thank you, *guapito*." I hugged around his waist and pressed a grateful kiss under his jaw. "Where did Grudge go?"

"He's next door, resting up with T-Bone."

"I'll leave him be for now, then. But I'll need him for this blood transfusion." I untangled from Jandro and went to dig through the bag.

"Transfusion?"

"Shadow needs non-infected blood and Grudge is a perfect match," I explained. "They're probably brothers. Or biologically related somehow."

"Huh." Jandro rubbed his chin. "Never noticed it before, but you're right."

"Help me with this IV? And I should drain him again."

Together, Jandro and I set up the IV drip along the headboard. Shadow woke groggily when I stuck the needle in the back of his hand.

"Hey man, welcome back," Jandro grinned at him. "Heard you took a hit and couldn't believe it. Had to see for myself."

"Jan…dro?" Shadow blinked several times.

"He's really here," I assured him with a hand to his arm. "Rode all day to help me take care of you."

"I wouldn't go *that* far," Jandro joked, then playfully thumped Shadow's shoulder. "It's good to see you, bro. I'm glad you're okay." He leaned over and kissed my neck. "That you're both okay."

"What's this?" Shadow turned over his hand with the IV needle attached.

"It's giving you nutrients," I said. "At least until you can keep food down, okay?"

He nodded. I noted that he didn't seem to be triggered by needles, only blades.

"I'm not sure if you were awake for this, but it turns out Grudge matches your blood type," I said. "So if it's okay with you, I'll take another pint of blood or so from you, then Grudge can donate his blood to replenish you. I think it's your best chance to beat the infection."

Shadow paled slightly. "You'll take blood, how?"

"With a needle and tubing. Just like when you first donated, remember?"

He nodded, relaxing against the headboard as he sat up. I caught myself staring when the muscles in his arms jumped. For as sick as he was, he didn't look one bit weaker.

"Okay." His odd-colored eyes lingered on my face. "I trust you."

"Thank you." I squeezed his hand, a gesture that Jandro did not miss. "Ready to get started?"

"Yes."

Jandro made a very capable nurse, as it turned out. He lifted the spirits of everyone in the room, without goofing off too badly. Seeing Shadow in the shape he was in was probably a sobering experience. Grudge came back soon after I started taking more blood from Shadow. Once I collected about a pint, Grudge rolled up his sleeve and offered his arm without hesitation.

All-in-all, the procedure was simple, and easy to do with the right equipment. Almost immediately after receiving Grudge's blood, Shadow began looking healthier and more alert.

"I think I can manage a shower," he said, after all was said and done. "I feel gross."

"If you can stand, great." I watched him warily swing his feet to the floor and push to standing. "But you should still rest tonight. We'll see how you feel in the morning."

As he took a towel and clean clothes to the bathroom, Jandro turned to me. "I'll go downstairs and see about getting us our own room."

"Oh, sure." I leaned over to kiss him swiftly. "I'll just be cleaning up."

It didn't take long for him to return. "No vacancies," he reported. "These fucking small towns, I tell you."

"Oh, okay." My eyes darted around the room. "Shadow should keep the bed. There a might be a cot folded up in the closet if—"

"Mari, don't be silly." Jandro approached me with a

curious expression. "The bed's big enough to fit all three of us."

I watched him, trying to get a read on his expression, while he did the exact same thing.

"I know you saw me," I said, my eyes locked onto his. "Why don't you just come out and say what's on your mind?"

Jandro's gaze flicked up to the bathroom door behind me, the shower still running, before looking back at me.

"Has anything happened that I should know about?"

"Nothing beyond what you just saw."

He folded his arms, one hand stroking the stubble on his chin in thought. "Do you want to be with him?"

Like the man we were talking about, the answer wasn't simple. It wasn't just about what Shadow or I wanted, but his comfort level. Maybe an affectionate friendship was enough for him, and there was no need to escalate anything. Maybe, like Gunner at first, he was not into the idea of sharing a woman.

"Or is it just a physical attraction thing?" Jandro tilted his head when I didn't answer right away.

"It's more than that," I said. "But I'm not sure what to tell you, because he and I haven't even talked about it. We're *just* getting comfortable with each other."

A boyish grin spread across his face. "I see. So you're just crushing on each other hard and pretending not a damn thing is happening. Fuck, that's adorable."

The shower shut off and my pulse jumped.

"I want to get to know him better," I said in a quick, rushing whisper. "As a potential partner, but not just physically. I want to take things slow, so he's never uncomfortable."

"But you *do* want his dick. You're imagining it right now, I can see it. You have dick-eyes."

"Jandro," I whined. "Please don't be embarrassing."

"Oh, *mi Mariposita*," he laughed, drawing me into his chest. "You're the cutest thing ever, and that's why I love you."

SHADOW

The hunger pangs rippling through my stomach woke me up. I wanted to eat an entire cow, and wash it down with a freshwater pond. But something was holding me down.

No, wait...

I lifted my head to assess the weight on top of me. It was Mariposa, sleeping on my chest.

She looked so pretty, my breath felt momentarily trapped in my lungs. Her cheek rested on my pec, parted lips nearly brushing my sternum. Her arm draped across me, hand resting on my opposite side like how she usually hugged me. Somehow, my arm ended up wrapped around her back with my hand resting on the side of her hip. I found it hard to believe we just ended up this way in our sleep, but how else could it have happened?

I lifted my other arm, propping it up behind my head so I could see her easily. Her eyes moved under her closed lids as she slept, dark eyelashes occasionally twitching. She sucked in a deep breath and stirred, her arm holding me tighter, but she didn't wake.

Taking in the details of her face, I struggled to remember the past day or two. Last night I felt better, more lucid than before. I felt good enough to shower and walk around a bit. Before that was a lot of feeling awful with hazy memories. I was either freezing or sweating my balls off. Thirsty, hungry, and weak, but unable to keep anything in my stomach. My body felt fatigued and stiff, like I wanted to sleep for weeks, but then I was too hot, cold, or nauseous to sleep.

Physically I felt miserable. I had no idea if I was sick for weeks or mere days. But for the first time ever, I had no fear of dying alone and discarded while being sick. Because Mariposa was always there.

Through the feverish haze, her face was the only thing I saw clearly. It might have been real or hallucinated, but I sometimes heard her voice telling me I was safe and okay. Once in a while I felt her hands holding mine and her lips on my forehead. That had to be just the fever dreams, but even so, I knew she would heal me. Even at a subconscious level, I knew she was safe, capable, and cared about me to some extent.

Looking at her now, her body glued to my side and resting on me so sweetly, I didn't just feel healed from the infection. This trip, this time we got to spend together, made me feel like something deeper inside had healed. Where there was once anxiety and shame, I now felt warmth and ease.

I was still fucked up. I would never be the same as other people. But a small something within me had shifted. My past didn't have the power over me it once had.

Mariposa sighed and began stirring some more. I lifted my arm away to give her space to move. Her cheek dragged along my chest, lips brushing my skin as she pulled herself away. That sensation, along with her hand sliding across my stomach, hit me with a rush of heat and desire. I wanted to draw her back into my side and taste how those lips felt on my own.

"Morning." Mari rubbed her eyes as she rolled to the center of the bed.

"Good morning."

She smiled groggily and warmth bloomed in my chest. Saying good morning became our daily ritual. She used to force it on me, saying it when I dreaded hearing the words because I was expected to answer back. When I finally did answer, she never stopped. Eventually I looked forward to seeing her, to having the opportunity to say two insignificant words to her. It was never insignificant to me, and I wondered if she knew that.

I just then noticed Jandro sleeping on his stomach on the far side of the bed. *Oh yeah, he got here yesterday too.* He accumulated some serious scars of his own, from the burns on his back. And yet Mari still loved him…

Don't start wishing for that. Be satisfied with what you have already.

"How do you feel?" She sat up and stretched, exposing a sliver of belly under the hem of her sleeping shirt.

"Better." My stomach protested loudly. "Hungry."

She grinned, scooting toward the foot of the bed. "I was hoping to hear you say that. Let's start you with soup, then see about introducing solid food."

While my soup heated on the hotplate, she checked my temperature and other vitals. "Fever's gone," she reported, then picked up her stethoscope. "Breathe for me." She pressed the dial to my chest and I looked down at her fingers so close to my skin. "Your resting heart-beat sounds back to normal. Lean forward for me." Once I did, she took one glance at my back and let out a soft gasp. "I guess I shouldn't be surprised," she muttered. "All signs of infection are gone and the arrow wounds are closing up beautifully. If you're feeling up to it, I don't see why you couldn't ride home today."

"Really?" I started looking at her, then four points of soft pressure on my legs drew my gaze down. "Good morning, Freyja." The cat chirped as she walked up my thighs, purring hard when I went to scratch the side of her face.

"She never left your side." Mari gave an affectionate scratch at the base of the cat's tail.

"Neither did you." I returned my gaze to the stunning woman sitting next to me, the healer of not just my body, but the toxic parts of my soul I once thought were beyond repair. "Thank you, Mari. For everything you've done for me."

Her smile was lighthearted, but the air between us felt tense and heavy. "I'm just so glad you're better. I hated seeing you so unwell." She looked down from my face, eyes traveling slowly down my torso.

It only hit me then how exposed I was. Sunlight

poured in through the windows, so she could see *everything*.

I'd felt self-conscious of my scars before, but never like this. Every doubt I thought I'd conquered fought and clawed its way back to the forefront of my mind. She was kind enough to not treat me like a freak, but I'd always be something *other*, a curiosity. It didn't matter that our bodies found each other during sleep and seemed to fit so well. In her eyes, I'd never be held in the same regard as her men.

And that hurt me more than I ever expected.

I wanted to wipe my skin clean, to erase everything that designated me as *other*, just to have her look at me the same way she saw them. But I was helpless to alter the past that left its marks permanently on me. In that moment, all I could do was find a shirt to put on.

Mariposa blinked, her cheeks flushing a delicate pink as her gaze returned to my face. "I'll check your soup." She stood abruptly. "Watch out for Jandro. He's rolling toward you and will try to smother you with cuddles."

I decided to stand too, much to Freyja's dismay, but it was funny to watch Jandro roll completely off of the bed to the floor.

"Fuckers." He rubbed his face, grumbling at Mari's cackles.

"We need to set up guardrails for you," she cooed.

"You know I can't be near an edge. Usually you or Gunner is there to stop me."

Mari wouldn't let me have solid food until I finished all of my soup. Once she was satisfied, she had Jandro bring up toast, eggs, and bacon from the kitchen.

"Don't eat too fast or you'll feel sick again," she warned me.

"It's so cute to see you fussing over him," Jandro teased her over his coffee.

She glared daggers at him, but otherwise didn't respond.

T-Bone, Grudge, and Larkan joined us for breakfast a bit later. The moment I saw Grudge, a strange urge pulled in my chest, which I ultimately decided not to question. I went up to him and pulled the silent man into a hug.

"Thank you," I muttered. "For helping Mari, and for giving me your blood." He looked stunned when I pulled away, and I was sure everyone in the room looked the same. Shit, maybe that was the wrong thing to do?

"Don't get used to that." I brushed it off with a wave of my hand and went to return to my food. But Grudge's chuckling laugh escaped and he thumped me on the back.

Once everyone finished breakfast, it was clear we all had one thing on our minds—heading home.

"You owe for the paint you scraped off in your spill," Jandro jabbed my arm. "Lucky for you, nothing was badly damaged. Your bike just looks ugly now."

"Yeah, yeah. I'll pay you back for the paint." I downed the rest of my coffee, eager to feel the speed and power of my machine under me again.

"Do you hear this shit?" Jandro was pointing at me, but looking at Mari and the Sons. "*Yeah, yeah*? Dude hit his head and woke up with Reaper's fucking attitude.

Mari, bring the old Shadow back. We don't need two Reapers."

Mari nearly choked on her own coffee. "It's not his fault you become an uptight dad when it comes to taking care of their bikes."

"An uptight dad?! *Dios mio*, you're supposed to be on my side."

"I am, I just love giving you a hard time." She grabbed his jaw to kiss him, and an odd sensation stirred in my chest.

It felt sharp, like how I remembered pain felt when I was being cut. But it wasn't because she was kissing *him*. I'd seen her being affectionate with her men plenty of times before. Maybe it was just cementing in the knowledge that she'd never see me that way.

Thankfully, T-Bone seemed just as antsy as me to hit the road. As Mari and Jandro joked and dawdled, he collected our dishes to return to the kitchen downstairs. "Meet you all in the garage," he called on his way down.

I collected my few belongings and followed after him.

———

THE OPEN ROAD and my bike felt like the final pieces of healing that I needed to be one-hundred percent better. Once I settled into my seat and felt the rumble of the engine beneath me, I remembered how I felt *more* than human while riding, not sub-human. The motorcycle became an extension of me, carrying me with speed and strength no one had with just two legs. And when we pulled into Four Corners at the end of a long day of riding, I was elated to be seeing a sunset again.

As we pulled up to the B&B and parked, I felt the desire to point out the sky to Mari, to just watch and enjoy it with her. Maybe, like with the Night-Blooming Cereus, share for the first time why they were important to me. But she was already off in search of her men.

"You're back!"

I turned to see Dyno walk up, clapping T-Bone and Grudge in a three-way hug. The three of them kissed and muttered affectionate words to each other, while I busied myself with removing my saddlebags from my bike.

"Shadow!"

I looked up. "Yes?"

"Come have a drink with us." Dyno tilted his head toward the bar up the street. "Since the other Demons are busy, you can hear updates first." He waggled his eyebrows. "It's official business from the governor. Trust me, you want to hear it."

"Uh, okay." I had nothing better to do, and rather than fatigued from the ride, I felt amped up and energized.

I set my things in my room, then returned outside to follow the Sons to the bar. Dyno seemed completely unable to wait until we were actually sitting and drinking to start talking.

"You got anything nice to wear, big guy?" He faced me, walking backwards down the sidewalk. "And I don't mean like, nice leathers, but *nice*. Fancy shit like a suit or something."

A sense of dread crept over me. "Do I look like I do?"

"Didn't think so," he laughed. "It's all good, I was just curious. Vance has tailors and seamstresses and shit, though they'll probably need a whole bolt of cloth for you."

"What exactly would these things be needed for?"

We reached the front porch of the bar. Dyno grabbed the door and held it open for us as he explained.

"The governor's throwing a dinner party in honor of us bringing his daughter back safely. It's gonna be one of those big, grand ballroom type of things. Dignitaries and officials from allied territories will be there. Other important assholes, I dunno. Yo, a bottle of whiskey! Shadow, what're you drinking?"

"Um, whiskey's fine."

Dyno slapped my chest as we made our way to a table. "We're heroes now, dude! Aren't you stoked?"

"What are we supposed to do at parties like this?" I asked. "I barely know how to be around people as it is."

"Relax, man." T-Bone had his arm around Grudge's shoulders, tangling his fingers in the silent man's long hair. "You're around people right now. Hell, you're hanging out with *us!* And you barely know us compared to the rest of your crew."

"I like you guys better than some of the Demons," I admitted. "And I can be in places like this," I gestured around me to the bar, "without much issue. It's ballrooms and important people who are complete strangers that I'm unsure about."

"Important people are just like normal people." Dyno pulled an empty chair over and stretched his legs over it. "Although, we might get a lot of weird questions from these fucking politicians because they know jack shit about our lives."

"They want to live vicariously through us," T-Bone smirked. "Like all we do is ride and fuck chicks. It's no big deal, Shadow. Just wear the fancy threads, drink the good shit, smoke the Cubans, and enjoy yourself."

"I'll try."

The whiskey bottle placed on our table called out to me to finish it, to numb the anxiety and retreat into the dark recesses of my mind. I knew if I did, I'd find another bottle and finish that one too. And then maybe another, however many it took to wrap myself in that protective layer of numbness.

But now I felt stronger in ignoring that seductive call. I managed to challenge myself before, when I trusted Mari to cut the arrows out of me. I hadn't felt that scared in years, and for a moment, thought I might not survive it. But I did.

I was changing. The meek, silent man who once clung to Jandro as his only friend was someone I didn't recognize anymore. Now I could hang out in a bar with other guys, hug a woman I cared about, and talk to her without issue.

When looking at it that way, a dinner party no longer sounded like the worst thing in the world.

I might even survive it.

GUNNER

They looked like ants marching through the dust, but we knew it was them. I urged Horus to fly closer, just to make sure.

He sailed overhead, the details of the riders becoming clearer as he approached. There was no mistaking Jandro's tricked out ride in the middle of the pack, or Mari wrapped around his waist. Shadow rode a few bike lengths behind them, while T-Bone, Grudge, and Larkan guarded the front.

My human body was moving before my consciousness slipped back into it, and I nearly tumbled over the small table.

"Watch it, bird brain," Reaper growled.

"They're heading back," I said. "Maybe three miles out."

He looked up from his maps. "All of them?"

"Yeah, everyone."

The president slammed his palms victoriously on the wood surface as he stood up. "Fucking finally."

It felt like they took three hundred hours to travel three miles. We stood anxiously outside of the B&B, our temporary home, while the roars of their bikes grew steadily closer.

My heart went nuts at the sight of them with my human eyes coming down the street. I bounced on my toes, eager to see my woman's smile and taste her kiss again. Reaper stood like a monument next to me, his emotions on a tightly-held leash.

When Jandro pulled up and Mari threw her leg over the bike, Reap was on her in a flash. Her helmet went crashing to the ground as he shoved it off her head and grabbed her nape for a rough kiss.

"Lark, Shadow." I nodded at our guys who were also dismounting. "Glad to see y'all back in one piece."

"Glad to be back." Larkan looked around, in search of Noelle most likely. "That territory was fucking weird."

I looked back at Reaper, still wrapped around Mari and playing tonsil-hockey with her like they were in their own little universe. Jandro saw me and laughed. "Give them a few seconds. He deprived her, remember?"

"Yeah, and whose fucking fault is that?" I crossed my arms.

Mari finally came up for air and looked at me, a dreamy smile on her face that made my heart leap. "Gunner!" Thankfully, Reaper released his hold and allowed her to come over to me.

"Baby girl."

I took her face in my hands and kissed her sweetly at first, but that single taste awakened just how badly I missed her. I pulled her sweet curves flush to me and devoured her mouth just as Reaper did.

"Never leave us again." The taste of Reaper's cloves and whiskey on her dissolved quickly, and my tongue found her sweet, feminine flavor underneath.

"I won't." She pulled at my shirt, nails scraping over fabric and skin as she devoured me just as hungrily.

A growl ripped from my throat as she nipped my neck, hands roaming under my shirt shamelessly. Meeting Reaper's eyes over her head, I knew we had to be briefed on what happened, but fuck it. Everyone was home and alive. It could wait.

Reaper walked up behind Mari, pinning her against me with his own body against her back. Dragging his fingers through her hair, he raked the dark strands away from her ear to growl, "Inside." Then he nipped at her earlobe and released her.

He didn't have to tell me twice. I pulled her by the hand to our room in the B&B, leaving it open for him and Jandro before I lifted her up. Knowing where I was headed, she wrapped her legs around my waist, arms around my shoulders.

"Fuck, I missed you." She let out a soft gasp when I pressed her back to a wall.

"Baby girl." With my hips anchoring her to the wall, my freed hands roamed my woman's gorgeous body. "You're about to find out *exactly* just how much I missed you."

I got her topless before the other two got there, Jandro nearly tripping on her discarded bra before he locked the door with a definitive click. "Remember to share, Gun," he smirked.

"Whatever, asshole."

I was too busy remembering how many tongue licks was the length of Mari's neck. And how far my hands slid up her ribs until her perfect tits filled my palms. My cock ached as it rubbed against her spread-open center. I could feel the heat from her there and it drove me fucking wild. Before she became mine, I hadn't fucked anyone in months. Now, I could barely go three days without her before turning into a rutting animal.

Mari's feet slowly touched to the floor and the other guys were on her like animals themselves, diving in to consume her. She shrieked with laughter as Reaper tossed her over his shoulder and onto the bed, swiftly removing her boots, and stripping her jeans and panties from those long legs. He wasted no time in pulling her thighs apart and diving in to give her sweet cunt a long, sucking kiss.

"Fuck." I palmed my cock through my jeans, trying to ease some pressure as I watched her thrash under his tongue. Jandro started tearing his clothes off and so did I.

He crawled on the bed toward her head, sliding a thigh under her head for support as he caressed down her body. Already panting, Mari had one hand on the back of Reaper's head between her legs, the other reaching up to find Jandro. He held her wrist, kissing her palm, when her gaze found me with a lazy smile.

"Don't tell me you're going to sit back and watch,"

she breathed, before shuddering as Reaper slid a finger into her.

"Not a chance," I grinned back, heading for the nightstand. She watched as I pulled the drawer open and took out the bottle of lube and toy we used last time.

"I don't want that this time," she panted, thighs clamped around Reaper's head.

I lifted an eyebrow, stroking down my length with an idle hand. "You don't want anything back there at all, or…?"

"No, I do." Her lips parted with breathy moans, tongue darted out to wet her lips as she watched me touch myself. She wanted me so bad and it was so fucking hot to see. "I want you. All of you."

Reaper released a long moan, his mouth still fixated to her pussy. He kept one hand clamped down on her waist, the other busy below his own waist to free his cock.

"You sure about that, baby girl?" I picked up the plug and held it next to my shaft. "You did good with this last time, but there's still a size difference."

"Quit showing off, bird boy." Jandro leaned over her to pull a pert nipple into his mouth, then released it with a loud sucking noise. "We all know you'll make it good for her, so get your ass over here." His lips wandered over her breasts and sternum as he spoke, hands following closely behind.

"Well if Reaper ever stops hogging her down there, who knows if I'll get the chance." I walked around the bed, tossing the lube in the air once before crawling to the other side of her. I brushed off Jandro's remark, but internally I swelled with pride. My biggest hesitation about being Mari's was not knowing where I'd fit, not knowing how or where she needed me. Now that I knew, I was going to put my heart and soul into giving her exactly what she saw in me—feeling safe and secure, especially in the face of doing something scary or new.

Jandro shifted to the side, kissing down her shoulder and left breast to make room for me. Mari turned her head, kissing me eagerly with soft pants and whimpers that grew increasingly desperate for release. Reaper took his time with her orgasm for once, eyes closed and savoring her, dining on her pussy like it was the finest meal he'd eaten in his life.

I ran my fingertips over the swell of her breast, dragging over her nipple and ghosting a feather-light touch on the underside. When she turned her head to kiss Jandro, I traced over the same movement with my tongue. The VP and I made a game of it, alternating who kissed her lips and her luscious body.

She was quivering on the razor's edge of release for minutes before Reaper finally sent her there with a vicious tongue-lashing. Her hands curled into my hair, nails raking across my scalp while Jandro smothered her cries with kisses. Reaper licked her through the crest of her pleasure and the aftershocks before he finally sat up, lower jaw coated her in arousal as he pulled his clothes off to join the pile on the floor.

"My turn," I announced, sliding down toward her legs. "You guys sit back."

"Gunner, I need a minute," she panted, limp like a noodle when I rolled her to her stomach.

"Don't worry, baby girl." I propped her up until she was on her hands and knees. "I'm just gonna play with you 'til you're ready to come again."

She was so wet, pink, and pretty with her ass in the air. Knowing how sensitive she was, I resisted the urge to take a long lick up her entire slit. Instead, I smacked both palms on her ass, making her jump as she took Jandro and Reaper's cocks in each fist.

"Don't distract her too much." Reaper's growl turned into a low purr, running a hand along her neck and upper back as she stroked him.

"Just getting her warmed up for the fun part," I promised, massaging down the backs of her thighs.

"I'm already having fun," Mari giggled, before her lips made soft sucking and kissing noises.

Jandro groaned, leaning his head back until it met the headboard.

"Baby girl." I brought my mouth even closer to her delectable pussy, knowing she could feel my breath on her tender flesh as I spoke. "We've barely gotten started on your fun."

Running my hands over her ass and thighs, I began with just kissing around her swollen lips, lapping up her sweet nectar without touching her directly. Already, she deepened the arch in her spine, pressing back into my face for more. I grinned against her flesh, and sucked a hard kiss right where her thigh met her butt cheek.

"Fuck." Reaper smacked his head back on the headboard now, while Jandro took in deep, ragged breaths.

Both of their eyes fixated on Mari, hands touching her anywhere they could.

I brought my mouth to her pussy, taking light sucks and kisses of her lips while avoiding her clit. Moving my hands to her lower back, I massaged lightly and moved down until my thumb grazed the tight ring of muscles.

"Mmm!" Her mouth was full of someone—Reaper, by the looks of it, but her reaction to me was immediate.

She wiggled her hips, pressing back eagerly into my face, and my dick flexed with need. She wanted *me* back there, where she never had anyone else before. I couldn't get over the high that she trusted me so completely, to ensure she'd enjoy it and not make it painful. Another part of me reveled in the fact that she chose me to do something more dirty and taboo.

I'd always been the sunny, good-natured, smiling guy. Chicks always went to Jandro or Reaper if they wanted something more depraved. So knowing Mari not only trusted me, but saw me as capable for things like this was an amazing fucking feeling.

Dipping my tongue into her pussy, I felt around on the bed until I found the bottle of lube. I flipped the cap open with my hand and poured a generous amount directly over her ass. Massaging the slippery liquid all around her hole until my fingers were coated, I started inserting them one by one, always pausing to gauge her reaction.

Once I was up to three and started moving them in and out, she came up gasping for air, both hands still working the others' cocks.

"How is that, baby girl?" I sat up, pouring more lube

over my fingers as I worked them in and out of her ass, then pressed a kiss to her back.

"It's…a lot." She lowered her head with a sigh, resting her cheek on Reaper's lap.

"Want me to stop? Or back off?"

"No, just keep doing that. It doesn't hurt, it's just intense."

I dragged my other hand over her pussy, finally coming to that hard little pleasure button of hers. Separating two fingers, I slid them back and forth on either side of her clit. "How's this?"

Her head threw back and a shuddering moan escaped her, the reaction making me grin like a madman. Reaper smiled down at her too, watching her fingers curl into his thigh and her eyes pinch shut as she rocked back on both of my hands.

"Gonna come for us again, sugar?" He stroked her face tenderly. "Gonna get yourself all nice and relaxed so you can take one of your men in your ass?"

Her thighs quivered with the effort of staying up and I knew she was close. I kept my hand on her pussy still, letting her rock back between my fingers to get what she needed. My other fingers kept stroking in and out of her ass, getting the muscles stretched and used to having something back there.

"Holy fuck, you're so perfect," Jandro moaned. She had returned to him, head bobbing and slurping loudly as his hands tangled in her hair.

I dipped my face between my hands, desperate for another taste as she grew wetter from her approaching orgasm. Her pussy was so sweet, I could never blame

Reaper for taking his time down here. She rocked harder between my fingers, her muffled moans with her stuffed mouth still reaching the ceiling.

She came with shudders wracking all over her body, her knees giving out beneath her. I followed her down to the mattress, my fingers still stroking the inside of her ass while my mouth chased her pussy for a taste of her orgasm. She ground against my hand, now flat against the mattress as I licked her.

I pulled both hands away from her then, just to give her a break from all the sensations while she caught her breath. But I couldn't stop touching her completely, and laid alongside her to plant kisses down her spine.

"Hmm hi, love." She gave me a dreamy smile, eyes all hazy from pleasure as she touched my face.

"Hi, baby girl," I grinned back, scooting closer to reach her lips. "I love you."

"Love you." Mari returned my kiss, warm and sweet, before pushing up to her hands. She crawled to Reaper and leaned in to kiss him. "Love you." He tried to hold her there for longer, but she leaned over to kiss Jandro next. "And I love you."

His flushed skin and giddy smile echoed what we were all feeling. She loved all of us, and we felt it, as sure as we felt this bed beneath us. Nothing about this was disjointed or unfair. This one woman somehow made three bikers want to please, satisfy, and hear those words from her like it was all that mattered. She was incredible for that alone, and for so much more.

"You're our world, sugar." Reaper cupped her chin

and pulled her back to him, love and adoration in his eyes. "Don't leave us again."

"Never." She accepted his demanding kisses this time, melting into him as he pulled her forward until she was straddling his lap.

He moaned into her mouth, hands digging into her ass as she rolled forward. Her pussy dragged along his length, leaving a trail of wetness from base to tip. I spotted her wicked smile as she pulled back to tease him with no entry.

"Sugar," he growled a low warning.

She finally paused, her entrance hovering over him. Still, he wrapped an arm around her waist, crushing her to his chest so she wouldn't move, then surged up to impale her.

"Oh, fucking god, I missed that…" He caged her in with both arms, forehead on her shoulder as he pressed into her with long strokes. Her arms went around his neck, mouth against his ear with her soft whimpers.

This looked intimate, something between only them. Jandro and I hung back, giving them space for a few moments, until Mari looked over her shoulder at me.

"Come here, Gun."

I scooted forward, running a hand down her back as Reaper's hold on her loosened. She turned to Jandro then, pulling a deep kiss from his mouth before kissing down his chest.

My fingers trailed down the cleft of her ass, circling her tight hole. "Still want this, baby girl?"

"Mm-hm…" Her mouth was stuffed with Jandro's

cock again, a hypnotizing sight, better than any porn film.

Reaper paused in his thrusts and slid down the bed, allowing me better access as I placed a knee on either side of Mari's feet. I lubed up my cock first, letting the head rest on her ass while I stroked the slippery liquid up and down my length. Her eyes were on me as she took long sucks of Jandro.

"Feel this first, babe." I reinserted my slick fingers in her ass, earning a moan from her as she began to move on my hand with Reaper inside her pussy.

"Mm, you feel tighter." His hands swept forward and I heard the wet sucking sounds of his mouth on her nipples. "But I bet you want more, don't you?"

"Mm-hm." She illustrated this by pushing back harder on my fingers.

I chuckled, pulling my hand away and resting my cock head on the same place. "Who am I to deny our girl what she wants?"

With a hand on her lower back to steady her, I poured more lube on her ass and my head, then began pressing through her tight entrance. A few inches in, she released Jandro from her mouth with a gasp.

"Oh god, that's…"

"Breathe, sugar. Relax."

I added more lube, pulled back until I was nearly out, then slowly pressed forward again. She hissed in a breath and shut her eyes tight, hands balling into fists in the sheets.

"Talk to me." I leaned over her back and brushed

kisses over her shoulder blades. "Good, bad? Pain or no pain?"

"Just…a lot." Her eyes cracked open at me. "It's intense. I feel so full."

"You are." Reaper kissed her. "Full of your men's cocks."

"Not *all* of them," Jandro smirked. His cock laid across his lower stomach, slick with her saliva.

"Easy, 'Dro. Give her a minute."

"I know, I'm just correcting your statement."

"Move on us if you feel like it." I kept smoothing my hands up and down her back, planting kisses on her spine and shoulders. "We'll stay still. You take what you need."

She wrapped so tightly around me, all my baser instincts urged me to move, to thrust and feel the grip of her body send pleasure through my dick. But she chose me for this because keeping her safe and unafraid was my number one priority.

A tightening of pressure made me hiss in a breath, but I kept still. Only my hands moved across her skin, reminding her I was here. I realized it was Reaper rubbing her clit, making her pussy flutter and respond to his touch. I felt the same response in her ass and it was incredible, almost making me forget where I was.

As Reaper coaxed another orgasm out of her, she did start moving. I sank my teeth into my lip, holding my breath as her twitches and movements of pleasure shot heat and intensity down the length of my dick. I wondered if this was what she feeling—so much, but so fucking good.

Gradually she made her movements bigger, riding Reaper as she pressed back onto me. I felt his cock move through her and it was fucking wild. From the look on his face, he felt her more intensely too, and like me, was struggling to keep his control on a leash.

When she leaned over to take Jandro back into her mouth, Reaper and I took over. We found it easiest to alternate our thrusts—as he sank into her pussy, I pulled out of her ass. It was fucking surreal, almost like I wasn't really there, but in someone else's body, watching. But how incredible she felt every time I slid back in was a hot dose of reality.

This was my life, pleasing and protecting this woman with two other men, in a world where others would use and discard her.

I leaned over until my forehead touched the tattoo on her back, the one that matched mine. Lost in the rhythmic, mounting pleasure, my body felt weightless. She grounded me, kept me right where I wanted to be.

"You feel amazing," I rasped on her shoulder.

"Fuck yeah, she does." Reaper watched her with rapt attention, and I knew he was just as concerned about her pleasure and comfort level as me. His green eyes were hooded, fixated on her like she was the drug we needed to feel an ounce of anything good.

Mari matched us in our movements now, her sweet ass bouncing off my hip bones as we crashed together, slamming down on Reaper as he drove up into her, and stroking Jandro into ecstasy with her mouth and fist.

It was amazing to watch and feel. We all came at her from different angles and positions and, with just a bit of adjusting, she took it all like she was made to be shared by us.

The pleasure was taking full control of me now, filling every pore in my body with a delicious ache. Every movement through her, every sound she made, and even hearing the other guys moan, loosened the threads of my control and I drove harder, deeper into her ass to chase it.

She got louder, her holes squeezing around us as Reaper sped up to match me.

"Oh fuck, that's so hot." Jandro squirmed as he watched, his body under the mercy of her mouth. "Fuck her good, guys."

Her moans turned to long, drawn out whimpers as Reaper and I drove into her again and again. I tried to listen carefully through the pulse pounding in my ears for any sounds of pain, but she rode us just as hard as we did her. Her hands clamped down on Jandro's thighs as she took him down her throat. I grinned at the sight of our greedy, dirty, perfect girl. The pleasure, the heat, the sensations of us filling every one of her holes was possessing her too.

"Oh, come for us, sugar."

Reaper's voice was barely more than a raspy whisper, like he smoked a whole pack of cloves in an hour. Sweat slicked across his skin from effort and restraint. He felt for her clit again, strumming it with a barely-controlled frenzy to get her off before we did.

She let out her loudest whimper yet before her ass closed around my length like a vice. Judging from Reaper's strangled moan, her pussy did the same to him.

"Fuck! Fuckkk…"

It took every last drop of my remaining control to fuck her through her orgasm, her ass pulsing with the tight convulsions that wracked her whole body. I couldn't hold out through her aftershocks though, and pleasure zapped through my whole lower body as I spilled violently into her. Through the thin wall separating us, I felt Reaper empty into her too, sending another jolt of sensitivity throughout my whole body.

We slid out of her with slow care just as she lapped up Jandro's release, licking the panting man's cock like an ice cream cone.

I fell to my side on the bed, utterly spent and blissed out. Mari stretched out long between me and Reaper like she was just waking up from a nap.

"How was that, baby girl?" I skimmed my fingertips down the side of her body, still helpless to keep myself from touching her.

"Intense," she breathed with a bright smile. She looked ready to face the day, save more lives, maybe. "But so, *so* good."

"Worth repeating?" Reaper kissed her shoulder, a wolfish grin on his face. "With me in your ass next time?"

"I'll fight you for that, Reap." Jandro moved around our stretched-out legs to rest his head on Mari's lap, his usual spot.

She smiled lazily, running her fingers over Jandro's scalp. "I just love feeling all of you at the same time. It really solidifies how good we all are. Together."

Reaper kissed her first, then Jandro slid up to take

his kiss from her, and then finally me. I held her chin between my fingers as I sipped love and affection from that beautiful mouth.

It was wordless agreement from all of us, because the way she said it was perfect. There were no more words to accurately describe the feeling as we snuggled in closer to her on all sides. Contentment settled over me as I closed my eyes and just sank into this feeling.

Together. Us.

TWENTY-SEVEN

MARIPOSA

"**Y**ou couldn't have told me *before* our crazy sexathon?" I huffed, rubbing the towel over my wet hair.

I wasn't really upset, though. I just didn't expect to attend a fancy dinner party in the company of the governor, while still feeling the ache of all my men inside every part of me.

"Really, *bonita.*" Jandro hugged me from behind, smacking a kiss on the crook of my neck. "When it comes to you, or being in a room full of peacocking politicians, where do you think our priorities lie?"

"Well, at least I got to soak in a long bath before the tailors came looking for us."

I turned to the dress hanging on the bathroom door. It wasn't quite a ballgown, more like a knee-length cocktail dress that hugged my form. Still, it was finer than anything I'd worn in years, maybe ever.

Governor Vance's tailors balked when I asked for the back to be open, but with my insistence, they made it work beautifully. Running my hand over the silky material, I smiled inwardly at the thought of all these politicians and dignitaries seeing a biker gang's tattoo on a woman in an expensive dress. We were honored guests and undoubtedly expected to play nice for the evening, but the tattoo would serve as an important reminder.

MC women had to be just as strong as their men to survive, albeit in different ways. I earned my tattoo, just like the men did. Hopefully it would remind the governor and his associates that outside his world, where women were little more than dolls to be dressed up and traded around, there were others like me who weren't so helpless.

Now, we were in his home by invitation. Our working relationship was off to a good start, but it wouldn't take much for our completely opposing worlds to clash. We would show him respect, but he had to return that same courtesy. Tattooed women and all.

I had to hand it to Vance's tailoring staff. Reaper and Gun told me about the dinner party after our sexathon, then a well-organized team of people with garment bags, measuring tape, bolts of cloth, and fabric shears knocked at our door. They got us fitted into semi-formal clothes that slid on like gloves within hours, before moving on to the rest of the party.

I thought I heard protests from Shadow's room as they measured and fitted him, but tried to keep my excitement in check. A party like this seemed like it was absolutely *not* his thing, but I really wanted to see him in a suit.

Once my hair was dry enough, I took the dress off the hanger and stepped into it. The built-in bra was snug and supportive without being too restricting. Reaper had looked like he wanted to murder the seamstress who measured my chest, but I was glad they sewed this in. It accentuated my shape nicely, and allowed my back to be completely bare without a bra strap ruining the look.

The guys wore slim-fitting slacks that paired well with their riding boots, and white button up shirts tucked in. They picked out blazer jackets to wear, but chose to forgo ties. Jandro was already undoing the top buttons on his shirt and pushing his sleeves up.

"Okay, as hot as you look like that," I folded his collar down and pressed it smooth, "this is a look for after the party, not before or during."

"I'm just making it easier for you to rip it all off me later." He ran his hands down my sides and took a step back. "Jesus, you're so fucking stunning."

Reaper came over from getting himself situated in the mirror. He had the top buttons undone too, teasing a bit of the ink under his neck, but he at least kept his sleeves intact. "I fucking swear, sugar, you're making it even more tempting to skip this whole thing."

"Not fucking happening." I imitated his tone, enjoying his smirk as I came over to run my fingers over the exposed skin of his throat. "You need this time with Vance, president. To have his attention as an equal, for the wellbeing of your club."

"It doesn't matter what I say, Mrs. President." He ran a hand along my side, following my waist to my ass.

"With you on my arm, I know exactly where his attention will be."

"I'm sure we can steal her away to prevent any distractions." Gunner walked up to check himself in the mirror, looking dapper as hell. He'd shaved, and brushed his hair back neatly so it fell to his collar in soft, uniform waves. Not only were his shirt buttons and sleeves intact, but he even added a pocket square to his blazer. Rather than his engineer boots, he wore a pair of polished brown loafers.

In his usual biker getup, it was easy to forget he came from money. But right then, he looked every bit the polished, private academy graduate. The others noticed too.

"You clean up nice, Gun." Jandro reached out like he was going to mess up Gunner's hair, but the blond demon shot him a scathing look.

"All of you do." I placed Gunner's earrings in my lobes, then adjusted Jandro's necklace at my throat. Reaper's ring sparkled under the bathroom lights as I finished touching myself up. "I'm going to be the luckiest woman at this party."

"These stuffy old farts aren't gonna know what hit 'em." Gunner slid an arm around my waist and placed a delicate kiss on my earlobe.

"Are we ready to go and get this over with?" Reaper hovered impatiently by the door. "They said the governor would send a car."

The guys spilled out into the B&B lobby, while I hurried to finish setting my make up. I heard the familiar voices of Larkan and Noelle floating in, then my heart jumped at the sound of Shadow's low rumble.

He's coming too! Be normal. Act natural.

What was natural and normal with him anymore? Treating him with polite distance? Hugging him or kissing his cheek? With closer friendliness, like with the Sons of Odin now? Something shifted between us since the rescue mission, and Jandro spoke aloud of what I tried and failed to shove down.

I wanted him. I wanted to sit and talk with him just as badly as I wanted to curl into that huge, strong body. I wanted to help him face his fears, to feel his strength like an impenetrable shield. I wanted him to know how amazing love could feel.

My whole body thrummed with nerves as I forced myself to quit stalling. I shoved some items into a clutch purse, made a final check of my hair and teeth, then headed for the door.

The tailoring staff politely informed us that animals would not be allowed at the party, so I gave Hades, Freyja, and Horus final pets before leaving the room. If I wasn't already nervous enough, I turned out to be the last one ready. Everyone stopped chatting to turn and look at me.

"Holy shit, girl!" Noelle held her arms out. She wore a simple, but elegant, white toga-style dress that made her red hair and colorful tattoos pop. "Are you ever not fucking stunning?"

My face reddened as she leaned in to kiss my cheek. "Thanks, Nellie."

She held tightly on to my arms, her lips lingering

near my ear. "Thanks for watching out for my man," she whispered. "I knew he'd be in good hands with you."

I returned her affectionate squeeze. "He watched out for me. He's a true Demon and you should be proud."

She released me with a beaming smile, returning to Larkan's side as he slid a possessive arm around her shoulders. They looked as adorable as ever, but my gaze slid over to the largest man standing with us.

Shadow's broad chest and arms filled out his suit in a way that made my knees buckle. His slacks could barely contain his muscular thighs, and if he turned around, I'm sure the same would go for his ass. Like Gunner, his hair had been brushed back and fell over his shoulders in soft waves. He'd clearly run his fingers through it, as evident by the strands pulled forward to cover the scarred side of his face.

He looked uneasy, and completely out of his element. But none of that took away from the fact that he just looked wildly masculine and beautiful. He would be even more irresistible if he didn't see himself as so ugly and unworthy.

I made a decision right then. Jandro knew, so the other guys had to as well, to some extent. If Shadow didn't know, I hoped it would be made clear to him soon.

With a smile, I crossed our small circle to Shadow's side. "You look so handsome." Even in heels, I had to stand on tiptoe to reach his face. Slowly, to not catch him off guard, I brushed away a strand of dark hair to kiss the scar on his cheek.

Everyone's eyes felt heavy on my back, but I ignored them, stepping back after the brief kiss to give Shadow space.

"Um, thank you." He looked equal parts stunned, confused and terrified. "You look…very nice."

"Thank you." I put him on the spot, so I didn't expect to get a compliment back. I just wanted him to know what I saw when I looked at him.

Reaper's dry chuckle rumbled in my ear, followed by his firm hand on my lower back. "Ready, sugar?"

I nodded, following his lead out to the front porch.

Two large black SUVs waited for us, Governor Vance's staff wearing dark suits as they held the doors open. The short drive took us into the heart of Four Corners. I thought at first that the event would be at Vance's cabin home, but our rides pulled up to a sprawling pre-Collapse building in the middle of the city.

The driver opened our door, with Reaper taking my hand as he stepped out. Jandro and Gunner followed, framing me protectively on all sides as we walked up the stone steps. A quick glance over my shoulder told me Shadow followed a few paces behind, as usual. More staff members pulled open heavy glass doors for us, and I could only blink in awe at the inside of the building.

The outside had been completely understated, if even unremarkable. But the inside had a beautiful dome ceiling as one big skylight, showing the early evening sky darkening above the chandeliers. Tall archways led to various spacious rooms for different functions. One was clearly a smoking lounge, another with drinks and hor d'oeuvres. Another room appeared to have a live band with a dance floor and its own private bar. The main banquet appeared to be straight ahead, and also the largest room, with a single long table elegantly set with dinnerware.

It was all very classy and clearly expensive, but was worlds different than what we saw in Blakeworth. There was a timeless, simple wealth to this place. It wasn't flashy, nor overtly trying to show off how rich the governor's family was. This place looked like anyone could dress up for a night and have a good time here. As nice as everything was, there was no clear class divide between people, and I found that comforting.

"Mari!"

I turned to see Kyrie floating elegantly through one of the archways. The fear and anxiety in her eyes was gone, only warmth shining through.

"Kyrie!" I reached out to clasp hands and kiss cheeks with her. "I barely recognized you. You look amazing."

"Yeah, damsel in distress isn't a great look on me," she laughed.

I squeezed her hands and leaned in a little closer. "You sure you're okay to be here?" I whispered. "You just got back yesterday."

She returned my hand squeezing and gave me a reassuring smile. "Trust me, I'm good. All I wanted to do was go back to my normal life, and this is exactly what that is." She laughed lightly and spread her hands.

"The life of a governor's daughter isn't for everyone, but it's the normal I know."

"Fair enough." I released her hands. "But if you need anything, even just someone to talk to, let me know."

"I'll do that," she said earnestly, before her eyes drifted over the men flanking me on all sides. "Now will you, uh," she cleared her throat, nerves creeping into her voice, "introduce me to your, um, husbands?"

"Of course! Where are my manners?" I slid my left hand around Reaper's bicep, my colorful ring flashing against his jacket sleeve. "This is Reaper, president of the Steel Demons motorcycle club." I wrapped my opposite hand around Jandro's arm. "This is Jandro, vice president and mechanical genius. The pretty one standing behind me and grinning at you is Gunner, captain of the guard."

Gunner laughed lightly, my assumption obviously correct as I felt his soft kiss on the back of my hair.

"You met Larkan and Shadow," I continued. "And the gorgeous woman on Lark's arm is Noelle, my sister-in-law."

"We are not her husbands, I just pretended to be one," Larkan winked, earning a playful smack on the arm from Noelle.

"It's a pleasure meeting you, Kyrie." Reaper's voice was warm and smooth as honey. "We're glad you're back safely, and grateful to your father for allowing our stay in Four Corners."

Kyrie's eyes dropped under Reaper's heavy gaze, her cheeks flushed pink. I knew exactly what she was feeling

—these men were just as hot as they were intimidating to those who didn't know them. It was the same intensity I felt the moment they burst into the Old Phoenix service center, which felt like an eternity ago.

"The pleasure is all mine." She composed herself with a bashful smile. "Mari quite literally saved my life. The Steel Demons are welcome here for as long as you choose to stay."

"We appreciate the hospitality," Jandro said charmingly.

Kyrie lifted her chin to acknowledge Shadow behind all of us. "It's good to see you feeling better, sir. I'm glad you could come."

He blinked in surprise at being noticed. "Um, thank you. Mari is the best at what she does."

Warmth filled me as I tried to keep my smile in check. I secretly loved that I wasn't the only woman to acknowledge and validate him. He might need more than just me to boost his confidence.

Kyrie's hand went to the pendant at her throat, a large tear-shaped stone with swirling colors in shades of red and white. I noticed Reaper's eyes fixated on it too. It was definitely a unique statement piece.

"Have you guys seen Dyno and the other two?" Kyrie asked as she looked around.

"They're coming, but may be a bit late." Shadow surprised everyone by answering her calmly. "Grudge needed some convincing to attend, so they're working on him."

"Well with you here, hopefully he feels better seeing a friendly face," Kyrie smiled politely at him. "Can I offer you all some drinks and appetizers? Everyone is just kind of milling about before the first course."

We followed her lead through one of the archways to one of the smaller rooms, which was still as big as the entire B&B we stayed at. I took the opportunity to poke Reaper and tease him.

"Staring at the girl's chest, were you?"

"No, her necklace," he muttered. "It's a lace agate. My mom used to have a bunch of stones just like it. Not many people wear jewelry like that and it just jostled the memory a little."

I rubbed his arm and pressed a light kiss to his shoulder. In turn, he brushed a kiss along my forehead.

The curious and heated stares began almost immediately upon walking into the room. My men subtly pressed in closer to me, my ever-vigilant shields. Gunner swept a hand along my upper back—a possessive, affectionate gesture which also exposed my tattoo. He was telling everyone, in no uncertain terms, that I was claimed.

"You must be the biker crew everyone's been talking about," a portly, older gentleman greeted with an extension of his hand.

Reaper's nostrils flared, but he accepted the handshake. "One and the same. I'm Reaper, Steel Demons president."

"Ah. Well met, R-Reaper." The man smiled uneasily. "I guess we'll find out tonight if the stories about you are tall tales or true?"

"If I'm in the mood to divulge," my husband returned coyly. "A good whiskey usually helps."

"Oh, please sir, come this way!" Another middle-aged man swept his arm toward the bar. "I promise you've never seen a whiskey selection like this. Do you care for cigars, Reaper?"

I chuckled and removed my arm from Reaper's when I saw his eyes light up. "Go on. Indulge in your smoke and booze."

"Keep close, sugar." He kissed my cheek and headed for the bar to peruse the selection.

Governor Vance's associates made more introductions and small talk with us, polite enough to not stare at me too much or ask probing questions. I struggled to remember all of their names and titles—every one was a John or a David and their titles were things like Minister of Finance and Secretary of Development. The Sons of Odin finally showed up, and the difference in Kyrie's mood was like night and day.

She nodded and listened politely to one of the older men rambling about something to her, then completely tuned out when T-Bone, Dyno, and Grudge walked into the room. Dyno's eyes lit up at her too, then he bit his lip with a silent nod to acknowledge her. T-Bone winked at her in greeting, but seemed preoccupied with Grudge, who looked like he wanted to bolt back out into the street.

Shadow also noticed his distress, and my stomach fluttered when he went over to greet his silent friend. He didn't just protect people with his strength, but also his softness. If only he could see that in himself.

"Yes, unfortunately General Bray couldn't make it," one of the men said to Jandro, cutting into my thoughts.

"His wife isn't feeling well so he stayed home to take care of her, even though they have house staff. Completely devoted husband, that one."

"As a husband should be." Jandro's arm tightened around my waist. "But we'll look forward to meeting him another time. Gunner's our strategist and I'm sure they'll have lots to talk about."

A tuxedo-clad waiter strode into the middle of the room at that moment. "If I could have everyone's attention," he projected his voice. "The first course is about to be served, if you would all follow me to the dining room."

MARIPOSA

Governor Vance waited for us at the entrance of the main dining hall. He accepted a kiss on the cheek from Kyrie before addressing me and my guys.

"President," he greeted Reaper jovially. "And Sons," he turned to T-Bone. "As my honored guests, I've marked your seats near mine at the head of the table."

"Thank you, governor. You're looking well."

Reaper followed him down the length of the long table, one hand in mine, the other holding a tumbler of whiskey. Jandro and Gunner trailed after me, while the Sons and Shadow walked up the other side of the table to sit across from us. I couldn't get over how endearing it was that Shadow stuck so close to Grudge.

"It's wonderful what restful sleep and the peace of mind of having my daughter back will do," Vance returned.

He did look much better than that sorrowful, shell of a man we first met in his cabin. His eyes were bright, and he'd just gotten a fresh shave and a haircut. He looked across the room to Kyrie, who was further down the table chatting with Larkan and Noelle. She kept sneaking glances down toward the Sons, but her father's attention had returned to my husband.

"Please, sit. Make yourselves comfortable." Vance dropped into his seat at the head of the table. "What whiskey did you select, president?"

"I like this twelve-year from, what was it?" Reaper dipped his nose in the glass. "Big Sky Distillery. Your friend told me it's the only above-board distillery running since the Collapse."

"Ah yes, still wild country up there in Montana," Vance grinned. "Not much has changed that far north."

"I hope this doesn't make you think I keep my business strictly legal," Reaper smirked.

"Wouldn't dream of it!" Vance laughed. "Working with the Sons has taught me to ask either the right questions, or none at all."

"Smart man."

The conversation paused as everyone leaned back to allow servers to place salads in front of them. My eyebrows lifted as I watched Reaper place his napkin in his lap, then reached for his salad fork. I wondered if my guys would eat like they were raised by wolves in a place like this, but it seemed I had nothing to fear.

"My daughter has taken quite a liking to you, ma'am," Vance nodded at me before his first bite of salad. "From what she tells me, you were the one who conducted the actual rescuing."

"You can call me Mari, sir. And thank you," I smiled at him. "I just had to get near her and stall for a distraction. I couldn't have gotten her out of there without the men providing firepower and muscle."

"She's being modest." T-Bone grinned from across the table. "She pulled a knife on Blake and his son, then put herself between them and Kyrie. And then they made a break for it when armed guards started shooting."

"My word." Vance leaned back in his seat, looking at Reaper. "I know things work differently in MCs, but I can't imagine sending my wife into danger. Medic or not."

"I tried to stop her," Reaper chuckled. "But we also work democratically, and I was outvoted. It's ironic that the women came out unscathed, while my best fighter nearly died."

"Ah, yes. I was told. Remind me his name?"

"Shadow, he's the big fucker—er guy, right there."

Vance leaned over his plate. "Excuse me, Shadow?"

His head jerked up from reading something on Grudge's notepad, eyes wide with confusion. "Um yes, governor?"

"A toast to you and your bravery." The governor lifted his glass, prompting everyone at the table to do the same. "The injuries you sustained on this mission were not in vain. I'm forever in the debt of the Steel Demons MC and the Sons of Odin MC for returning my only child to me safe and unharmed."

"Daaaad." Kyrie hid her face behind her hands, earning soft laughs from everyone in attendance.

"You're all heroes to Four Corners," Vance continued. "Wherever your travels may take you, you will always have a home here. Cheers!"

He turned to clink his crystal wine glass against Reaper's tumbler, the sound rippling down the table as politicians toasted and celebrated with outlaws. How often did that happen these days?

"I expect you to hold me to that, president," Vance leaned over to talk directly into Reaper's ear. "I want to assure you I'm not making empty promises as a figurehead. I'm a grateful father, who happens to have a bit of wealth and some power. Tell me what you need and I'll make it happen."

Reaper set his salad fork down and swirled the remainder of his drink, ever thoughtful and methodical. "I appreciate that, governor. First I'd like to know, are you concerned about Blakeworth declaring war on Four Corners since they see your daughter as their stolen property?"

"My general has already been informed and is preparing our troops," Vance said lightly. "I'm not especially concerned because of how quick citizens are to desert Blakeworth. I imagine we'll have plenty coming to our side once they see Four Corners as a place of refuge."

"Mari mentioned Blake may be in alliance with General Tash," Gunner jumped in. "Even if Blake's army deserts him, Tash is a force to be reckoned with. He's why we had to leave our previous home."

"I've heard stories about this man, too," Vance mused. "They call him the phantom general around here. He strikes quickly, then disappears and sends others to do his bidding, is that right?"

"Sounds like him," Gunner said. "He tried to use our club as one of his pawns, but we caught on and fought back. One of our best men died in his last attack on our home."

"My deepest condolences," Vance offered. "I'll let General Bray know about this possible alliance. He's very resourceful himself and has his own crafty methods of gathering information. It's a shame he couldn't be here tonight, he's quite the life of the party."

The next course came out, a light and delicate carrot-ginger soup that made me want to drink from my bowl. I resisted, keeping my table manners ladylike as I decided to shift the conversation.

"How is the hospital faring, governor?"

"Oh, it's always short-staffed with so few people medically qualified these days. But Dr. Brooks does the best he can. On top of being the only one trained as a surgeon, he's also running a teaching program in hopes of having more doctors available."

My heart soared at the same time Jandro squeezed my knee under the table. "I don't have a certificate to prove it, but I was trained as a labor and delivery nurse. Plus, learning things on the fly for the past three years. I'd be happy to help in any way that I can."

The governor nodded enthusiastically. "That would be brilliant! Forgive me for not suggesting it sooner. I'm afraid we've grown accustomed to women not taking initiative to such roles in recent years."

"That's all right," I smiled politely. "Maybe it can serve as a reminder to the women of Four Corners that we're capable of more."

"Indeed, indeed."

But I noticed the governor's reservation in that answer, and so did the men sitting around me.

Dyno wiped his mouth with a napkin. "Kyrie sure is born into a fortunate situation. There must be plenty of opportunities for a governor's daughter that not everyone can afford."

Vance swallowed a mouthful of soup, taking the time to choose his words carefully. "She has never wanted for material possessions, not has she had to worry about her education or safety—at least I thought so until recently." He set his spoon down in his empty bowl. "But the unfortunate reality is that there aren't many opportunities for women of any stature, no matter how well educated or financed they are. Unless, and forgive me, I don't like it, but this *is* the truth," he took a deep breath, "she marries another governor or his son to forge an alliance between the two territories."

"So we have come full-circle," T-Bone scoffed. "Back to the dark ages."

"Of course it's barbaric, but it is…the current reality," Vance sighed. "I've never pushed her to marry anyone. Frankly, I'd be happiest if she spent the rest of her days here, safe, unwed, and far away from the eyes of any men." He chuckled, elbowing Reaper. "Once you're a father, you'll understand."

"I do in a way, but my…upbringing is somewhat

different from yours, governor." Reaper's fingertips trailed the inside of my thigh. "A girl deserves multiple fathers to protect her, dote on her, and show her examples of what a man really is. When she's a woman, she'll know what kind of treatment to accept, and will choose the best men to please and protect her as an adult."

Vance chuckled politely. "Different worlds indeed, president. But I respect it. And if I may say, Mari, you certainly look satisfied with your ah, *arrangement.*"

"I am, governor," I smiled. "Very satisfied."

Jandro started to laugh, then coughed, choking on his soup until Gunner whacked him on the back. Across the table, Dyno and T-Bone still wore surly expressions.

"I'm just curious, sir," T-Bone stroked his beard. "What if Kyrie wanted to marry someone completely below her status? Say, a bricklayer. Or some other tradesman. Would you support the relationship if she loved the guy?"

Vance took a long time to answer. The soup bowls were taken away and the next course replaced it, but none of us were looking at the food.

"My daughter's wellbeing and happiness is what's most important to me," he said finally. "If such a man can give her everything she needs, and provide a good life for her, who am I to tell her no?"

Seemingly placated by that answer, the Sons dug into their meal.

The rest of the dinner conversation was lighthearted. Drinks poured freely and the whole table was soon abuzz with laughter and lively conversation. Plates were cleared and replaced swiftly. I lost track of how many courses the meal was, but was completely stuffed by the time dessert was placed in front of me.

"Help me with this," I begged Jandro, sliding the brownie topped with vanilla ice cream and hot fudge toward him. "I can't eat another bite."

He sliced his fork through and took a heaping mouthful, looking at me like I was crazy for not having any room left.

Dessert was barely finished before the men started putting their napkins on the tables and pulling cigars out of their jacket pockets.

"Won't you join us, gentlemen?" Vance gestured toward the slim case in the hands of a waiter, displaying an array of smoking options.

"Ooh!" I leaned over, spying a slim, feminine-looking cigarillo in the box. "May I?"

Reaper laughed as he made his own selection. "You sure about that, sugar?"

"Just for tonight, while we're celebrating."

Vance seemed caught off-guard, but quickly recovered. "Cigars after dinner is usually a men's tradition, but why not? I have a final gift for the heroes of Four Corners and that certainly includes you, Mari."

"Governor," Reaper coughed. "You have been far too generous already——"

"Nonsense. Follow me to the patio, will you?" Vance turned to see who would be coming along. "Shadow, will you be joining us?"

"Um, I appreciate it, but smoke doesn't always agree

with me, governor." Shadow stood behind his chair. "I think I'll turn in for the night. Thank you for the dinner."

"Of course, I'll arrange a ride back for you. Ah, Remy?" Vance called over one of his staff and leaned in close to whisper instructions in the man's ear. It took several seconds, ending with a wink and a slap on the man's shoulder from the governor. "Have a good night Shadow, I've arranged a small gift to meet you back at your room as well."

"Sir, you don't have to—"

"Not another word! You bled for my territory, my family, and it will not go unrewarded. Off with you now, sleep well."

The rest of us stepped out to a cool, picturesque evening through a set of double doors at the end of the dining room. A bonfire was already lit, with patio furniture and another bar outside. Water rippled over a dark lake just beyond the seating area. Moonlight and stars reflected in streaks of silver over the water's surface.

"Mrs. President." Reaper flicked open his lighter and held it in front of my slim lady-cigar.

I smiled, leaning in to puff the other end as the flame embraced it. "Thank you, Mr. President."

He just smirked, the warm glow dancing in his green eyes as he lit his own. We accepted another round of drinks and took our seats next to the governor.

"Martin," Vance called to another member of his staff. "Will you turn on the lights on the other side of the lake?"

"Certainly, governor."

A minute later, warm lamp light steadily grew brighter across the water. A shape took form against the darkness—the form of a house. As my eyes adjusted to the light, I saw it was a two-story cabin, much like the governor's own residence.

"I admit I don't entirely understand your dynamic, except that there's four of you," the governor said. "And that you currently don't have a permanent home. The floor plan is the same open concept as mine, but can be adjusted if you wish."

I sucked in too much smoke and heat burned my throat as I coughed. Someone pressed water into my hands and I drank it greedily.

"Sir," Gunner breathed. "Am I understanding you right? You're giving us…

"A house, yes. You can live in it part-time or full-time, whatever your plans are. I meant it when I said Four Corners will always have a home for you."

A stunned silence fell over us as we stared at the home. Fantasies immediately began flitting through my head. While it had been nice that everyone had their own place in Sheol, a single home for all of us would be so convenient. We'd be cohesive, a real family unit.

I could see Jandro making breakfast with fresh eggs every morning. Gunner watching Horus hunt over coffee as the sun rose. Reaper and I sleeping in and making love before the day began. And Shadow—

My thoughts stuttered before the realization screeched them to a halt. I was getting way ahead of myself, already thinking of Shadow as mine, let alone picturing him in my household. He needed to decide if that was what he wanted, and so did my guys.

"Governor, it's not that we don't appreciate this." Reaper stared across the lake, and I wondered if fantasies similar to mine played out in his head. "But it's not just us. I have an entire club—twenty-five people, including women and kids to look out for. They're spread out in the town now in various rooms and taverns. I can't accept a place like this while my people still need homes of their own."

"I thought of that as well," Vance grinned. "My architects are planning a new development along this lake, I can give you a tour tomorrow. But we're thinking of a community playground, a garden, and around thirty homes, depending on lot sizes. You can all stay together that way, if you'd like."

"Sir," Reaper coughed with a shake of his head. "I don't mean to be rude, but it's too much—"

"Four Corners doesn't have standardized currency yet," Vance clapped him on the shoulder. "So this is how I'm paying you and your men for bringing my Kyrie back to me. Offering a basic human need, such as shelter, is the least I can do. Please," he shook and squeezed Reaper's shoulder a little harder, "don't think the homes come with strings attached. We can draw up a contract if that would make you feel better. But I'm forever in your debt, Reaper. Not the other way around."

"If you would just let me think about it," my husband said cautiously, though still starry-eyed with disbelief. "It's just...a lot."

"We're not used to gifts like this," Jandro explained.

"We're used to taking, stealing the things we value most, then fighting like hell to keep them."

"It's not a gift, it's payment," Vance insisted. "Your men risked their lives and returned what's most dear to me."

"No disrespect, sir," Gunner chimed in. "But men like us are also not inclined to trust politicians at their word. I've seen firsthand the corruption brought on by wealth and power because I was born into it. Most outlaws have been a victim to it at some point or another."

"I understand," Vance nodded. "Well, after we have the time to get to know each other, I hope we can come to a place of trust. I think the Sons of Odin would vouch for me."

"It's because of them we agreed to come here." Smoke curled around Reaper's mouth. "They've been loyal to you longer than us and have lost a lot more. If anyone deserves home and community, it's them."

"They're good men. I think of them like my own sons, in a way." Vance lifted his eyes to where Dyno spoke to Grudge in a low voice a bit further away from everyone else. "It's a tragedy what they've endured."

He couldn't see, but I spotted T-Bone talking to Kyrie near the patio doors. Her eyes were wide and dreamy looking up at him, their heads bent together in an intimate conversation.

Reaper followed my gaze over Vance's shoulder and huffed out a quiet laugh. "I'm glad you think so, governor. Keep that in mind for when they do things with no apparent explanation. Bikers are unpredictable, and we mourn our losses in different ways."

"Fair enough," Vance shrugged, either not noticing, or ignoring what we saw behind him. He lifted his drink instead. "To remembering those we've lost and forging new, lasting friendships."

"I can drink to that," Reaper grinned.

SHADOW

I breathed for what felt like the first time in hours. The governor's car dropped me off at the B&B and I was finally alone. Blissful silence was freeing. Spending hours rubbing shoulders with men who wanted to do nothing but talk was suffocating.

But I did it. I made it through the night and lived. Now quiet and solitude were my rewards.

Once in my room, I undressed for bed, kicking my boots off and undoing the buttons on the crisp shirt like they were ropes binding me. I pulled my sleeping pills from the drawer, then sat on the edge of the bed, ruminating on the evening as I untucked the shirt from my slacks.

Mari looked amazing. Every man in the room stared at her like some exotic pet bird and it brought out a bloodthirst I'd never felt before. She wasn't theirs. What right did they have to gawk so openly?

I huffed out a dry laugh to myself, knowing I wasn't any better. At what point did I change? My whole life had been spent in fear and avoidance of women. Now I wanted to gouge out the eyes of strange men over one, as if I had any right to her myself.

Look at me. Pining over an unavailable woman and dining with politicians. You're moving up in the world, Shadow.

I thought back to when Mari first told me she was proud of me. She had that same look when the governor toasted me, drawing everyone's attention to me. I thought I handled it okay, but poor Grudge looked like he was the verge of a panic attack the whole time. Only looking at Kyrie, the governor's daughter, seemed to bring him any sense of calm.

What was it about women that had such an effect on us?

A soft knock on my door pulled me out of my thoughts. Dread filled me at the sound. I had exceeded my limit of socializing. It didn't matter if it was Jandro or someone else familiar, I was done for the night.

The knock came again and I bit back the growl of frustration. Maybe if I pretended to be asleep, they'd get the hint.

"Sir?" a feminine voice called through the wood. "I'm here on the governor's orders."

I was puzzled enough to stand and crack the door open. The woman on the other side had a face caked in makeup, her dress like a second skin as it hugged all her curves. She smiled coyly at me and I remembered.

Fuck.

The governor had sent a gift. And here she was.

"Um, hi."

"Hi," she giggled, tossing a lock of red hair over her

shoulder. The color looked fake, like Reaper's sister's hair. "You gonna stare all night or let me in?"

I stepped back from the door and she pushed her way in, closing it with a swing of her hips. Damn it, she was in my space now. A stranger in my room when all I wanted was to be left alone.

My mind raced, wondering how I should get her out, but my body was much slower to move. She walked straight up to me, confident and unafraid as she pressed her chest to mine. That was different. Did I suddenly become approachable? Or was she handpicked by the governor for her boldness?

"What's your name, big guy?" Her hands went to the buttons at the bottom of my untucked shirt, long red nails swiftly finishing the work I'd started.

"Uh, you don't have to do that." I backed away, holding the sides of my shirt closed. I had an undershirt on, so she didn't see the full extent of my scarring yet. As much as I didn't want to sleep with her, I also didn't want to deal with the fear and disgust I'd seen so many times before.

"That's a funny name." She snickered at her own joke, hands coming to her hips. "Well, if you'd rather keep it on or do the honors yourself, it's all good with me, cowboy. I'm Morgan, by the way."

With that, she hiked up her dress and pulled it over her head, now completely naked except for her heels. Like most service girls, she didn't bother with lingerie.

"How do you like it, big guy?" Morgan's voice took on a husky whisper as she stalked toward me. "I could climb you like a tree. You can fuck me against the wall, show me how strong you are."

"Um…" I kept stepping away until it was my back that touched the wall.

"Aw, you nervous?" She reached out and trailed her fingertips from my chest to my waistband. "You seem a little shy. You can lie back and just let me take over. I'm cool with that, too."

She stepped one leg between mine, and just started to rub her thigh against my crotch when I stepped to the side.

"Um, no. No, thank you."

Fuck, why did she have to press against me and get so close? Her presence in the room felt so invasive and I just wanted some fucking space.

"All right," she scoffed, annoyance now lacing her voice. "Tell me what you like, so I have something to work with here."

God fucking damn it. There was no getting rid of her, was there? And how bad would it look if I refused a gift from the governor? I'd have to get this over with, just like I always did.

"You can just, um," I swallowed, "get on the bed. On your hands and knees is fine."

Morgan grinned, heading for the bed like I requested. "See, now was that so hard?"

She assumed the position and waited. I went around behind her slowly, dread sinking into my limbs. My feet felt like lead dragging across the floor. I didn't want to do this, not with her. Not like this.

Glancing up, I realized she faced the mirror—the

perfect position to watch ourselves. That made me want it even less.

"Uh, can you face the headboard, please?"

"You're a picky fucking bastard," she huffed, but turned in the direction I asked.

Now I could just stare at the wall like I always did, and not the shame in my own face. I pulled my zipper down slowly, with reluctance. This might be over with quicker if I thought of someone else, the only person I wanted to do this with.

But that didn't feel right either. I didn't want *her* like this. I wouldn't want her facing away from me, just a body to invade. I'd want to see her face, to feel her hands on me. Not that any of it mattered.

Overtly aware of Morgan waiting for me, I began to stroke myself. After a whole minute of trying to get things started, my own hand was failing me. So I stared at the strange woman's opening, spread open and on display. That wasn't working, either.

"Need some help?" She sounded utterly bored.

"No." I ran through every scenario in my head that had gotten me hard before, every one but *that* one.

Nothing did it for me. I knew it the moment I saw this woman standing outside my door. As Jandro put it, I might as well try to shoot pool with a length of rope. Nothing that had previously worked for me could any more. Only *she* did.

I released my limp dick with a sigh, tucking it back into my pants. "I'm sorry. This isn't going to happen."

"Well." She didn't hesitate in sliding off the bed and

picking up her discarded dress. "Thanks for completely wasting my time."

"I'll make sure you still get paid," I told her, looking away as she got dressed.

"Uh, yeah," she scoffed. "I better be." She paused once she got her dress on, looking at me from head to toe. "Gotta admit, I'm kinda bummed," she mused, her voice softer. "You look like you could be a good lay if you weren't in your head so much."

Sure, like that was going to happen.

I grabbed the doorknob and swung the door open. "Sorry to waste your time. Have a good night."

"You too, big guy." She cast a coy look over her shoulder as she walked out. "Good luck."

It felt like I couldn't close the door fast enough, and I forced myself not to slam it. My room was blissfully empty of other people again, but my relief was gone. I thought of *her* and my cock stiffened instantly.

I leaned against the door, letting the back of my head hit the wood as my hand cupped over the front of my pants. The room wasn't just empty now, it was lonely. I did want someone here with me, but only if that someone was *her*. I wanted those lips that smiled at me and kissed my cheek. I wanted the only hands that ever touched my bare skin like they desired me.

MARIPOSA

"Holy fuck, I'm exhausted." Gunner laid his head on my shoulder as soon as the car door closed behind him.

"Same here." I ran my fingers through his soft hair, watching blankly through the windshield as we pulled away from the building. "I have a feeling I'll be too wired to sleep, though."

"Right?" Jandro's voice was raspy from cigar smoke. "Just like that, we could have a house gifted to us by the governor of Four Corners? Shit's fucking wild."

"If we're all losing sleep over this, that's a sign we shouldn't accept it," Reaper called from the passenger seat.

"Or you're just looking for excuses not to," I pointed out. "I'm glad you brought up the club, though. Everyone else, like Tessa and the boys especially, need a stable place more than us."

"Yeah, I dunno what to think," Reaper admitted. "I

don't get a slimy vibe from him, but I didn't from Tash either."

"Sleep on it." I leaned forward to kiss the back of his shoulder. "Or try to, at least."

The short ride back to the B&B was in comfortable silence. My feet ached once the car pulled up and we stepped out. I couldn't wait to shed this dress and heels.

Under the porch light's glow, I saw the silhouette of a large man sitting in one of the patio chairs.

"Sup, dude," Jandro greeted Shadow as we walked up. "Thought you'd be in bed by now."

He got a noncommittal grunt in reply. "Just felt like some fresh air."

"All right, well," Jandro was already yawning. "Good night."

We slipped inside and quietly made our way to our room. Taking my shoes off was a huge relief, as was getting out of the dress. But I wasn't ready to turn in yet, albeit for different reasons than fantasizing about a home to share with my loves.

"I think I'll sit outside with Shadow for a bit." I pulled on a long-sleeved shirt and lounge pants.

"Okay." Reaper didn't seem fazed as he pulled me in for a kiss. "Goodnight, sugar."

Already falling asleep, Jandro murmured a response in the same manner. It was Gunner who approached me with a tight-lipped frown and a knitted brow.

"What's wrong, handsome?" I wound my arms around his neck.

He ran his hands across my sides, touching his forehead down to mine. "You'll come to bed with us, right?"

"Yes." I kissed him deeply, savoring the rough cigar flavor mixing with his usual bright, sweetness. "I'll only ever go to bed with *my* men." I slid a hand down and grabbed his ass on the emphasized word, and that finally brought a smile to his face. "I love you, Gunner. I'll remind you in any way I need to."

"You shouldn't have to," he whispered, lips on the bridge of my nose. "I'm just being—"

"I will, anyway." I leaned up, catching his lips again with a possessive bite. "Because you're mine, and I'm here to give you what *you* need."

"You do. All I need and more." He sighed, running his hands up my back. "It's just my head being a dumbass. Old habits, you know."

"You're not dumb. This is just strange to you." I pushed his hair back to look into those sky-colored eyes. "So don't let your head talk itself in circles. Talk to me. Talk to them."

"I know." He cupped the back of my neck, thumb massaging gently at the base of my skull. "I love you, baby girl. Thanks for being patient with me."

His kisses were warm and sweet, a gentle rain pouring over my lips and face. This warmth and affection was one of my favorite things about him. My heart was jumping at the chance to talk with Shadow, but he wasn't mine yet. If Gunner needed me, he was my priority.

"Want me to stay?"

"Nah, go hang on the porch with the big guy." He swatted the side of my hip, the easygoing smile returning to his face. "But come cuddle with me when you're back."

"You're sure?" I kissed his throat, licking lightly over his pulse.

"Yes." He grabbed my shoulders and playfully held me an arm's length away. "But not if I let you keep doing that."

"I'll be right back," I promised, dropping a kiss to his knuckles on my shoulder before he released me.

"Mari?" he whispered.

"Yeah?"

Gunner stroked his thumb over his bottom lip as he thought. "Just know that Shadow better appreciate you. He's never gonna find another woman like you, so I hope he realizes what you're worth. If he doesn't, we won't accept him."

So my guys did talk. It was on their radar, at least. Part of me wanted to argue that I could make my own decisions about who I wanted to be with. But I knew how important trust was, not just with me, but between each other. Reaper had already trusted Jandro and Gunner, but Shadow was a bit of an outlier. If I got too deep in my feelings to see clearly, they could have clarity that I didn't. Now I had to listen to their concerns too, because it wasn't just me Shadow would be spending time with.

"I understand, Gun." I closed the distance between us to stroke his cheek. "You all want the best for me, and I love you for that."

He kissed my palm, then playfully shoved me away again. "Go talk to your new boyfriend."

I held back a snort as I left the bedroom, closing the door silently behind me. The whole B&B was quiet and dark as I tiptoed out the front door. But not even being as quiet as possible could get past the assassin sitting outside.

Shadow turned his head as I crept out the front door, the porch light bringing out his cheekbones and deep lines cut into his face.

"Mind if I sit with you?" I asked before moving any closer.

"Um, no." He shifted in his seat, the bench creaking under his movement. "Go ahead."

I lowered down next to him, mindful to keep some space between us. "Couldn't sleep?"

"You could say that." He started to fidget, hand curling around the armrest of the bench. "How was after dinner cigars?"

"Smoky," I laughed. "All the guys are raspy and I'm sure I'll be regretting it tomorrow. But the governor showed us a house he wanted to gift us." I shook my head with a deep inhale. "We're not sure if we'll take it. It feels like too much, but if it was one of our kids we almost lost, we'd probably feel similarly. So we're thinking on it first."

"Congratulations," he said a bit stiffly. "If you do decide to take it."

"We'll see." I lifted one shoulder in a shrug. "There's still everyone else that needs homes. And Reaper's not entirely sure about settling here." I curled my legs underneath me. "How are you liking Four Corners?"

He shrugged. "I'm fine just about anywhere. I

wouldn't even mind being nomadic. As long as I can ride and see the sky." His throat worked in a deep swallow.

"I'm sorry you didn't feel up for joining us out back. I didn't know cigar smoke bothered you."

Shadow smiled, a sight as rare as the night-blooming flower he showed me, and just as dazzling to see. "It doesn't. I was just tired of being around people."

"Ooh, naughty," I teased. "The wounded hero of Four Corners dipping out on an invitation from the governor. That takes balls of steel."

"Unfortunately, mine are still fleshy and vulnerable."

He said it with such a straight face, the first peal of laughter burst out of me loud enough to wake the entire B&B. I slapped a palm over my mouth, trying in vain to smother the laughs that followed. Shadow's broad shoulders shook with quiet chuckles as I blinked back tears and tried to compose myself.

"Oh my god," I panted, wiping the corners of my eyes. "I think you leveled past Jandro with that one."

"I learned from the best." He appeared more relaxed now, slouching against the bench, hands no longer fidgeting and his knees wide.

The distance between us was gradually closing, so I took my chances scooting closer until my leg brushed his. His eyes flicked to where our bodies made contact, but he didn't pull away. When our laughter faded to quietness, I voiced the question that had been on my mind for days.

"Can you tell me about your tattoo?"

He looked puzzled for a moment. "This?" His hand hovered over his chest.

"No, this." I touched my index finger once to his thigh, then returned my hand to my lap. "I saw it when you were sick."

"Oh." He returned his gaze out to the road in front of the B&B, his mind somewhere else. "It was the first one I ever did. I wanted to practice on myself before tattooing anyone else."

"Are the hieroglyphs upside down so only you can read them?"

"Yes." Amusement crossed his face as he looked at me. "It's such a shitty piece of work, I'm surprised you could tell."

"I mean, it's clearly roughly done, but it's not *that* shitty."

"I did it in prison," he shrugged. "I worked with what I had, but since this one, I've only gotten better."

"That is definitely true." My next question hovered on my tongue, my heart accelerating for some reason. "Will you tell me what it means?" His brow furrowed, that expression making me backtrack immediately. "You don't have to, of course."

"You *want* to know?"

"Sure I do." I held his gaze, fighting the impulse to push his hair back and kiss that scar again. "I want to know more about you in general."

He stared at my mouth and I wondered if we held the same train of thought. "It means, *the sky is my reason*."

A simple phrase that clearly held so much weight.

"Your reason for what?"

"For living," he said softly. "When I was confined to my cell, the sky used to feel like another planet, some place far away that I would never reach. I could only see it through a crack in the wall. But seeing it, how the sky changed colors right before nightfall, it gave me a reason to keep waking up again."

My throat felt uncomfortably tight. "You mean when you were in prison?" I asked.

"No," he shook his head. "Before that." He let out a scoff. "Prison was a wonderland compared to that place."

"Shadow?"

"Yes?"

Our eyes locked and I felt frozen in place while also being thrashed around by a storm. My pulse crashed wildly, every cell in my body crying out to touch him, to give him another reason. There was no turning back from this point, and that both terrified and emboldened me.

"I don't want to pretend like nothing happened between us."

His chest lifted with an influx of breath. I remembered the warmth of his skin on my cheek, the gentle rise and fall as I watched him sleep.

"I don't either."

We moved toward each other before the words were fully out of his mouth. His arm lifted and I slid over to nestle into his side, my feet tucking underneath me as I leaned into him. I'd been craving this like a drug ever since the first time, feeling like I was protected by the strongest shield, while also melting into his gentleness and warmth.

Only this time was different, and we both knew it.

I lifted my face to his. He kept his arm along the back of the bench instead of wrapping it around me, his lips hovering close enough for me to taste the soft puffs of breath. Some guys doubted a girl's intentions down to the last moments, and I knew Shadow second-guessed himself plenty. So I decided to leave no room for doubt, and closed the distance between my mouth and his.

Shadow's lips were soft, more pliant than I imagined. But he didn't move, didn't respond to the soft presses of my mouth.

I pulled away for a moment, finding his eyes. "Is something wrong?"

"No. I…just…"

I reached up, finally giving in to pushing his hair away and exposing his beautiful face. "You've never kissed anyone?"

His eyes dropped from mine, stiffness entering his body as he started to pull away from me. That was all the answer I needed, but I wasn't about to let him withdraw this time.

"I can teach you." I wrapped a hand around the back of his neck, gently stopping his retreat. "How does that sound?"

He leaned into my hand on his neck, but didn't pull away further, despite being plenty strong enough. "Okay."

A smile pulled at my lips. God, he was so hot. Sexy,

dark, and dangerous, yet adorably innocent. "Okay. Just follow what I do. This is stage one."

I leaned in until our mouths touched again, then pursed my lips to press a closed-mouth kiss on his top lip. He copied the movement on my bottom lip, and it sent a jolt straight to my heart. I had a feeling he'd be a fast learner and that proved to be true. He caught onto the rhythm of exchanging soft pecks after only a few tries.

"Stage two," I whispered, keeping my lips parted as I pulled his top lip between mine.

He released a soft groan as he sucked lightly at my bottom lip, his kiss in perfect sync with mine. My lower half was thoroughly jelly now, while my top half pulsed with heat, with desire I was sick of holding back.

I didn't even have to say stage three. Our tongues simply met in the middle, gentle taps and exploratory licks growing deeper, bolder as this heady rush carried us like a tidal wave. My leg slid over his lap as I came to straddle him. His hands came to my hips, then quickly dropped away.

"Yes, please. Touch me." I grabbed his hands and returned them to me. "I want you to."

A moan came from deep in his chest, our teeth clicking from our hardest kiss yet, as he wrapped one arm around my waist and the other caressed up my spine. I couldn't get enough of his hair, running my fingers through it as my other hand rested on his chest. His heart pounded like a drum against my palm, matching the beat of my own pulse.

"You're a natural kisser," I murmured, pausing for a breath despite wanting to kiss him until I passed out.

Still, he looked puzzled. Uneasy, despite his body language proving he wanted this just as much as I did.

"What's wrong?" I pressed a deliberate kiss to the scar cutting through his eyebrow.

"Why are you doing this with me?" That question and his resulting flinch from my kiss sent a painful ache through my chest.

"Because not only do I like you as a person, I'm also ridiculously attracted to you." I wrapped both hands around his neck, my fingers pressing into the knots behind his shoulders. He still had some stiffness there from the arrows tearing through his muscles.

"How?" Despite his bewilderment at what I said, his hard expression slackened with my touch.

"How can I not be, is a better question." I leaned in to kiss him again, his lips catching and savoring my mouth in a way that sent fluttering down to my toes. "You're strong, you're caring. You're smart and creative. You're loyal and selfless." I rested my forehead on his, letting my mouth hover an inch away. "And you're so fucking hot. Why do you think I stared at you so hard that I spilled beer on your table that day?"

"Because my scars are ugly and make me look like a freak."

"No, love." I kissed between his eyebrows. "Because you were the most handsome man in the room to me."

His hand on my back drifted forward, pushing my hair off my shoulder and gently stroking along my jaw. "You don't mean that."

I leaned into his touch, encouraging him to cup my cheek. "Do you trust me?"

"Yes," he answered quickly. "With my life."

"Then you know I wouldn't lie to you." I brought his hand to my chest, over my pounding heart. "There's no faking this. This is real, Shadow." I returned my palm to his chest, feeling the matching beat of that muscle through his shirt, skin, and the tattoo that bound us together. "It's always been here, and I don't want to fight it anymore."

"Neither do I." His gaze lowered, the arm around my waist running down the side of my thigh.

"But you're still uncertain," I ventured, clasping my fingers over his on my chest. "Tell me why."

"Your men," he admitted, meeting my eyes again. "They…they *know* how to do this. Take care of you, treat you like you deserve." He swallowed. "They know how to…to please you. Why would they share you with me?"

"Oh, Shadow…"

I leaned in, dropping a kiss on his brow. He released a sigh, eyes closing softly, so I kissed each of his eyelids. I kissed his cheeks and his nose. When our mouths met again, his lips were parted, waiting. I melted into his taste, curling up small as his arms came around me in a tight, protective embrace.

When we parted for air, he kissed my forehead, stroking my cheek with his thumb. I expected him to be gentle, maybe even overly careful and a bit clumsy, but these touches damn near brought tears to my eyes. His tenderness sent my heart and hormones running wild and I wanted to drown in it. I wanted to peel back the layers of him with kisses instead of violence, to uncover and protect this man who deserved all the love in the world.

"My men," I whispered, tucking my head under his chin, "care about both of us. They're letting us explore this because they want us both to be happy. Is it so hard to believe that can happen if we're together?" I skimmed my fingers along the collar of his shirt, touching the skin around his throat. "Jandro is your best friend. He loves me. Don't you think he might want this for us?"

Shadow's broad chest rose and fell with each deep breath, his caresses soothing and delicious on my back. If I hadn't promised Gunner I'd come to bed, I could easily fall asleep on him like this.

"I just never thought I'd be good enough." He shifted his weight, but held me in place against him. "Never normal enough, I guess."

I raised my head with a soft laugh. "If I wanted normal, I never would have hooked up with those three in the first place."

"Yeah, I guess you're right." He smiled again and my heart skipped. Jesus, he was just so beautiful.

Our lips touched together again, but I pulled back at the last moment. "You *are* enough," I whispered, bringing my hand to his scarred cheek again. "And whatever you don't know, I'm willing to show you, okay?" I couldn't help the grin that followed. "Although if your kissing skills are any indication, I don't think you'll need much guidance."

"Hm, I don't know." His eyes brightened as he cupped the back of my head. "I think I need more practice."

He kissed me through my laugh, his confidence shining through as he pulled me close. Not a stitch of clothing was removed, and our lips didn't travel anywhere beyond each other's faces. There was an innocence to kissing Shadow that I loved, like we were two teenagers learning the basics. We had already crashed together once and it burned us both. Now, coming together slowly, organically, seemed like a much better idea.

We kissed until my lips felt thoroughly bruised and my eyelids could barely stay open. I must have dozed off for a moment because Shadow was rousing me with kisses in my hair and gentle shoulder shakes.

"Should get you to bed," he murmured with a kiss to my temple.

"Mmhm, I promised Gunner…"

My legs slid to the floor, the rest of my body peeling away from his warmth, his solidness. I didn't like this, the feeling of cold night air with no solid bodies sandwiching me, but crawling into bed would soon alleviate that.

Our fingers intertwined, Shadow led me through the front door of the B&B, through the open front room, and stopped in front of my door. He didn't let go of my hand, and my half-asleep brain considered just dragging him in to snuggle with the other guys.

One day. Not yet.

"So." Shadow stared at our hands, his thumb

sweeping over mine. "It'll be okay if I kiss you good morning tomorrow?"

I grinned, leaning my chest against his as I stood on tiptoes. "Only if you kiss me goodnight first."

He grinned back as he bowed over me, bracing his other arm against my back. I would've swooned if he hadn't pinned me against him. In the dark hallway, with his face fully uncovered, long hair falling over his shoulders, and his bright white eye glowing like a cat's, he was every woman's fantasy when it came to late night kisses in the shadows.

The kiss was long, sensual, and lingering. I saw stars as he returned us upright, his fingers reluctantly untangling from mine as our bodies separated.

"Goodnight, Mari." He walked backwards toward his door, eyes never leaving me.

I leaned my head on my door, hand on the knob as I watched him back away. My legs could barely hold me up from fatigue, all the drinks at dinner, and everything this gorgeous man did to burrow his way into my heart.

"Goodnight, Shadow," I breathed before opening the door and quietly slipping inside.

Epilogue

REAPER

The air was warm, the sun pleasant on my face. Desert stretched out in all directions, the sky a perfect royal blue with fluffy clouds. My gas tank was full, so I accelerated and felt the power of the motorcycle kick underneath me. The road was empty and smooth, with no potholes.

That was how I knew this was a dream.

I pulled over at the edge of a canyon, parking under the sparse shade of a Joshua tree. Ancient rock formations stretched out as far as the eye could see, their ribbons of color too vivid to be real.

My instincts urged me to turn around at the footsteps behind me, but I stayed facing forward while the last bit of uncertainty left me.

"Took you long enough, Daren."

"You always were an impatient bastard, Reaper."

I turned slowly, all expectations gone at what I would see standing there.

It was just my brother.

He was still in his riding gear, russet brown hair pushed around by the wind, those cheeky green eyes we shared bright and full of life.

That was what brought my breaths to a stutter, he looked so *alive*. More than that, he looked fucking good. Nothing at all like the lifeless, pale, clammy body I held as he faded away.

"What's the matter, Reap? You choking up on me?"

"Man, you just…" How could I be dreaming? I could *feel* my throat closing up. "It's good to see you, that's all."

"I'll visit more. Noelle's mind is a little hm, distracted, shall we say?"

"Yeah," I barked out a laugh, still staring at him in disbelief. "Yeah, she's all wrapped up in that guy."

"I saw everything that happened on that mission." Daren hooked his thumbs through his belt loops, propping his foot up on a rock. "Larkan's good people. You should patch him in."

"How did you see everything?"

"Freyja showed me." He smiled lightheartedly. "She's like an anchor that we all come home to. Sometimes I'm tethered to her, other times I'm free to make visits as I please. Like this one."

"They said I had to…to be open to letting you visit me."

"Right. It's a two-way street," he grinned. "Talking animals have a way of opening you up to things, don't they?"

"Heh. I'm a stubborn ass, but yeah, I think it was my old lady's cat that sealed the deal."

Daren's face grew dreamy at the mention of her.

"Mariposa," he breathed. "What a name. What a woman."

"Yeah."

I didn't feel the need to elaborate. If his spirit, consciousness, or whatever was in Freyja's domain, he must have seen plenty. And knew exactly what kind of woman she was.

"You did good, Reap. Mom'll be proud."

Wait. Did he say *will* or *would* be proud? If she was dead, he had to know, right? I opened my mouth to ask, but his face darkened and what he said next made my stomach drop.

"You have to break down the door."

"What?" I blinked. "What door?"

"You *have* to break it," he repeated, his tone grave. "She'll die if you don't."

"Who, Mari? Or Mom? Is Mom okay? Is she with you?"

"It's gonna hurt, man. It's gonna hurt like hell for a long fuckin' time." His brow pinched with pain at the vision he was seeing. "But it's the right thing to do."

Goddamn my brother and his fucking predictions with no fucking context.

"Daren, please." I moved closer, close enough to touch him, but afraid he might disappear if I did. "You have to give me more than that. What's gonna hurt? What door am I breaking?"

"Listen to Hades," he continued as if I hadn't said anything. "No matter how badly you want to, do *not* disobey the command."

"What command?" I demanded, fear now slicing through my veins. "Who is he going to make me kill? Daren!"

But my brother was already gone.

TO BE CONTINUED IN HEARTLESS - STEEL DEMONS MC BOOK 6

PRE-ORDER HEARTLESS HERE

Acknowledgments

They kissed! THEY KISSED! I've been wanting to write that scene for at least four books and it finally happened! But the best part is I'm so lucky I get to share it with all of you SDMC readers. Thank you for coming along for another leg of this ride! Hold on tight, because the road is only going to get bumpier from here.

If you'd like to hang out with me regularly, join my reader group, Crystal's Coven. We're a friendly bunch, and I'm always posting teasers and new excerpts there before anywhere else online.

A big shout-out to my pack babes, Kathryn and Aleera, for hearing me vent, cheering me on, and enduring my teasing—*cough-torturing-cough*—about the events of this book.

Brandy, I just heart your face so much. I swear you've been supporting me since Day 1, and I appreciate you endlessly.

Telisha, Danielle, Janet, and Izzy, you all make my job (and life!) easier by ensuring these books are ready for the world to see. Thank you, thank you, thank you!

See you all in the next book!

-Crystal

Also by Crystal Ash

Harem of Freaks: The Complete Series

Say Your Prayers

Steel Demons MC

Lawless

Powerless

Fearless

Painless

Helpless

Heartless

Senseless

Ruthless

Merciless

Endless

Shifted Mates Trilogy

Unholy Trinity: The Complete Series

For a complete list of books by Crystal Ash, visit her Amazon page.

About the Author

Crystal Ash is a USA Today Bestselling Author from California. She loves writing steamy, heart-wrenching romance with tortured heroes, especially if they're in a reverse harem. Crystal's other loves include animals, mythology, and well-crafted alcohol, most of which can also be found in her stories.

When she's not writing, she's probably drinking craft beer with her husband or trying to coax her feral cat into accepting affection.

crystalashbooks.com

facebook.com/Crystal.Ash.Romance

instagram.com/crystalashbooks

amazon.com/author/crystalash

bookbub.com/profile/crystal-ash

www.ingramcontent.com/pod-product-compliance
Lightning Source LLC
Chambersburg PA
CBHW021342310726
48971CB00001B/246